Temples

A novel

Latha Viswanathan

WILLOW BOOKS

Detroit, Michigan

Temples

Editor: Randall Horton
Cover design: Aquarius Press

ISBN 978-0-9992232-4-6
LCCN 2018935201

Willow Books, a Division of Aquarius Press
PO Box 23096
Detroit, MI 48223
www.WillowLit.net

Printed in the United States of America

Never the spirit was born
The spirit shall cease to be never.
Never was time it was not
End and beginning are dream.
There was never a time when you did not exist.
Nor will there be any future in which you and I cease to exist.

Bhagavad Gita

Acknowledgments

I would like to thank my friend Patricia Menon for her careful reading and useful comments.

Thank you to Randall Horton and Heather Buchanan for believing in my work and making this book possible.

Contents

1. Signs from Saturn   9

2. Shrine Under the Banyan Tree   26

3. Incident at Mayapuram   43

4. Lotus of the Heart   67

5. Watergate and Churchgate   90

6. Blue Hills of Ootacamaund   116

7. Churning of the Ocean   143

8. The Conch and the Discus   168

9. Auspicious Beginnings   200

10. Arjuna's Penance   215

Chapter One
Signs from Saturn

Last night in bed a lightning pain flashed in the upper region of my body. By the time I opened my eyes it was gone, that fleeting sense of helplessness replaced by irritation; always something with this whining body. I treat all aches and pains with contempt, putting old age symptoms in their place. But it had succeeded in spoiling my sleep. It was one thirty according to the clock on the stool behind my cot, four hours before I get up normally. I closed my eyes and tried to sleep but all I managed to do was travel to Mahabalipuram in my head, the sea wall stretching like a gray serpent before me; the shore temples and sculptured rocks to my left, the turbulent-soothing ocean to the east; all of these were calling out to me. They used the voice of an old friend when they spoke to me.

Perhaps you found it strange or maybe you think the old man has lost his marbles giving rocks and crumbling structures human quality. It was not like that, let me assure you. I went to the temples, rested my eyes on those wondrous rocks, meditated for a while watching the waves, and it was as if I was born again, my spirit vibrant, that feeling of bounce in my brain, and I was ready to do what had to be done, my small temple restoration projects and book. Work gave meaning and kept darkness away from me.

I retired officially on my sixtieth birthday to satisfy bureaucratic requirements. Now I continued to work as a consultant, a role that evolved into a full time job because there were few experienced men like me. Even that idiot boss of mine, (whom I called "Sub-Optimal" meaning less than satisfactory) Subbudu, admitted this on several occasions. For example, at my retirement tea party, he read: "…many of us in the department including myself, your sub-ordinates, Vadivelu and Dharmaraj, among others, have the highest regard for your expertise in the field of temple renovation. This A-1 asset of yours coupled with top notch reputation for honesty and credibility make me want to hold my palms together and say namaskaram Sathya Saar and offer you this sandalwood garland as a token of our appreciation cum admiration…" The fellow was a windbag prone to murdering the English language among other things but more on that later.

It was possible that some people thought my work useless, this obsession with the past but after careful consideration I have abandoned the alternative, the life of a retired man. To retire was to withdraw and I was not one for such things; I have always enjoyed making myself useful. Perhaps, in a moment of weariness, I have felt frustrated because of the bureaucracy and corruption of the Indian system and the ignorance of most people, but there was no alternative. As I said before, I did not want to be an old man waiting for death, waiting for Yama to come and take me. It was good to be this obstinate person, I thought, doing what I can for people; there was such splendor in and close to this dirty city of Madras.

When I was younger, I used to think wait till I am older and have finished with these Indian Institute of Archeology government fellows then I will do some traveling, go to the hill station Coonore, buy myself a small tea estate, and plant dahlias and cosmos, and read and read and read. Now I cannot stoop long enough for gardening; the slightest drop in the temperature makes my rheumatic problem misbehave; and as for reading, I still like to do that but even that has become tiresome, too many people going yodley yodley, how much to take in; the gray matter was no longer obedient blotting paper, it was also talking back saying, enough enough now let me be. So I have decided finally to admit it, yes, my work, simply put, is who I am and what I am and this so called Indologist and healer of temples is all I really want to be.

***

The temple restoration project at Periamalai began tomorrow and I needed every ounce of energy. Willing myself to sleep, I played that old trick on myself, staring at one thing so long and hard that it became something else. I focused on a minute portion of an object, in this case, the top of the walking stick which hung from the coat rack in the corner, something at seventy-five I carried out of habit but thankfully didn't use.

On the northern wall of this room was the diamond shaped rosewood shirt rack from which hung my spare dhoti, and an American T-shirt gifted to me by Cookie, my niece's daughter who came all the way from Houston to polish her dancing at the famous school, Kalakshetra. I suspected it was also for a period of Indianization and cultural immersion since she was engaged to be married.

There was the built-in bookshelf with my favorite books, a few inscribed with my name Sathya. My eyes rested on the calendar from the marketing savvy Periamalai village Mogul Store owner, Yusef Ali.

Sometimes, I was astonished and proud thinking of all that I had done, the places I had been and the people I had met. Temple restoration projects in Angkor Wat, Cambodia; Borabadur in Indonesia; Ayuttha in Thailand. Not to forget the trips to America, where I consulted for non-resident Indians with advice on idol installation, played liaison and introduced them to the finest sculptors in Tamil Nadu.

All these I saw in spite of the darkness in my room, for these features and objects were as familiar to me as the geography of my own body. My mind moved away from this room to the hall and beyond, pushed out through the front door and past the covered verandah, leaped across the driveway and garden out into the busy city. It pulled me higher and higher so that I was on par with the coconut trees and mango trees, so I could reach out and pluck the black bees clinging to young fruit. I saw the strip of land behind the house with the slums. Washermen and women were sleeping in their thatched huts—dark huddled shapes with blankets drawn over their heads and ears, to keep the dew from entering their chests. We Indians have a horror of the cold air entering the orifices of our bodies and making us sick, which was why you see many a well dressed Indian man or woman attending even formal functions with balls of cotton stuffed in their ears. Block the openings, keep the wind out, that is the philosophy.

***

Early next morning, the shore temples beckoned and I knew nothing else would do. I had to drag my body there and smell the salt in the sea air, feel the texture of rock against the skin of my palm for comfort. My black Morris Minor was parked in the portico in front of the house. I saw that my neighbor Venkat's house was completely dark. He had turned off the light in his room upstairs. A night of reprieve from his usual insomnia meant he could not see or hear me.

It had been a few years since those corrupt and useless government people finally followed the recommendations in my archeological report. They had erected a wall around the sea-ravaged temples. I liked going there when the city slept and I had the place to myself. Besides, the idea of driving myself there, this added to my adventure. Young people like Cookie and Venkat associated slow reflexes with old men. Pity they had not peeked inside my agile mind. There was nothing slow there. But you, O great silent one, you already knew that I, Sathya, have never had a slow thought in my life. Who was this person I was talking to? Never mind, I reminded myself, I talked to myself these days, a sign of intelligence or advancing years, I did not care, you may choose to believe what you like.

I felt at peace with myself in the vicinity of a temple, maybe because as a child I had run to the village temple frequently in times of trouble, seeking solitude and shelter in the hot afternoon when the heat was unbearable; inside, the smell of coconuts and overripe bananas mingling with the fragrance of flowers, incense and sandalwood soothed and comforted me. The warmth of the arati flame near the skin of my palm and the sound of temple bells transported me outside myself and this world.

These days I was also working on a book of South Indian Temples, a coffee table book with Venkat. He took the photographs, I provided the text. This was the way we had worked together before on several articles and pamphlets, during our trips to Southeast Asia. I knew Venkat from when he was a little boy. He emigrated to Canada thirty years ago and now he was here to work on his projects and spend time with his ailing mother.

I drove past closed shops, deserted streets, the hush of the night thick in the air. The window was rolled down on my side and the wind rushed in, its touch sharpening my alertness, helping me concentrate. My feet performed the familiar dance steps of stepping on the clutch, shifting gear, moving onto the accelerator, then stepping on the brake as a stupid stray dog decided to run across the road. On the pavements, fruit and vegetable carts were covered with cloth as their owners slept nearby.

In the shore temples of Mahabalipuram, at high tide, powerful and foamy white surf became an invisible giant hand, an unseen sculptor, shaping gray black rock. Now the waves hissed and surged and sang their song. I could taste the salt in the spray and feel the grit of sand in the sea breeze. As I stood there on the shore, waiting for dawn to break, the receding waves sucked at my flat and slightly swollen feet.

I stood before the two foot carving of Lalita, most benign and beautiful aspect of the divine mother. The design at the base was the wheel of light and radiance, the Srichakra that represented cosmic energy. It had the power to grant the devotee anything he desired. I reached out with my right hand and caressed this and prayed that my forthcoming projects would go well. My eyelids began to twitch so badly that I had to close my eyes and place my fingers over them. I could feel the beating of my heart get stronger for I knew the answer to my prayer was here. It was a superstition only but who is to say that such things are not indications of the future, of things beyond the control of mortals? Just then, as if to confirm my suspicions, I heard the cawing of a crow and felt the whoosh of its wings as it flew past my head.

***

Driving back from the temple, I was almost home when all of a sudden there was a terrible racket, a rattling noise emanating from the engine; the vehicle began to choke, sputtering hopelessly as I continued to apply pressure to the accelerator. Out of the corner of my eye, I saw an animal munching grass near the oleander bushes in the garden. The car was half-way into the portico when the bloody thing died and became silent. I did not know what the problem was. Usman, the driver, would have to take care of it as soon as he came. I did not want us to be late for our appointment and meeting at Periamalai. That much was certain. I shooed the goat that had got into the garden.

Seven o' clock in the morning. The air was pleasant in the terrace where I sat on the corner cement bench, the way I always did, with the Eagle flask full of milky coffee and a stainless steel tumbler by my side. I rolled my shoulders, then turned my neck this way and that, enjoying the temporary relief from pressure in the small of my back, that concave portion of my spine that needed much coaxing to relax. My skin felt damp because I had just finished doing the ten yoga postures with which I began my day.

I heard the bore well motor go fut fut and I knew Nagu, my servant, had turned on the switch. His wife, Paru, began to sweep the entrance to the house, the area that lay just beyond the gate. Bala, my cook, hurried in the street wearing his usual dingy dhoti and shirt. My neighbor Venkat's terrace was to the left at the same level. I heard a cough and saw a glowing fiery tip of a cigarette. We understood each other well and did not usually chat unless there was something important to exchange.

The Radhakrishna house across the road came to life as their old servant, a stooped and shrunken man, lit incense sticks and did arati by lighting a piece of camphor for elephant-headed god Ganesha who was sitting in an alcove in front of the house. Above Ganesha was the name of the house: "Misty Glen," the name given to the house by its former owners, an English company that used it as a guesthouse. "Misty Glen" suggested the English moors. Reality spoke otherwise. I saw the same servant fill a mud pot with cold water, placing it on the empty alcove below Ganesha. An aluminum tumbler was placed upside down on top of the lid. Mr. and Mrs. Pattabhiraman, a.k.a. Mr. and Mrs. Awesome, the owners of the house, were generous sorts who liked to provide thirsty passersby with cool water. I called them Mr. and Mrs. Awesome because after a brief visit to see their daughter in Chicago, Mrs. Pattu (short form for Pattabhiraman) had taken to shouting "awesome" whenever she had a fit of hysteria. Seems her daughter and son-in-law had left the children's channel, Nickelodeon, on full blast to baby-sit mother and father when they went to work.

I turned around and looked at the slum behind the compound wall of my house. There was a communal tap to one side. Two children were cleaning their teeth with their fingers while a woman filled her bucket with water. Soon the washermen would twist their sheets into long ropes and thwack them on the washing stone. The sheets would be spread everywhere, on the roofs of the huts, on the ground; a few favored ones hung from rusted metal clotheslines. Buffaloes took turns fanning their tails under asbestos sheet sheds at the end of the slums. This explained the prevalence of mosquitoes on our street.

The sky was slashed by two horizontal stripes as pigeon colored clouds parted to let the sunlight through. I squinted as I sipped my coffee and looked southwest towards the distant cremation grounds where a thin funnel of smoke was rising up. Perhaps the first body of the day. "Om Shanti, shanti, shantih," I muttered.

When my turn came, it would be the electric crematorium, no stray dogs and puppies sniffing at my charred bones and flesh.

The coffee tasted warm and good against my tongue. Paru had finished sweeping the garden and sprinkled the entrance to the house with water to wash away the film of dust and mud that settled there overnight. I saw the slight bulge in her stomach and realized anybody could tell she was carrying. Must be three months already from what Nagu told me. He was watering trees and plants to the side of the house. I looked at Paru and the cremation grounds again; life and death was evident everywhere in this city.

I liked to watch her do the threshold design, the kolam at the entrance of the house. In the olden days, these designs used to be drawn with rice powder prescribed by the Dharmashastras to feed insects and ants. But of course, these days, powdered quartz glinted in the sunlight.

In preparation for the festival of Nagpanchami, Paru had forsaken the usual dot design in favor of a nagamandala. There was a small separate drawing of a baby snake near the big snake. The symbol of the snake, constantly revitalizing and regenerating itself, spoke of the eternal cosmic cycle.

***

In my bedroom I pushed the play button on the cassette player. M.S. Subbalakshmi, the nightingale of South India, was singing verses from the religious text of Vishnu Sahasranamam. This was part of my daily routine, I said my prayers out loud in the adjacent bathroom as I poured water on myself.

At the end of my bath, I felt something fall plop and crawl on the skin behind my right shoulder, an unnerving sensation that broke my concentration on the prayer and before I knew it, I dropped the bucket on the floor, shook myself like a rattle and stood staring at the cement floor. A striped baby lizard tail twitched madly near my right foot. I lifted and moved the bucket a few inches to see the khaki colored body minus tail dart towards the windowsill. The tail continued to dance as the body raced away. I watched till the tail became still. Last week, I referred to the astrological handbook, the Panchangam, for rahukalam hours, periods considered inauspicious to start any new project because of planetary configurations. After noting the rahukalam hours, I glanced at the page where it said a falling lizard on the right shoulder was a bad omen.

The sound of water falling into the empty bucket drowned M.S.S's sweet voice but I continued reciting the mantras and rubbed the oval shaped cake of sandalwood soap on my skin. Then I used the plastic mug to pour water and rinse myself. The water pressure dropped suddenly, the tap sputtered and made choking sounds. I opened the adjacent tap and it too produced nothing. The water pump had been switched off too soon. Usman, the driver, usually took care of this because Nagu, my servant, left early for his job in the post office. I thought of the car and remembered that the driver was the only organized and mechanical minded fellow in the whole-blessed house.

M.S. Subbalakshmi was not waiting for me; she was racing ahead like she always did. I willed my mind back to the job of the moment, reciting Vishnu Sahasranamam.

I stepped into the bedroom with a damp towel tied around my waist. The ceiling fan was rotating wildly to keep the heat and humidity under control. Nagu had hung my freshly starched and ironed dhoti, kurta and angavasthram, the material I wound around my neck, on the back of the rattan chair. For a hot place like Madras, this was the best cotton clothing worn by sensible chaps like me. I adjusted the sacred thread on my chest using the right thumb and forefinger and finished chanting two more verses before moving towards the small oval mirror in the corner. The breeze from the fan blades hit the moist skin of my body and I closed my eyes at the pleasure of it. This was Madras; such a sensation was fleeting, and I knew that within ten minutes, when I sat down at the dining table, I would be sweating again in spite of this bath. I shook talc all over my chest and under my arms, squirted a few drops of Parachute coconut oil from a bright blue plastic bottle onto the middle of my left palm. Then I vigorously rubbed my palms together and flattened the wing-like tufts of graying hair on either side of my head.

Dressed in my dhoti, I walked towards the puja room. I dipped my fingers into the Monaco biscuit tin on top of the old English safe. Deftly, expertly, I drew triple vibhuti, holy ash stripes with my fingers on my outer arms, chest and forehead. Watching me apply vibuthi ash on myself, Cookie, my grand niece from America asked, "What does it really mean when you do that, Sathya Thatha?"

I explained wearing ash is based on the idea that the world is governed by three principles—creation, preservation and destruction—Brahma, Vishnu, and Siva.

"You mean, like the dust to dust idea?"

"Exactly. We wear it because of this," I gestured at my body, "the mortality of this. We must struggle to overcome the ego. Do you understand? Remember my name Sathya means truth. I try to follow that." I looked at her face and saw that she was no longer there. Her eyes had that glazed look, typical of people that age, never staying in one place, running here and there in their minds. How could she appreciate this ego problem, which was something I struggled with all the time?

Paru finished sweeping the prayer room and poured ghee into the brass lamp. The wicks burned steady, four golden drop-shaped flames facing north, south, east and west. I had given her free rein over the puja room since her pregnancy. Menstruation and its associated pollution would not be a problem for the duration of nine months. Of course, this had never really been a problem for a liberal chap like me. The monthly business was a scientific process in the rational sense, but she and I both understood that occasionally, I observed some of the old ways out of respect for tradition.

I pressed a red vermilion circle on my forehead and brushed a bit of fresh ground sandalwood on my Adam's apple. Then I continued with my prayers to neutralize the effect of the lizard landing on my back.

***

As I finished my prayers in the puja room, Bala, the cook, heated milk in the kitchen. He was vigilant about the monkeys that sometimes appeared in the garden and entered the kitchen looking for food. I could hear the shrill whistle of the milk cooker. Bala said Paru had gone upstairs to check if Cookie was still sleeping. I remembered only then that Cookie's dance school Kalakshetra had given their students a three-day holiday. Some Muslim festival or the other. Another one of those newfangled politically correct observations. Majority of the students were Hindus and nobody worried about their lack of spiritual development. Throw in a few Christians and Muslims and we were full of concern for them. I could not understand such imported western hypocrisy.

Cookie and I had decided she would call me Sathya Thatha though I was not really her grandfather. "Grandfather's brother is close enough, I figure," she said, making me smile and agree with her. Nobody had called me father and it felt oddly pleasant to have a young woman call me Thatha, grandfather. It felt as if I had had a double promotion.

I told Cookie that I would call her Kamala, lotus, the flower of the goddess. This was her real name. "I'll not call you Cookie like the others. What kind of name's that?"

"Hey, I go by that name," she pouted. "I'd prefer it if you'd call me Cookie if you don't mind. We tried Kamala when I was in kindergarten. They kept calling me Camela as if I was some humped animal."

Then it was time for breakfast, idlis, soupy sambhar with onions of the small variety and coconut chutney. Cookie was already seated at the dining table, sipping her first cup of tea; eyes still veiled with sleep, staring nowhere in particular.

In my head, a tail twitched this way and that then became motionless. The lizard was supposed to be a resilient creature; it would grow another tail. But my worried mind was anticipating problems.

Bala came to me with a tumbler of buttermilk diluted with water and seasoned with salt and crushed lime leaves. "Usman is not here," he said.

"Where is that idiot?" I asked. "I told him to be here early. None of these fellows has any sense of time. Always some bloody excuse."

I checked the Panjangam text again and confirmed that in four hours, it would be rahukalam, the beginning of inauspicious time when Saturn exerted its negative influence priming opportunities for things to go wrong. Only the other day I read that scientists in America have discovered more moons around Saturn. Whether this was good or bad I did not know. I hoped some slight adjustment in my favor could be made because of this.

I stood near the window with the rosary in my hand, murmuring mantras to calm my nerves when I saw Usman enter the garden on his bicycle. He dismounted and began his hand wringing, "the bus did not show up..." I raised my hand as a signal to make him stop with this foolishness.

"We don't have time for this," I told him. "I don't know if we can make the trip with this problem in the car." I saw that he had already got the bonnet gaping open and was peering inside seriously. He assured me there was a way to fix the problem; it was only a minor inconvenience.

When I returned with my papers and documents, Bala and Usman had conferred over the fan belt problem and come up with a solution. Bala was standing behind me with the dosa/idli lentil and rice grinding machine's belt, swaying it excitedly as Usman said, "Best and fast substitute belt, good idea no?"

"Isn't it a bit too big?" I asked suspiciously. Usman was confident of his ingenuity; he had always managed in the past this way, throwing sand on the engine when small flames leapt up, sticking his arm out of the car when the signal failed, willing to sacrifice a body part if necessary.

In our country where even dung was made into patties and used for fuel, everything was put to good use, double and triple use if possible, assuming many roles; nothing was thrown away; no disposable society here. The new big belt made a racket as we backed out of the house. Usman reminded me the village of Periamalai was only two hours away, we would manage getting there on time.

Venkat had slung his camera from his shoulder and was carrying a bulging case with all the lenses and things in one hand and holding a tripod in the other. I had completely forgotten about him accompanying me today. An odd number setting out on a journey was not the best idea. Even numbers were harbingers of good fortune. Odd numbers were tricky business. Too late to make a fuss now.

The substitute fan belt vibrated like a child's wooden top inside the bonnet. As we pulled out of the portico, I looked down and noticed the design Paru had made that morning. The tires erased part of her effort as we drove over it. Cookie waved to me from the front verandah where she was sitting with the sweet lime vendor.

We had reached the end of our street when I realized that idiot Bala had forgotten to give me a bottle of boiled water, something I always took on my trips. We drove past the slums, the huts behind the houses on our street.

My servant Nagu's mother, Ayah, was leading a small group of old women who searched through mountains of rubbish. They searched for saleable items that were discarded by the careless: plastic milk packets, bottles, newspapers, old notes or magazines. She recognized our car and flashed a toothless grin. Her family and ours had remained tied through the generations, way back from our village days.

I remembered her as a young woman, coming to our house on oil bath days, massaging our heads and bodies with warm oil while we stood there in our underwear. The old woman had magic in her thumbs; she could iron out any kinks in your body, stretch and relax muscles with the pressure of her hands.

***

We began the trip with the enthusiasm of leaving the chaos of the city. The roads became wider and less crowded and the trees we passed had wider canopies of green. We drove past stretches of fields and two women carrying bundles of firewood, swaying their buttocks as they balanced the weight on their heads. They crossed the road without bothering to look on either side. How lightly these people took the worth of their own lives.

Usman clucked his tongue and sighed heavily when we passed through village areas because it meant driving in slow motion. He liked to pretend that he was a pilot, maneuvering some airborne craft hurriedly through the skies. Down here on earth, we had to dodge big mats of chilies drying on the road, the wheels crunching over the edges. There was, of course, no question of overtaking any other vehicle.

At last, a good stretch of road and no interruptions for a while. Venkat had closed his eyes and covered his face partially with his Blue Jays baseball cap to keep out the sun. I too felt my eyes growing heavy and gave in for a bit.

A screech and a bump as we came to a sudden stop. Usman was shaking his fist and shouting at the men and women outside. They had spread rectangles of hay on the road, leaving it to dry in the sun without any thought of motorists. We all had to get out. The men and women huffed and puffed as we watched them pull a big rope of the stuff from around the front wheels. We Indians did not understand how to use the road. The concept of civic sense was non-existent among the masses of this country.

I noticed that Venkat lit a cigarette and was taking pictures of two urchin children running behind an older child spinning a metal circle with a long stick. After several clicks, he turned to me and said, "It never ceases to amaze me how happy these kids are with so little. You should see the kids I normally photograph in the so-called developed countries. They're so bored with the world; they depress the shit out of me." I saw briefly two expressions on Venkat's face merging in that moment he spoke to me. A look of surprise followed by fleeting pain as if some distant memory haunted him. I remembered our time together in Cambodia a couple of years back and the little boy he had befriended there.

"This word for excretion, I know it is very fashionable in your part of the world. I notice Cookie also using it every time something is not to her liking."

Venkat smiled sheepishly and said he did not mean to offend me.

"None taken," I said. "I too use gutter language occasionally, especially when I am by myself. By the way, I'm curious, what do you know about Shani?" I asked.

Venkat looked puzzled. "You mean the planet?"

"Yes. It is partly because of Saturn, the dreaded planet, that we have had so many difficulties. It sends out negative energy. "

Venkat threw back his head and laughed. What did he know about my intuition? He was a non-believer.

Usman was signaling that the car was ready. He assured me that we would make it on time. I was not so sure, I felt some discomfort in the pit of my stomach.

I was remembering a conversation I overheard between Cookie and Venkat, both of them sitting on the cane chairs in the front verandah. They did not know I heard every word in my bedroom, their voices coming through the one-foot gap above the doors leading from the verandah to my room. Cookie said there was a Hindu smell about me, a mixture of sandalwood, vibhuti and coconut oil, the same smell that emanated from the corners of temples, (except that in the case of temples the oily underpinning was much heavier because of rancid oil in many of the wick lamps) I added mentally as I overheard her talk. I was not upset by the description but quite flattered. It seemed very apt to me that I should be thus described.

I was a hirsute man, gray everywhere. I did not mind anymore since I read in an American magazine that body hair was a sign of intelligence. Better to be a hairy chap with something upstairs than a smooth and vacant idiot. The small hair in my nostrils and on my ears I chopped off when I remembered to look closely in the mirror, something I did not do often, for what was there to look at?

The reflection in the mirror showed my face to be long and clean shaven. The bifocal glasses with the tortoiseshell frame was something I could not do without. First thing in the morning, I reached for them. There were a few things I wore and carried almost always – this old Rolex watch on my wrist, a good Parker pen in my shirt pocket, the sacred thread with the gold Vishnu coin across my chest.

My skin had always matched the color of dried tamarind, thinning now especially on my arms and fingers, creasing in places like a layer of cream on hot milk. The body betrays us so easily; it always comes down to the common denominator, wrinkles and problems. It is only the mind that distinguishes in the end. I had crooked and rather large teeth, some of which were missing but the ones that remained were strong. My parents, unsophisticated people that they were, did not know or care about things like dentistry; it was enough that I was a boy and could make my own way. A few physical shortcomings were not seen as impediments to a man's progress. They hoped that such things built character in their sons. I noticed that my ankles and wrists were small like most South Indian Brahmin men. Our vegetarian diets predisposed us to slight frames and feminine-sized bones.

***

I tried hard to distract myself, but the strange augury of the lizard in the bathroom was burrowing into my brain. So far, there had been a mixture of both celestial and earthly omens. The position of planets at the commencement of a task told us the shape of things to come.

An hour before we reached Periamalai, my throat felt parched and I longed for something to drink. I looked for the usual water bottle, then I remembered it was not in the car. When we passed the next roadside shop selling tender coconuts, I told Usman, the driver, to stop. All of us, I noticed, had needed that break, as Venkat, my photographer neighbor and friend, along with Usman, hurried behind trees on the roadside to do their business while a young man chopped away the husk of a good sized coconut for me. I told him to prepare a few more for the others also.

The coconut juice was good and sweet, some of it dribbled down my chin. I noticed two sad faced children staring at me without blinking their eyes. That was a dirty habit some of these people had. Spoiling the little pleasure you derived from eating or drinking; they hounded you all the time, sending daggers of guilt into your heart. I finished the last of the juice and handed over the empty coconut to them so they could eat the flesh. I told the others to do likewise and decided to wait in the car. No point in being too accessible to these children in case they decided coconuts were not enough.

I had settled into my seat in the car and wiped my spectacles clean when I noticed a monkey in the distance, carrying what looked like a coconut, out into the fields. Soon everybody was in the car, and Usman said we would be there in half an hour. I felt a great sense of relief. "You better get this thing fixed properly," Venkat referred to the fan belt. "I have never in my life heard of something so bizarre. Using an electric rice and lentil grinding machine's belt for a car, whoever heard of that?" he said and shook his head.

"That is why this is India," I told him; "We are specializing in ingeniousness, from the time we are young. You see our daily life, how every little thing is a big problem, power cut, water shortage, cement shortage and what not. But we are not crying, we are smiling and managing, is it not?"

Venkat had his baseball cap on his face and did not answer me. I too decided to squeeze in a little nap. The breeze from the window was a gentle lullaby and I heard Venkat snoring before I myself fell asleep.

Next thing I know Usman pressed the horn and made the brakes screech and we came to a halt. Venkat was swearing, "God damn it," as we were both pushed forward and his camera bag fell to the floor of the car.

"Bloody hell," I heard myself shouting. I almost kicked the bucket (I liked to read Zane Grey from time to time) and hit my chin on the front seat. I touched the chaffed and tender spot to see if it was bleeding. Usman opened the door on his side and I saw him run behind the car. "What is it?" I asked Venkat. Already, there was a small crowd.

"He hit a monkey," Venkat said.

A monkey, my God. My heart was thumping suddenly when I heard the chattering of many monkeys; some of them swinging wildly from branch to branch of the big tamarind tree adjacent to the road. Venkat and I got out of the car and pushed our way to the center of the small crowd. The poor creature twitched on the ground. It was one of those red-bottomed, straw colored monkeys, a puzzled frown creasing the hairy forehead. A minute or so and then it was all over, the animal was still. The eyes turned glassy, the tongue slipped out. "God," I said. It felt like a stone had grown in my throat.

Two monkeys struggling over a coconut leaped onto the middle of the road from a tree, Usman said. So many of them about in these rural roads, how to keep track of all their movements? This one, it seemed, had appeared suddenly in front of the car. "No more reckless driving, all right?" I said and waited till he nodded his head.

Somebody else in my position might have said something about the innate cruelty of Muslims or something crass like that. I knew this was not the case with Usman. The chap was gentle. But like most drivers, he used the vehicle as a weapon of sorts, using it to create thrill and drama. He drove rashly and braked hard at the last minute. It was insane. A treacherous thing to do in a country where even driving normally was dangerous.

Saturn had sent many signs today. Rama, Krishna, I beseeched, show me the way please. My chin was stinging badly. It would swell into a bruise. I was not going to think about that, I had bigger things to worry about.

"Bloody things don't belong on the road," said Venkat.

"The place is theirs too. According to Darwin, they were here before us. The place belongs to them as much as it belongs to us."

"Inga vappa, Come here," I called to one of the fellows standing and gawking. I asked him if he would be good enough to cremate the creature. I gave him ten rupees. He said it was not enough. Venkat, acting like a Canadian, handed him a fifty-rupee note. "What did you do that for?" I asked. The fellow had no idea of how much to pay for anything in India. Useless, I told myself, these non-resident Indians, NRI's who came here and turned everything upside down. They made life difficult for people like us who earned salaries in rupees.

Naturally, fifty-rupee note man was all movement and action now, hurrying to get a rag with which to wrap the monkey, his wife ordering the children to go to their hut nearby and fetch kumkum to mark the forehead. "We should be leaving," I reminded everybody. "There is not much left that we can do."

As the car began to move, I saw that fifty-rupee man had deposited the dead animal on the ground by the roadside while he was urinating behind a tree with anthills on either side. Then and there I made a silent vow. I planned to request my cook Bala to make a vadai malai, a lentil doughnut garland, and take it to the Hanuman temple to propitiate the gods. What a terrible sin it was to inflict violence this way on an innocent creature minding its own business. Even if the monkey was doing so on the road where the silly thing did not belong. What a life we lived these days, filled with so many transgressions. All this rush, rush and rush took us straight to trouble. The image of the twitching monkey was imprinted on my brain and one day I knew that I too would disappear that way, if not on the road then at hospital or home, all the same difference, as Cookie, my grandniece said in her American English.

Chapter Two
Shrine Under the Banyan Tree

We were in front of Mogul Stores, the corner shop that served as a social center for the residents of Periamalai and its neighboring village of Mayapuram. Yusef Ali, the marketing savvy Muslim owner of the shop, always donned grimy cotton pajamas, kurta and a cloth cap on the crown of his head. He smiled incessantly as he handed out change and goddess Saraswati calendars to his Hindu customers, displaying betel stained teeth. He directed the goings on of his busy empire along with two assistants, Pillai, one of those enterprising chaps who had left his home state of Kerala for greener business pastures in Tamil Nadu. Pillai had six toes on one foot. I remembered this from last time I was in the shop, picking up a mango drink for Usman and myself. I looked down as Pillai pounced on an unsuspecting insect with a shout. He was always doing that-- stomping on a roach or beetle with the ball of his foot and announcing his deed loudly for everyone to hear.

The other younger assistant of Yusef Ali, the owner, was a mere slip of a boy, Thomas, whom I gauged to be in his early twenties. His face had the expression of a savant or an idiot, depending on your point of view. The brown eyes were vacant one minute, then the pupils darted wildly next minute if you happened to catch his gaze. He weighed lentils and rice and wrapped packages with string for the customers. As he worked, he laughed and smirked to himself as if there was some comic reel running in his head. He was an untouchable turned child of Yesu Cristo, thanks to George, the American missionary. I knew George and his wife Claudia, a doctor who tended to the welfare of these people. They had settled in the village two years ago.

Mogul Stores carried all sorts of provisions, sacks of various lentils, rice and wheat lined up in front; plastic mugs and buckets in garish colors hanging from the eaves, brooms tied in bundles and stacked in one corner, rose colored peppermint and orange crescent candy in bottles on the shelf next to Ali's cash and change drawer.

Usman slowed down so we could pick up packets of Frooti, a sweet mango drink we both relished. Yusef Ali flashed me a grin and his young assistant Thomas offered us straws along with our drinks.

We passed the usual landmarks before turning into the main street of Periamalai village—sugarcane fields with straight stalks rising like bamboo poles, the small stretch of road from where the view of the big mountain to the east was best, the vegetable and fruit market that catered to the two villages of Periamalai and Mayapuram. As we waited for a cow and several sheep to move across the road, vendors sold baskets of hairy yams, snake gourds tied with string and hung like curtains in front of a stall, fly covered sliced yellow pumpkins.

Far away, the metal crowns on the spires of the Shiva Vishnu temple in Mayapuram temple dazzled in the sunlight. As we approached our destination, the Periamalai Kali temple with the mother goddess, I saw that the government jeep was already there, parked across the road at an angle in front of a tea stall.

The two junior fellows from my department waved to me. The department for Conservation of Cultural Property studied ways to save and maintain ancient monuments and antiquities with support from the department of History and Culture. I explained to the men who were waiting by the jeep why we were late and suggested we get on with what we had come to do. We had to replace the old stone tablets, nagapratishtas, with substitutes that could withstand the elements. The original pieces would be sent to the museum. "Where are the new stone tablets?" I asked one of the junior fellows from the department, S.D., the initials standing for Sputnik Dharmaraj, so called because he fired his speech in sputters as if a rocket was about to take off.

"The nagapratishta tablets are in the boot of the jeep, Saar. We covered them with cloth, Saar. Vadivelu and I wanted to prepare the ground, Saar; we got ready to excavate the present ones under the tree but you can see,

Saar, the women, they are praying, some special ritual on Tuesday, Saar. So patiently we are waiting, only fifteen minutes more then we will begin, Saar."

I could see the trajectory of his speech going on and on, lot of yodley yodley coming out of this windbag so I raised my hand and said, "Enough enough, S.D. Land your rocket and cool down; I can see the women for myself."

Vadivelu, the other fellow from the department, was an emaciated chap whose intake of nutrition seemed to go straight to his hair. He had an abundant, well oiled mop that rose in an impressive wave above his forehead. The fellow was better known as Puncture because he accentuated his speech with a big hiss after every sentence as if he had to empty out his lungs and fill them up again before he could find words for the new sentence taking shape in his head.

Since this Periamalai Kali temple was not a Brahmin temple, animal sacrifices were sometimes offered here by the villagers. Abstract notions of a higher power did not interest practical village people who only sought explanations for facts and troubles of daily life. Their agricultural deities were mostly female, ones who had power over disease and calamity related to the harvest. The Kali in the village temple was also Plagueamma, who protected against cattle plague, cholera, and malaria, any epidemic, human or animal.

S.D., Puncture and I walked towards the tree shrine where the women worshippers had gathered. The scene was hauntingly typical of rural south India. A large banyan tree with roots that hung like giant matted hair from the branches and women gathered around the base. On closer examination, nagapratishtas rose like promissory stone fingers, signs left behind by aliens from a bygone era. These tablets and live snakes were worshipped by women who wanted children. Villagers had built a circular wall around the base of the Banyan tree with bricks and filled the raised bed with mud where the old slabs were embedded. These nagapratishtas were large slabs of stone with figures of cobras mating, two snakes intertwined, carved in bas relief. The stone tablets were marked with blotches of red kumkum powder, the color of blood, symbol of fertility. Flowers lay scattered and piled in front of the tablets, along with bowls of milk and incense.

There was an older woman leading a younger one and they circumambulated the tree. Two cobras glided through the gnarled roots that protruded above the ground around the base of the shrine. I noticed that the older and younger women who had been circling the tree now stood in front of the tablets with their palms clasped in devotion.

The younger woman, in a bright maroon sari, had shiny silver toe rings that indicated she was a new bride. Poor woman, recently wed, perhaps only for a few months and already there was the pressure to produce an offspring. Useless people with their stupid ideas; how will our swelling population be checked under such circumstances? Our idiot men in villages and cities could not seem to find other ways of entertaining themselves than sticking it into their wives.

The older woman whispered in the younger one's ear and a few seconds later, the young woman moved closer toward the shrine. Her body was against the brick base of the tree and she looked left and right for a few seconds, her eyes wide open, face rigid, before she stepped back a bit, knelt and bent her head on the soil, barely five feet away from the tablets. We stood transfixed as one of the cobras slithered towards the girl's bent head, lifted its hood in the form of a question mark and then brought itself down on her dark hair like the palm of an elder touching a young one in blessing. Everybody turned attentive and quiet, hypnotized by the sight.

I was holding my breath and my nails were digging into the flesh of my palms.

***

S.D. and Puncture began preparations for the removal of the large central tablet. The new replacement nagapratishta was a lighter gray because it was as yet untouched by the elements. I noticed that bits of loose mica made the carved bodies of the snakes shine in the sunlight. The zigzagged crack in the second older tablet bothered me. I prayed that it was superficial and no harm would come from careful digging. I reminded S.D. and Puncture to pack it and send it to the Museum of Indian Art in Madras where it would be restored to good condition.

After half an hour, I was getting restless from doing nothing and standing around so I myself went to get the quilted khaki blankets we had left rolled in the boot of the car. When I returned to the shrine, Puncture stood gingerly in the middle of the raised circular bed, his toes clutching the gnarled roots of the tree, staring nervously at a coiled form.

I heard a hiss and the cobra's hood shot up like an arm. "Ayyo, Ayyo," Puncture shouted and jumped right down to the ground beside S.D. hissing, letting out air as though his lung had been slashed. Then the snake lowered its head back to ground level and circled itself as if preparing to sleep again. Fed up with all this delay and hissing by snake and man, I grabbed my walking stick with the lion head. I used the curved head part to prod the snake hoping to send him on his way. The snake proved smart, he took the hint fast and slithered down the raised bed, onto the road as people gaped and clucked their tongues. He danced his way past the road and disappeared into the ditch under the tea stall.

A few men had gathered around the shrine. They murmured the way people do when they are generally dissatisfied with things but do not know exactly what is wrong. I was vaguely uneasy for mob psychology was something to watch for in a country like India. Especially where superstition and religion and people's beliefs and faith were concerned.

S.D. and Puncture were taking immense pains to dig as delicately as possible. As they stopped to wipe the sweat from their faces, one old crone with no teeth and sunken gums said to everybody and nobody in particular, "This napagpratishta was put here when my great grandfather was born, before the village temple was built. It has survived the British and two world wars. What does the new government do? Send their people to snatch our past?" Having finished her small speech, she unwrapped a wad of tobacco and betel leaf from a knot in her sari and stuck the thing in her toothless mouth.

Her heavy earrings had managed to enlarge the holes in her ears to such an extent that her lobes grazed her shoulders. The longish oval hole in her ear was big enough for me to see through. The fellow behind her had a bad case of leucoderma, his face an angry map of brown and pink. The blotches were akin to North and South America; it was as if a part of the globe was rotating on his skin. If I stood there long enough, and he turned slightly to the right, would I see Asia, Australia appear moving under his nostrils, spreading on his chin with their contours?

Puncture and S.D. had stopped their work and looked at me for reassurance. S.D. had started his firing of "Saar, Saar, what do you say we do?"

I motioned for them to continue when I heard a man call me "Pappan thatha," Brahmin grandfather. I turned to see Mr. Australia behind me, saying "My own son was born after my wife offered her prayers here every day for a month. Who knows how many of our children were born as a result of praying to this holy shrine? Why take them away?"

Another man piped up saying, "We heard what you're doing in Mayapuram with the navagraha, nine planet statues outside the Shiva Vishnu Brahmin temple. You're building a protective roof of some sort, is it not? Why can't we have that here?"

I raised my hands for attention. "We're not taking away anything of yours," I explained; "We're installing another pair, newer tablets that can better withstand the elements. See the crack that runs jagged across the old one we are digging out? The tablet will fall apart in a couple of years and you will be left with nothing but rubble. On the other one, see the discoloration here from the elements? It also has the beginning of small cracks in corners where the stone has chipped off. In the museum, they will be restored carefully and preserved for eternity, for your children's children. Can you understand that?"

The old crone with the extended earlobes shrugged her shoulders. I gave a nod in her general direction indicating thanks. She pulled at the border of her sari to use it as a handkerchief. As she did this, she exposed one of her sagging cinnamon colored breasts. The nipple resembled a squashed date. It was her third eye, staring down at the ground as if sulking with the weight it had on its back. The others in the crowd murmured among themselves and moved away from us.

The older assistant from Mogul shop, six-toed Pillai, caught my eye and I saw that he spat into the gutter and crossed the road. He joined the men who were across from us, observing Puncture and S.D.'s movements carefully.

***

I saw my friend, the American Anglican missionary, George Atkinson, affectionately known as Brother George by his flock, wave and hurry to have a few words with me. "How are you, Mr. Sathya?" he asked.

"Fine, thank you. I see that you've become Indian, Brother George," I joked, "You've taken to calling us by first names only."

"Yes, I'm happy to be Indian that way. It's a warmer way, is it not?"

"Yes, yes," I agreed heartily. "And how are you doing? Are the folks in Periamalai and Mayapuram treating you well?"

"Not bad," he replied, crinkling his blue eyes against the glare of the sun. "I would like to talk to you in private," he said, lowering his voice and moving his face closer to mine. My legs were tired from all the standing so I suggested we sit in the jeep while I waited for Puncture and S.D. to return from their tea break. We climbed into the back seat and I slipped my feet out of my sandals and rubbed my throbbing left heel.

"What is it?" George needed encouragement to talk. For the two years that he and I had been friends, I noticed that he employed a circuitous way of talking and always went round and round the bush till I got impatient and fired off questions one after the other like a lawyer. Today, I was determined not to let such a thing happen. I nodded encouragingly and forced a weak smile.

"You know it's wonderful to see the fruits of one's labor. Do you know how many men and their wives and children have walked into my church? They show up for mass every Sunday, bless them. Only last week one of my men presented me a home-grown pumpkin. A huge, beautiful thing. It really got me, Sathya, that feeling when you're afraid to utter a single word because you may spoil the moment. That's how I felt when the sweeper and his wife did namaskaram as I held this thing in my hands."

"They know you're a sincere man. And they respect you for that," I said craning my neck to turn back towards the tea stall. Puncture and S.D. were smoking cigarettes and talking to Pillai from Mogul Stores. Near the shrine, I noticed the older woman stood waiting for the younger woman who walked to the back of the temple with priest Chandran's son. I supposed the priest was going to give her some sort of special offering from the inner shrine. Desire for offspring always made for persistence in women.

George continued in his circuitous way, "You know that when I offer a place for anybody and everybody in my church, I mean to say to all the people here you have a choice. You know that I don't believe in anything but voluntary conversion."

"Yes, the gentlest methods to increase the flock," I teased.

"You should see them, Sathya, once they're baptized. They are free of the stigma of their caste, something over which they had no choice. There is lightness to them, as if they've dropped a great weight. Their faces, their eyes are bright with love for such a compassionate God. And it is my great pleasure to arrange that meeting. "

"But George, after they become Christians and you elevate their status, what else changes?" I knew he offered the children seats in his school and gave them food, but in what way had he affected change in the long run? "You know they'll continue with their Hindu beliefs and superstitions; generations of such practices cannot be removed overnight," I persisted.

He stared at my face for a few seconds, his blue eyes moist with earnestness and feeling and sighed in an exaggerated fashion. "That may be the case but it's something else I'm concerned about. But before I get to that..." Now it was my turn to sigh and turn inward, seeking replenishment from my small supply of patience.

George lowered his voice though there was no need to do this since it was only the two of us in the jeep. "There was a bad incident in the house when my wife was alone with the boys." He explained that his boys were home from the American International School in Kodai for a long weekend.

Puncture and S.D. appeared just then outside the vehicle looking very diligent and anxious and informed me that everything was ready for the ceremony to be performed by priest Chandran. Under the tree, I noticed that a crowd had gathered again, the old woman minus the young woman standing ready for the priest with her hands clasped in the prayer posture. There were the same few belligerent men and noisy children.

"I'll tell you about it over lunch," George said. I was jolted into reality when I saw that my wrist watch said it was indeed close to one o' clock. I had hoped to be on our way back by this time, but now everything would have to be pushed back at least two hours for who knew what else lay ahead?

George had to go to meet one of his flock. I walked towards the shrine with S.D. and Puncture following behind. Priest Chandran was murmuring mantras in a most unpriestly way, as if he were saying it solely for himself. The priest, father of the chap who had disappeared with the young woman to the Kali shrine at the back, was a big fellow, one of those chaps who had breasts like a woman, jiggling with the joy of their own fat. I saw that most members of the crowd had their hands folded and that empty, transported expression on their faces. Given my experience, I had no qualms about saying I knew most such expressions to be fake. Some of those minds were ticking away dwelling on thoughts about work that had to be done, things they planned to do to other people, some of them even despicable, and others dreaming of food, drink and what not.

The new stone tablets were anointed with turmeric and kumkum, powders of yellow and red congealing on the stone in dark blotches as milk, honey and curds were first sprinkled then poured over the stone in holy cleansing rituals. A plate of incense and camphor was offered for blessing as everyone in the crowd murmured their final prayers and the temple bell clanged in the background. The ceremony was finally over and I congratulated Chandran on a job well done, making sure the troublemakers in the crowd witnessed what I did.

Puncture and S.D. were ready for lunch. Always the same story with these fellows: Minimum work, maximum pleasure. George returned from the store, and S.D. and Puncture gave us a lift. They were on their way to some hotel to eat biryani.

The small street on which George's house stood looked the same as last time except for the water tap in the middle of the street. George told me there had been much excitement last month when the tap had finally been installed. It was a Danish international agency that was responsible for this modern convenience in ten of the villages in this part of Tamil Nadu. First they bought taps of the wrong size and then followed up with failure to procure a water permit from the municipality with its endless bureaucracy of forms and under the table transactions. "You know," I said, "I have this theory that once the Whities come here they also slow down and say what is the point of all this efficiency and hurrying, better to relax and realize we are in India. You know the Brits who came here all enjoyed their roles of Sahibs and Memsahibs and many of them did not want to go back to their frigid England and freeze their buns off. Besides, nobody gave a hoot for them there. Here they had lots of Brownies saying 'yes, Saar, no, Saar, three bags full, Saar, and salaaming them and fanning them with punkah. They were eating vindaloo and mangoes and lichees and getting fat. Jolly old England offered only bangers and mash."

In the drawing room of George's house, a woman and her malnourished child squatted in the corner. Claudia was bending over them, talking in hushed tones. She was a slight and graceful woman, speaking in a shivery voice. She reminded me of Katherine Hepburn, her quintessential American style. I was looking at her thin lips and her stubborn chin that jutted out. "I've got to give her a tetanus shot," Claudia said, "I wish these women would take to wearing footwear. Please excuse me for a few minutes, Sathya, I'll join you in no time."

"The women and children from the families involved in the construction of our new church are all under her care," George said to me, a touch of admiration and pride in his voice.

The family dog, Monty, a lively German shepherd, bounded into the room and came towards me. As was the manner of our relationship, I raised my hand and said "Om Mahadeva," a mantra that made the dog stop in his tracks. I had discovered that he was peculiarly affected by the prayer; the words made him freeze at a respectable distance from me so that he sat on the floor and panted amiably without coming forward to lick and greet me.

Through the window, I saw where the new church was being built. Since it was lunch time, there was not much activity going on, but I could imagine the men and women who dug and carried mud on baskets on their heads, their bodies covered with dust, the racket that arose from the endless hammering, shouting and talk as they toiled. Somebody had left a transistor radio blaring a cinema song called Pettai rap.

"Let's go out into the garden; there is somebody I'd like you to meet," George said. We walked past the dining room into the back verandah where a man sat on a piece of wood that had been fitted with small rubber wheels, a contraption that helped transport his legless body. The bandages on his fingers told me immediately that he was afflicted with leprosy. His face seemed relatively unscathed while the rest of his skin looked thick and leathery, but there was no evidence of lesions or scabs. "This is Gopal," George said. "I was hoping you could give us the name of the wonderful doctor you mentioned in Vellore. Claudia feels there is hope for him, that he could be cured with the right sort of care."

I mentally jotted down that I should contact Dr. Raghuraman and tell him of Gopal.

We adjoined in the verandah after lunch. "I want to tell you about an incident that happened a while back in our new church. Somebody went into the boundary of the church, the area that had been blessed, and desecrated the area we had marked for the altar," George blurted out.

Claudia faced me, knitting her brows, "It could be that somebody did not understand, right, after all, a lot of them relieve themselves pretty much anywhere, is it not?"

"They understood that it was off limits, honey," George said. "They saw me bless the ground. So many of us prayed together there during the first service."

"We Indians have no civic sense. All that throwing rubbish out of our houses onto the streets, throwing dirty water out of apartment balconies, squatting and showing bottom to the whole world, it is a disgusting thing really. But then, as you can see, there are no public facilities, so what to do? I don't know what to say. It is possible that there are some elements here in the village who do not like what you are up to. A strong possibility, you must take that into account."

"Did you tell Sathya about the conversation you had with the members of the village council, the Panchayat?" Claudia asked.

George explained that before mass one Sunday, the men had shown up asking to speak to him and expressed concern about the number of people working on the new church construction project. The men said the construction workers were unfit to work on a holy project because many of these fellows frequented the village toddy house. Among them, many had been unemployed precisely because they were useless fellows; a few had been cobblers, one or two had operated cycle rickshaws, a handful were latrine cleaners. The fellow who sharpened knives was now laying bricks;

the man who used to take old bottles and newspapers to Mayapuram was the new head cook, coordinating efforts to feed the children and families. George stopped talking and looked at me.

"The men from the village council were angry that regular services had been disrupted. They now have to pay more for the same jobs to be done by fewer people," he said.

"And they feel the clustering of so many lowlifes, as they put it, was paving the way for some sort of calamity in the community," Claudia added.

"The main thing that is bothering them, I think, is that these people are no longer stained with the stigma of caste. I have told them as Christians, we're all children of God, equal in the eyes of the Indian and spiritual laws. I explained that there is no involuntary conversion here. Everybody comes to us out of their own free will." George had spoken with passion and I saw that Claudia threw him a look of fleeting tenderness.

"Your work here is controversial in nature, my friend. You realize that you are upsetting age old traditions of hierarchies. These chaps are suspicious of you and your ideas. I'd be careful. These fellows are not rational. Not all of them can grasp your ideas. They see the potential for change and don't like it. Understand?" I asked.

"Yes, of course. It's as I thought. But I cannot be ashamed and frightened to do what I do," George said.

We had differing views on proselytization and this was no time to go into that. There were too many of these so called Christian priests manipulating people and using caste and religion in a most un-Christian way.

"George, you forgot to tell Sathya that you will be visiting Madras in a few months? He is going to see the sculptor you told him about," she said. I remembered that I had referred George to Krishna, a man who breathed life into wood. Between them, they had decided that the cross would be made out of teak and that the stained glass would be designed and made by an artist in Ooty, the famous hill station that used to be popular with the British.

George was driving me back to the temple. I waved to Gopal in the garden, reminding myself again about Dr. Raghuraman in Vellore.

"I suppose that is the village arrack house?" I pointed out a thatched place with mud colored walls and small windows. As we came closer, I saw that the windows had metal bars and there seemed to be only vague shapes and dark outlines of men inside. I knew that my neighbor Venkat found his way into such places wherever he went. It did not seem to matter which part of the world he was in; the bottle beckoned seductively. It was the same way all those years ago when we were in Angkor Wat. He did not seem to care that the local concoctions might be adulterated and dangerous to consume.

Addiction was like a fire licking everything clean in its way. On the way back to the city, Venkat would be talking rubbish, a consequence of his time in the arrack house. There was pain beneath that hard shell of his; I knew the source of it.

As our car halted in front of the arrack house, I spoke to a man who squatted on the side of the road, asking him to fetch the man from the city. Venkat would be easy to spot because of his clean bush shirt and Nike shoes. The man looked defiantly into the sky and then past us, as if he had not understood what I had said. He met my eyes and continued to sit there stubbornly. "Those two are village council Panchayat men," George whispered to me as we saw a couple of men come out of the arrack house. We decided to leave.

I looked back and noticed the man squatting on the ground had not budged. If a man had done that in Periamalai during my grandfather's time, he would have been whipped. But it was my time now, and things were the way they were.

"The school connected with the temple—how are things going, do you know?" I asked. George's face clouded slightly, I thought, watching him squint as if to mask what he really felt. "Are they still segregating the children, the Brahmins inside and the others outside?"

"I'm afraid so, Sathya. You know how I feel about that arrangement. Some of the parents are still uncomfortable with the idea of an anglicized education. They watch all that rubbish on T.V. You know, the sensual thrusting of hips on MTV, the kissing in our Hollywood movies. You'll find a perpetual crowd outside Mogul Stores. Thanks to the owner's capitalist leanings. Yusef Ali is such an American at heart. You know, that bottom line fixation as if nothing that matters occurs on top." I watched my companion grin at the cleverness of his own joke.

"Have you seen the song and dance sequences in our Indian movies? All those wet clothes clinging to female bodies? We're not lagging behind. Just park here and let's go to the back, George. I've been meaning to take a look at the Kali shrine since they lime-washed the walls."

"Yes, of course. I'll join you later. I have to run across to the store."

At the Kali shrine, I turned my eyes to the walls. There were cobwebs in the corners near the ceilings and a startling stripe of betel juice rising up from the floor to waist level. Nothing changed with us Indians. Using national treasures as spittoons and urinals. Some of us needed to have our mouths sewn up.

"Why do you stare like that?" one of the men who had created trouble before was standing behind me. It was the chap with leucoderma, the fellow with Australia crawling up his cheek.

"I am an Indologist; I stare at everything in temples. It is my work, what I do every day."

"You folks have an answer for everything don't you? You think you know it all because of your education. The wisdom of life comes from living also. We don't want that white man here. Why do you suck up to that Christian? Are you not aware of what he's doing? It's people like him who don't belong here, all these do gooders, we don't need them here." I smelled more people behind me and confirmed this with another look. Two surly faced fellows who had not bathed in a while stood on either side of Mr. Australia.

***

George was hurrying towards me.

"Let's go to the priest's quarters at the back," I said. I need to talk to priest Chandran and explain to him that we should continue with the puja ceremony for the new tablets for all of this week. Devotees and priests should know that we government servants look after and respect their needs."

"Yes, yes, of course. I'd like to go along with you. Claudia would like me to tell him that she'll be offering free vaccination for all infants in Periamalai and neighboring villages.

We walked through the wooded path to the small brick house. The sun had been bright during our little walk and we shielded our eyes in the sudden shade. There was no doorbell for us to ring but there was a half open window and I went towards it intending to call out.

Though my vision was still cloudy from the sudden change of light, I saw the edge of a brightly colored carpet, the kind that was used to protect the base of a bed. Human forms seemed vaguely outlined and then I realized somebody was lying on the floor. I saw movement and called out. "Chandran, we're here." Nobody answered though the person on the floor stopped moving and got up. That was when I realized there was somebody along with this fellow on the carpet, another form that darted to the corner of the room, away from the length and breath of my sight. A pair of hands rushed towards the window and slammed the window shut. I stepped back in surprise and saw from the frozen scowling expression on George's face that he had witnessed the scene as well.

The front door flew open and I saw that the priest's son stood before us with a snarl in his face and the thin fabric of his cotton sarong bulging slightly at the center. I surmised quickly that this was evidence of recent activity. The young woman I had seen before in the company of the older woman, the newlywed woman who sought and received the blessing of the cobra, she appeared suddenly and ran from behind the house. The young man, his hair disheveled and his left eye twitching, scratched his bare chest. I finally asked, "Where's your father? I need to talk to him."

"Father's gone to bring provisions from the store. Mother is visiting my sister for her confinement in Mayapuram and we are cooking for ourselves these days."

"What's your name?" I asked.

"Mani," he muttered and banged the door shut. George and I walked back the way the woman in the maroon sari had run, towards the wooded path.

The fellow who was supposed to uphold all the beliefs and values, be a moral leader of the people, the same idiot was taking care of fertility problems by letting his son sow his non-Brahmin seeds into these unfortunate women. Or perhaps fortunate in the case of the woman whose face I had glimpsed. There was no evidence of pain or regret there. She looked satiated, like she had got what she came for. Probably married to a loafer, a sterile goat to boot.

***

In the car, Venkat was stinking of toddy next to me, talking about his grandfather. "He was a randy old fellow, like all of us Brahmins," he said. "He prayed diligently to the gods every morning. All those pujas and mantras. We're all the same, every one of us." I did not like the fact that this just returned foreign fellow should badmouth the dead. I scowled and tried to shut him up by placing a finger on my lips. I pointed to S.D. and Puncture in the front.

"Thatha went to the coconut and sugarcane plantation we had in Chinnakolam and always stayed overnight. When I was fourteen, the servants there told me why. They said Brahmin men liked their women. Taut bodies burnt by the sun. You could see the muscles ripple with health. Bold eyes that looked at you as you made love to them. They were with you, not just lying there."

"Enough, enough. Go to sleep and leave the rest of us in peace," I hissed.

Venkat's toddy breath was close to my face. "What's the matter?" he said, "Didn't you go along with your father to the plantations? Your grandfather and mine went to the fields together; they did the same things. They were best friends after all. The traditions are the same."

Tell me, O great silent one, when we had a staring contest as children, why was there that urge to blink and look away, what was it that prevented us from looking deep within each other? Were we afraid of something we might find in the other person that we did not have? The other person was more than a mirror image, for we knew instinctively then of the vastness of the universe, the possibilities and dangers that lurked within and we were scared of what we saw there. And because the other person was also like you, this meant you were also scared of yourself.

I took a deep breath and tried to recite verses from the Gita but my heart was not in it.

When I turned to look at Venkat, I found him slumped and asleep, his head against the window to my left. S.D. and Puncture had decided to stop for tender coconut water at a roadside stall. I supposed they wanted a drink again. Were these men buckets? How much could they hold? While we waited outside the shop, I looked at people on the street and caught Mani's piercing eyes across the road. Was he following us? He stared as if I was a woman he had to conquer into submissiveness. Then he turned abruptly and walked away.

I thought of Cookie and what she might have said. "Yikes. He gives me the creeps." That would have been her reaction.

Chapter Three
Incident at Mayapuram

I was in the verandah. "What are you doing, may I ask? What's that?"

"Nail polish. Haven't you seen a bottle like this before? This shade is called Pearly Pink. See?" Cookie held out her left hand and wiggled her fingers in delight.

"What do you need that for? You're beautiful without all that stuff."

"This way, I'm even more beautiful," she said, then smiled and pouted reminding me she was still a child. "I'm going to a concert tomorrow evening with my friends. We're going to watch Ravi. He's the best male dancer at Kalakshetra this year."

This fellow Ravi had been here along with Cookie's other friends on weekends. Since the chap had a lot of hair on his head, I thought of him as Basket Hair. Of course, Cookie did not know that.

***

Bala appeared from the hall carrying a tray with a stainless steel tumbler of coffee and cardamom cream biscuits. "Are there any leftovers from the morning? That yellow noodle and chutney?" Cookie asked Bala. As always, he said little but turned back and walked away to return with what she had asked. His so called white dhoti, really a murky grayish color, had spots of brown and red at the back as if he had been menstruating and had forgotten to protect himself. Cookie's eyes widened and she turned and caught my eye. "The fellow has piles,—what do you call it in America, hemorrhoids?"

Bala brought Cookie her sweet lime juice and noodles and I reminded her, "If your friends are coming for dinner tonight, you should let him know. He needs to prepare." I told Bala that he needed to change his dhoti. He muttered to himself as he left. I turned to the task at hand. I picked up the folder from the windowsill and looked at the few photos Venkat had given me. He had promised to hand over the others later. The first one had the old, zigzag crack snake tablet from Periamalai under the big tree; then a dappled shot of the temple from across the road (I surmised it was taken from the tea stall as he smoked one of his innumerable cigarettes); and then a few shots of the navagraha, idols representing the nine planets before and after we had erected the pavilion in Mayapuram.

The Shiva Vishnu temple at Mayapuram was an old structure, built during the Chola period. The navagraha statues there were valuable for their unique sculpture style, and the department and I decided we did not want them getting damaged further from exposure to sunlight and heavy rain.

I jotted down a few points in my notebook before they flew out of my head.

Cookie sat next to me, eating and looking at the photographs.

"Finish your eating business and then I will tell you about these, " I told her as a single yellow sevai noodle fell into my lap.

I decided on the order of the photos for the second section of the book and wrote the captions. Cookie put down her empty plate on the tray and pulled her chair closer to me.

"See this photo of the navagraha? It shows the nine planets that appear in all important temples of South India. We Hindus have always been big fans of the cosmos, so it is natural that we found a way to represent the planets of the solar system. The planets assume the forms of gods and goddesses."

She peered closely and asked, "What's all that piled like little dots?"

"Offerings of sesame seeds or rice or any of nine grains that are made by devotees to ward off negative effects caused by position of the planets. The accompanying prayers are supposed to neutralize things. On Saturdays, the brass lamps are lit with sesame seeds for Shani, Saturn. He can be a troublemaker if you're not careful."

She smiled.

The next photograph was a close-up shot. "You see the sculptures, how they are placed carefully so that no two planets face each other? See how Surya, the sun, faces east?"

"So a lot of people go to the temple and pray to the planets?"

"Yes and no. Nothing is that simple in Hinduism. It is not as if they're praying directly to the fields of energies emitted by the heavenly bodies or anything like that. You see the idea has always been to make things specific, filtered down to take away some of the abstract that comes along with the pure concept of God. Eternal consciousness or Atman does not come to mind as easily as forms and shapes of gods. We are sensory beings after all. So the idea is filled out, given shape as it were."

I saw that Cookie only half listened to what I had been saying by the way she was tapping her right foot on the floor. She did that a lot. A part of her mind unconsciously practicing some dance step. She reminded me of myself at such times. I too was always partially thinking about the temples, while I talked to people about other things.

I decided I must give her my full attention so I touched her shoulder. She turned toward me, startled. "How is your dancing going? Why not show me what you have been learning recently—maybe a performance on the terrace next week one night? You will have an audience. I want to ask my dear friend Iyer to dine with us and I think Venkat will also be joining us. What do you say?"

Her eyes dilated and then she said, "I don't know if I'm ready but okay, I have to learn to perform in front of people. Okay, no time like the present I guess."

"Good, that is decided then."

"What if I don't feel like dressing up, is that okay?"

"That's all right, you always look fine the way you are."

"Really Thatha?"

"Of course, why should I lie?" She got up and asked me to look again closely.

"You don't think I am too fat here?" she asked, sliding her palms down her hips.

"Believe me Cookie, everything is in the right place in the right proportion. You don't want to look like everybody else? I thought all you

Americans were great individualists. Why not apply that principle in this department also?"

She smiled and said, "You're impossible, Thatha."

We were both silent for a while after that. It was the kind of silence that made you fully aware of where you were and what was going on. I could hear the drone of a music box, from the house beside us. One of the children from the extended family that owned the cashew estates in Kerala. A sudden fishy smell came and went like an animal pausing in front of the house before moving on. I was sure it was from the shacks at the back where cooking was done in the open at all odd times of the day and they cooked rotten stuff—dead fish, animals and birds and eggs of all sorts, making their bodies a kind of graveyard. From the south side of the garden came the sound of a man shushing an animal—Bala and that itinerant monkey, I guessed. That rascal was probably at it again—eating guavas or eyeing the banana bunch on the banana tree.

"I want to talk to you about something." It was Cookie. Her voice surprised me and brought me back to where I was.

"Did my mother tell you part of the reason I am here? Other than polishing my Bharath Natyam?"

She had caught me off guard with the question. I did not know how to respond. Should I plead ignorance or tell her the truth? What would be the best strategy? My niece Jaya had requested that I not talk to her about it. "Let her decide for herself," she said on the phone. "Distance will help her perspective. She'll come to her senses and grow up." I had not replied. In matters of the heart, I had learned from watching others, the less said the better. People really did not want your opinion because deep in their heart they thought you could not possibly feel what they were feeling. The depth and urgency of it. The pure fire of it. It was best to shut up and listen. This had been my motto all along and I thought I should follow it again this time.

"What do you think of arranged marriages?"

I was relieved. She had decided to take a more general route. "What is there for me to think about? It's been working for generations."

"Yeah, but that doesn't mean much. Indian women have been putting up with all sorts of things."

"Maybe in some cases, not all..."

She looked straight at me and our eyes locked. Her face was blazing fiercely with the beauty of youth. The eyes bright and big, the hair on her head inky black, skin shining with health and all those white-after-American-braces teeth, what was not to like?

"Why didn't you ever get married?" I was somewhat taken aback by her cheekiness but I was impressed by the straightforward approach.

"It's an old story and a long one. Maybe I will tell you sometime. The marrying impulse in me was not strong enough. I always had my work." She threw a skeptical look my way and sighed. "What is it you want to talk about?" I prodded her gently, hoping to set her mind at ease. I could tell she was anxious as her left eye began twitching. Her hands were moving nervously as well; she was twisting and untwisting a small corner of her kurta.

"Kumar, he's my fiancé, he wants us to set the wedding date, but I need more time." I thought it best to look out at the road, to give her the impression I was not too curious. I stared at Misty Glen, at Mr. And Mrs. Awesomes' house and their Radha Krishna statue.

"When we first met, I thought the way we felt would change as time went on. I thought feelings would multiply in breadth and depth and there would be this rapport. We'd be kindred spirits, soul-mates or something. At the end of our engagement, I was sure we'd feel differently. But things are the same, everything feels the same." She looked at me and then down again into her lap before whispering, "Everything feels so right and practical and boring." She was barely whispering towards the end.

Aha. The child wanted roller coasters and volcanic eruptions and firecrackers blooming in the sky. All that rubbish in Hollywood and Bollywood cinemas and gyrating private parts on MTV that she watched. The symptoms were universal, the disease rampant and the prognosis doubtful, I thought. In such cases, O great silent one, it was always a good idea to change the topic. Luckily, there was a fellow coming down the road, carrying a big basket on his head. I recognized him. "Hey, come here," I called out.

Soon we were eating warm charcoal toasted peanuts and puffed rice out of paper cones. Cookie was talking about Alarmel Valli and Yamini

Krishnamurthi, dancers she admired and loved. Finally she got up. "I'm going to practice in my room for a while," she said.

I turned to the pile of work on the window sill.

The sound of a man shouting, the voice approaching nearer made me close my notebook, get up and look out. Mr. Awesome from across the road was walking extremely fast from the entrance of his house towards the edge of his garden. He kept looking back nervously and that was when I heard the softer shriek of a female voice. Mrs. Awesome was after him. Mr. Awesome, I gathered, hid behind the Radha Krishna statue because he suddenly disappeared from sight.

Mrs. Awesome liked an audience; she waited for the neighbors to come out onto their terraces and balconies. A group of drivers and servants huddled near the gate, all pretending sudden thirst and crowding near the mud pot and the Ganesha shrine. The usual domestic drama that was played out in public for all the world to see every few months was unfolding again, I guessed.

Last time they fought, I found out, she had been grinding coconut and chilies for chutney when he declared breakfast was late. The coconut had been plucked too young; it would not grind easily she said and suggested he wait a few more minutes. Mr. Awesome said he would grab something from the hotel near the office where the idli, chutney and vada was always great. Mrs. Awesome got so angry that she chased him out of the kitchen in his full office costume, starched dhoti and shirt, towel over his shoulder etc. He had run out with his kudumi, the knot in his hair, undone and creeping down his back like the tail of a rat. I remember spotting him from the terrace while having my morning coffee. He was holding the ends of his dhoti in one hand and running like a madman.

Being a good neighbor, I went down to help and saw that Mrs. Awesome came after him, somewhat slowed down by the weight of the object in her hands, the stone canon shaped pestle of the mortar and pestle which she used to grind chutneys. There was also the length of her sari which she had not tucked into her waist and which I suspect hampered her normal, nimble speed. Just past the gate of their house, Mr. Awesome slipped on a patch of mossy ground and I heard a cry as he cut his lip. I went to help him and watched as Mrs. Awesome caught up with us and her eyes glinted like black diamonds and her mouth quivered in delight. How captivating the woman looked. Her breasts rose and fell, the way they do when properly endowed women get all worked up.

The neighbors and I soon found out what it was all about this time. He had come in late yesterday smelling of non-vegetarian rubbish he had eaten at the Cosmopolitan Club. Garlic and mutton on his breath, he dared to approach his wife. Loafing around, going to Cosmopolitan Club where he mingled with all castes of people! "I'm not a fool," she said, "I know that you have alcohol, rum or whatever it is called; what sort of man are you, what sort of example do you present to our sons?"

We strained our ears and heard nothing so I imagined Mr. Awesome was doing the usual, pleading with her to stop this public display; "Let's take it inside," he would say. He would explain to her that he had to do all that club thing in the name of business, public relations, mingling with clients and what not.

Based on what I heard in the past, this much I knew. Whatever he said in his own defense, Mrs. Awesome was not impressed. She complained about him leaving early in the morning while she was in her bath, before they had a chance to talk. Last night, there was no point in talking to a husband who was drunk and had a case of terrible breath. This was the first chance she had had to see and talk to him after the deed was done. "Remember that you are polluted now and cannot touch me," she yelled. "It is bad enough that we were both polluted by crossing the seas to America. Swami had made a single exception but this problem cannot keep recurring, she said. Even Swamis had their self respect to think about. Then came the dangerous part. She turned to all of us, her audience, and sought our support. As usual, all the other neighbors shut their doors and went inside.

Next thing she always did was cross the road and come to me. I had tried staying inside, not opening the door, but it did not help. In spite of her madness or hysteria or whatever it was, she knew I had a soft spot for her. Her beauty and volatile nature always charmed me and this was something she made the most of.

Mr. Awesome jumped into their white Fiat and drove off, shooing the servants and drivers near Ganesha. Sure enough, there Mrs. Awesome was, approaching my house, tucking in the end of her sari to her waist which said she meant business.

Cookie had joined me to see what all the noise and shouting was about. The story about America, her time in Chicago, was related again to me by Mrs. Awesome. I usually managed to placate her with a few distracting comments about this or that but this time I wanted Cookie to hear the story firsthand.

Mrs. Awesome's dark glinting eyes were shiny again. She told us how she and Mr. Awesome had gone to visit their daughter in the Chicago area. "Cheekago," she emphasized to Cookie, making sure the child understood.

"The time in America served my husband right," she said; "he had to learn a few things. They put food on the table in the middle and you have to help yourself," nodding her head approvingly of this strange American practice. "For the past thirty years," she continued, "I had bent over my husband sitting on a wooden plank, waited for him to sprinkle water on his banana leaf, then waited again as he dropped a little water to make a circle around the leaf so ants could not climb into his food. Then I would serve him his favorite foods and he would not utter a word of thanks just stick his palm out when he had had enough as if I was stupid or something, as if hand signals were all I deserved, as if I was deaf. Not a single kind word. I watched how American husbands in all the T.V. shows kiss their wives before leaving for work. I don't need a kiss, but a kind word is nice before you leave for the office. This way, I want to ask, do you want me to send tiffin with the driver or are you going to some wretched hotel to eat meat and biryani made by Muslim cooks so that you can turn towards me at night when sleeping and breathe your stinking breath?"

Cookie had covered her mouth with her palms and her eyes fluttered in surprise. In the garden, Nagu turned on the tap and pulled out the hose to take care of watering the plants and his wife, Paru, appeared with a broom to sweep the front of the house.

Mrs. Awesome shifted in her chair and twitched her diamond studded nose like a jeweled rabbit. "Every day of every year," she said, "I wake up when it is still dark, bathe and cook and serve him food with my hair still wet. Remember that before going into the kitchen, I have said my prayers to the goddess after gulping down the healing urine of the cow. All those years I menstruated, I was very happy to be in the room upstairs, the one with the huge pink bathtub which I climbed into pretending it was bed or easy chair. Those three days, sometimes four, depending on my flow, I got into the tub and read back issues of <u>Kalki</u>, <u>Ananda Vikatan</u> and <u>Reader's Digest</u>."

Cookie was having a hard time sitting still so she got up saying she would get us tea and biscuits. The child had caught on to our Indian hospitable ways quickly, I thought.

As suddenly as Mrs. Awesome had come, she got up and left without saying good-bye. Such was her usual exit. Cookie came by with a tray and tea pot and no Mrs. Awesome there in the chair where she had sat.

Five minutes later, Mr. Awesome parked his car in front of the house and came towards me. Following their custom, it was his turn now. "My wife has hysteria," he said to Cookie by way of introduction. He was a fan of American rock music and exchanged CD's with Cookie. Such music bamboozled me for the words made little sense to me.

He took out his betel leaf box and the elaborate ritual associated with making an edible packet of the leaf gave him something to do with his hands while he complained about his tempestuous wife. He smeared the leaves carefully with pink limestone and placed pieces of areca nut and a pinch of tobacco. Then he deftly tucked the leaf packet into his mouth. Now he would talk with his chin tilted slightly backwards as saliva increased and pooled in his mouth.

"She is a tigress in disguise," he confided. "She is goddess Durga riding the tiger at night."

Across the road, I saw that Mrs. Awesome had retreated into her quiet shell after her outburst. She waved incense sticks in front of the Ganesha shrine. This, I supposed, so he would remove any further obstacles in her way. These husband wife fights always seemed to give her added vim and vigor and her face glowed in radiance for days to come. Mr. Awesome, on the other hand, who got up to leave, managed to look crumpled and wilted like a green stalk toasted on an open flame.

Nagu was leaning against his bicycle reading a newspaper. Usman had finished washing the tires of the car with Surf like he did once a week. He came towards me and asked if he could use our ration card for sugar, rice, wheat and other provisions his family needed since we bought all these items from Maharajah store in Adyar. I told him to ask Bala for the card. "How many children do you have now?" I asked.

"Four saar. Three daughters and a son."

"Don't you think that is enough? You need to educate all of them and give them a good life."

"My wife would like to have one more son, Saar. I am telling her it is enough but she does not listen. "

"Hmm," I said, not believing one word of it. Too many of these fellows put the blame on the wife, on the mother, on the uncle, on anybody but themselves. The deciding instrument came attached to him and he acted as if he did not know that. But then Muslims were heavily sexed. Everybody knew that. They wanted to populate the world with their mutton eating children.

"What is that you're reading, Nagu?" I asked.

"Dinamani, Saar. The Tamil newspaper."

"What are they writing about today?"

"There may be a bandh, everything shut down in protest next Monday."

"The slightest hint of a problem and the answer is always a bandh. Close everything down, halt all business and the solution is at hand? When has this strategy worked? The only time was when the British were here. They used the divide and conquer tactic and now we Indians are doing the same amongst ourselves. It's a disgrace, that's what it is."

"It's just like the plot in the Kamlahasan movie, Saar."

I raised my hand as a signal for him to stop. "I'm not interested in all these things. Have you taken Paru to the doctor? Are you buying her vitamins? Making sure she eats properly?"

"Yes, Saar," he said in a sheepish tone as Paru joined him, turned to me and said the brass lamps in the puja room had been washed and dried, the string of flowers placed in the basket. "Ayah will be here soon," Nagu reminded me.

I nodded my head and they walked towards their home in the garage. Usman appeared from the side garden with the ration card and held a grimy looking cloth bag in one hand. He too mounted his bicycle and said goodbye.

"Ayah, you will live a hundred years," I said to her as I watched her enter the house from the road. "I am sitting here thinking of you, and you show up right away." She laughed in that cackling way of hers and came towards me asking if I was ready for my massage and bath.

In the bedroom, I was sitting on a stool and there was another smaller stool beside me on which Ayah had placed a cup of slightly warmed coconut oil. My spectacles were on the bedside table. I was wearing a loincloth. This was what my father wore when he took a bath near the well. Ayah was stronger and so much younger then.

I remember her lowering the brass kodam into the garden well and the creaking of the wheel as the vessel came up filled with water. Her body in those days was taut and firm, not an ounce of fat visible anywhere. I remember admiring the rope of muscle that rippled under the skin of her abdomen and ribcage like an undulating eel on the surface of her body.

Ayah lifted the vessel and poured the water on my father's head. He sat on the washing stone near the well. The expression on his face at that moment one was one of pure bliss, his eyes closed and body still, as if he was there but not really there, traveling somewhere else. There used to be a time when I could not help wondering if there had been a special relationship between my father and Ayah. Maybe, maybe not, I never found out.

Ayah was telling me about her older son, Siva, whose wife and daughters lived with her. The daughter-in-law was sickly and needed expensive medicines all the time. "Siva sent money and a letter which my granddaughter read to me. He says it is a hard life living there by that fetid beach. The work makes all the men sick, but they have to keep going. For the sake of feeding the family, one has to do many things." Ayah's voice turned gravelly talking about Siva, her first-born, Nagu's older brother. She worried that he was lonely, not eating properly. Siva worked as a ship breaker in Seshasamudram with hundreds of others who took apart contaminated foreign ships. Iron and steel scraps were sold by the new Indian owners.

"You know I got him that job in the hospital and the other one in the ceramics factory. Getting drunk and disappearing for days on end is not the way to hold onto anything," I said gently.

"That is his fate, that is what is written on his head," she said and poured oil on my scalp. Her fingers moved the skin on my head back and forth and side to side till I felt the warmth and pressure of her fingertips had burrowed into my head, kneading everything inside me as well. I immersed myself in this cradle rocking moment when the world and people in it were wiped out. Ayah moved her hands to my neck and shoulders and I opened my eyes.

"Ayah, I told you many times. Your son should get out of there. Am I not willing to give you what you need for medicine for your daughter-in-law? The children are coming here every month to collect money for school fees. Siva should come here and find a job. That place is dangerous."

"He has to do whatever it takes to support his family. What can an old woman like me do?" she asked.

It was frustrating to try and explain that her son was working in a toxic wasteland and endangering his health. "That place, Seshasamudram, it is terrible. The ships they take apart contain materials that can make healthy men sick. Do you understand what I am saying?"

"That may be so. But what are people like us to do? Who will look after us if the man of the house does not work?" I sighed loudly because talking to Ayah about such matters was like talking to a bloody tree. That useless son of hers had been given many chances by me and my friend Iyer until a year ago. He discarded every opportunity by showing up at the job site with red eyes and slurred speech and sometimes, disappearing completely. I breathed in and out deliberately trying to remind myself that this massage was meant to relax me. Ayah did not approve of my lectures and began talking about something else. She said she had begun collecting discarded plastic milk bags from roadside garbage bins and sold these for money. Sometimes she found cans and bottles too.

She squatted on the floor next to the stool. I looked at the loose skin on her chin and neck, the way it swung cow-like as she moved. I saw the shrunken breasts that she attempted to cover with her cotton sari. There was that benign face, that toothless mouth as it attempted to smile or speak, and it shocked me because I suddenly realized that she could die anytime, maybe even tomorrow. She looked as if she was ready. But I could not imagine Friday evenings without her touch. Her whole family was a part of my life and there were times I felt a lump in my throat when I saw my servant Nagu driving his bicycle to the post office in the mornings. I had managed to save one of her sons. That at least had been accomplished.

"My daughter-in-law Lakshmi's T.B. is a little better now. She washes sheets and irons them using the big coal iron. When the coughing fits come, she cannot lift the iron."

"And the children, do they go to school?"

"They go to school all right. They learn all sorts of things there. Impatience. Anger. City children are spoiled. I began working when I was eight."

I moved the stool to the bathroom where buckets of hot water stood ready. Ayah filled a mug full and poured it over my head. She had made sure that some of the coconut oil that she rubbed on my face seeped into my eyes. It drew out the heat in the body and made the system cool again. This I knew from years of experience, an oil bath being a grand South Indian tradition that made you slough off all tension from the body so you were made clean and whole and fresh again, ready to face the battles of the world. Such a bath invited the most refreshing sleep known to man. How to explain the beauty of it to one like you who has not been initiated into this? Or perhaps you have? O Silent one, why do you not say something once in a while? Who is this person I am talking to? Never mind, I talk to myself, self-conversations livened and clarified things in my mind.

Ayah poured mug after mug of hot water on my head till I was traveling within myself, watching myself shrink into a child beside my sister and brothers. We were children standing there in our underwear as Ayah took turns to spread the heated oil on our bodies. We complained and ran away saying we did not want to be touched by this dark woman who pressed so hard and tickled us sometimes. Then my mother would drop roasted rice into the oil and Ayah would spread this on our bodies, on our pudgy stomachs. We were too busy eating the grains to realize she had finished her job. There was nothing left to do but follow her obediently into the bathroom where she brought out split pea powder and used it in the place of soap. Then she used soapnut powder to wash our hair. The tips of our fingers wrinkled like raisins and our eyes turned red from the heat of the body that was drawn out. Soon we were yawning, our mouths open like MGM lions. How hungry the whole process made us. We would hurry into the kitchen after the bath to eat Amma's dosas with ghee and sugar.

***

One friend who was my true mentor, a man I admired for his honesty, insight and intellect, was Iyer. I liked him all the more for I felt he liked me as well, offering me advice and help as I needed. He saw me as a younger brother and we relied on each other through the years for support through the usual ups and downs of life. Iyer, real name Poochi Iyer, had a doctorate in Indian philosophy from Presidency College.

The Theosophical Society was a favorite place of ours, one of the few remaining green patches in the city. The large trees and silence of the grounds of the Theosophical Society lent an ideal environment for our conversations. The ground under the trees crunched as we walked. Our usual practice was to walk through part of the same path, back and forth, back and forth as we discussed many points of interest. We liked walking for it helped clear our heads.

I heard the car horn and realized he had arrived with car and driver.

Iyer was outside the car, looking natty in his cotton khaki pants and white bush shirt, holding his teak walking stick like an Indian Johnny Walker.

"Why are you outside? You could have waited for me inside the car like you always do." I said.

"Do you have a bottle of Scotch in your Godrej cupboard? I've been dreaming of a good size shot. I want to meet that famous grandniece of yours."

I promised him that I would invite him soon as we got into the car.

"How is she coping, Sathya? All this dirt and poverty must be quite a contrast from the life she is used to?"

"Cookie is enjoying the experience here. What about all the culture, the music and dance that goes back hundreds of years? That is easy to get used to, no?"

We both laughed.

"She has not told me anything negative so I'm assuming she likes it all right. Jaya, her mother, had written before the child arrived. There has been an engagement ceremony. The child is not yet sure about the match. This is her time for reflection. Mother and daughter felt it best that she maintain some distance from the situation."

"How old is she? Twenty-four? She has plenty of time."

"I have a suspicion something is going on with her. It might have something to do with that fellow Basket Hair she brought home with her friends last time. I sensed this thing between them. You know the signs: the acute self-consciousness, the mood swings."

"Ah," Iyer said as we pulled into the Theosophical society compound where we usually walked, away from the crowds.

"How is the temple work?" Iyer asked.

I sighed. "I 'm trying to do this last thing you know—the projects at Periamalai and Mayapuram. These consultant years are crucial, you understand that. They are not to be tapering but more urgent because of the limited time I have left. These villages are so close to where I grew up."

Iyer and I walked in silence for a few minutes. A mynah hopped to my left and a striped squirrel leaped and crossed our path.

"I want to restore and protect the snake tablets in Periamalai and the nine statues of the navagrahas in Mayapuram," I stressed.

"I hear what you say Sathya. You know of my devotion to Srirangam. I have helped them restore the doors of that temple with advice and donations."

"Sub-Optimal Subbudu, my young boss in the office, S.D. and Puncture, my assistants, others, they don't seem to feel so strongly this way."

Doc sighed and said, "Our generation understands these things. With youngsters, who knows?" He shook his head.

"Your support means a lot to me, you know that?"

Iyer nodded and wiped his spectacles with the edge of the cloth towel he wore over his left shoulder in typical South Indian fashion. "I will do what I can to help. It is a good idea to ultimately move the navagraha statues like the nagapratishtas to the museum. Do it step by step."

I smiled warmly at him.

"Am I right in saying you see this as the final feather in your cap?"

"Yes. You could say that."

"So what's the problem? You're getting what you want?"

Iyer watched my face carefully before he spoke again. "You cannot expect these people to understand what belongs in a museum based on antiquity. After all, this is India; old habits die hard."

I stared at him with knitted brows.

"What I mean to say, dear man, is the villager does not realize the necessity to preserve art for future generations. They only want to do what they have been doing before—pray to the same gods in the same temples."

"I was prepared for resistance, but it's still a shock. In Mayapuram, for example, we built the pavilion to shield the navagraha statues from the elements and human hands. The number of people touching those statues, some of the subtle carving was gone, smoothened out like a baby's bottom."

"One must not look for perfection in anything including love. Pity one does not know this when young," Iyer said, shaking his head. He pointed to the bench where we usually sat. Though we had been friends for a long time, he played the guru and I remained the pupil, although we didn't always agree. I had noticed that Iyer shifted mental gears fast and jumped from topic to topic without any logical link. I could not help wondering if perhaps there was a touch of senility creeping in; it would be perfectly understandable in a man of his age. After all, he was eighty five, ten years older than I was. Other times, the man was so incisive, his memory so sharp and his reasoning so acute, he took me by surprise. I suppose we both nursed a small amount of denial about the ravages of age and time. It was perfectly normal, was it not?

"What are we talking about?" I asked, hoping to bring him back to where we were before.

"What am I telling you that for? You know nothing of these things. I am saying that the search for perfection in anything is a waste of time. But it is useful in the sense it takes you to the next step."

"What is that?" I asked puzzled. He spoke in riddles that were not always easy to decipher.

"Restlessness eventually leads to a kind of rest when the mind is filled only with awareness. This is all one can hope for."

I was not sure I understood what he was trying to say, but I let him ramble on. Sometimes, during these periods of conversation, I would catch a glimpse of something, a view of wisdom that I knew instinctively was vital but I had no use for it at this stage of my life. Besides, I already had a calling; there was a job to be done and I was doing it. That's all I really cared about.

"The Mahabharata says lack of fulfillment is a common condition of man," Iyer said, turning to me.

"Then I am glad I don't have that problem," I said.

"You like cutting your nose to spite your face, don't you?" he murmured.

I was not sure I had heard him right. The words seemed terribly unfair. But Iyer had become an old man and I was bigger than that. One must show a little tolerance towards the slightly senile.

"You know, Sathya, I have always been aware of the great privilege I have been given. I have managed to live in a world of ideas when most people around me are struggling to survive. One hopes the opportunity has been used well. Modern people feel there is no place for Sanskrit and philosophy in their lives. But I wanted my students, both rich and poor, to know there were options to misery. The best ideas are all there in our old books, you understand?"

I nodded. What was left for me to say? We sat in companionable silence hearing the crickets begin to sing in the trees. The streetlights came on. It was time for us to go home.

During the drive home, Iyer wanted to know if I had learned to use computers and what was that thing they called e-mail? I told him I had no idea. "Cookie knows," I told him. "She has this thing they call a laptop." Her mother and her friends from America were always writing to her and she wrote back. We both marveled at the child's supple mind. Young people had a lot more fluid intelligence, we consoled ourselves.

"I want to meet her," Iyer reminded me again. "Remember to keep the bottle of Scotch and Remy Martin also ready for me. I look forward to visiting you soon."

I invited him over for dinner the following Friday.

Sitting in the terrace before dinner, I looked up at the sky and the clouds at dusk. Lights came on in the windows of houses around me, Misty Glen with Mr. Awesome and Mami, the large extended family from Kerala to the east, owners of cashew estates and then of course, there was Venkat's house to the west. I could hear a child practicing Carnatic music, the svaras, the notes stacked like she was running up and down the stairs—sa sa, ri ri, ga ga, ma ma, pa pa, dha dha, ni ni, sa sa.

The streetlights still looked buttery yellow because of lingering light from the sky. I could smell a cigarette being lit somewhere and I saw that Venkat was sitting in a cane chair on his terrace. He usually sat there when he took breaks from long sessions in the dark room, waiting for film to develop. He cleared his throat before he spoke. "The pictures I took in the village, the ones you do not have, I think they'll turn out fine." I was happy that he was pleased with his efforts. He remained relatively sober when he worked. This I knew from observation.

"How is your mother?" I asked. His mother was an invalid, an old woman who had been a powerful figure once. A freedom fighter in her twenties, she had belonged to the old Congress party and marched with crowds singing nationalist Bharatiyar songs. Now, a stroke had left her right side partially paralyzed and her speech was garbled, her mouth twisted to one side. Venkat had spent the last decade going from one international assignment to another. Last year, he decided he needed to spend time with his mother before she died and he wanted to work on the book, a personal project.

"The same," he said and shrugged. I squinted as I looked at him closely. He lived a hard life. All that work and drink and no woman watching over him, he must have been lonely in all those strange places he visited, watching chaos and conflict and being part of so much grief. The fact that I did not have a woman watching over me really did not matter. You see, men belonging to Venkat's age group were vulnerable to all sorts of problems. After all, in the west, with that fast paced lifestyle, when one is immersed in one's career, where is the time for anything else?

"I had a visitor today with an interesting proposition. A real estate developer. He wants to build flats. Seems your friend Iyer has sold his house and is renting it now for a year." I stared back at Venkat in surprise.

"I was with him this evening and he didn't say a word."

"Maybe the deal hasn't been finalized. These bloody developers, I don't believe anything they say," Venkat said. There were always rumors about owners of big houses selling the land to somebody who wanted to erect big buildings with several floors of flats. Many had done this in adjacent streets of our neighborhood, ruining its character. Since last year, a cloud of construction dust hovered permanently over our heads. "The French institution I told you about has sent a letter," he said. "They want to exhibit my Angkor pictures."

"That is good news, isn't it? We want people to see the work that has been done and how much more needs to be done."

"You think I should say yes?"

"Definitely," I said. "Those pictures were good. I remember shots you took of the Bayon, the restored apsaras, the bas relief of the churning of the ocean. And then there were those shots you had of the boulders clasped by roots. Am I right? That was a wonderful time, what a great project in Cambodia. Our time in Borabadur was also memorable, was it not?"

"I'm going in," Venkat said suddenly. I supposed something was waiting for him in the dark-room.

In the fading light, on the terrace upstairs, a few feet away from where I sat, a chameleon lay still in a crevice between an arrangement of rocks. My niece Jaya had designed a corner rock garden last time she was here from America. I could see the bulging eyes of the chameleon and the head outlined. The body and tail were a shiny reddish brown. The creature seemed stuck to the spot, not moving any body part. Do chameleons sleep this way I wondered?

Bala came upstairs to tell me dinner was ready. I had forgotten that Cookie was having three of her friends over, including Basket Hair. The energy of twenty-four year- olds; wide eyes, sensuality and emotion in the air -- chances are I would be exhausted by the end of the meal. I hated to admit it, but I was fickle when it came to dealing with youngsters. I liked watching groups of them from a distance but disliked being stuck amongst them. Unfair or not, I found their conversation tiresome most of the time. If I was in a happy mood, I empathized and managed to laugh kindly inside.

There was rice, baby onion sambhar, tomato rasam, papads, snake gourd curry with coconut, grated carrot salad with lime juice and mango chutney. To finish off the fine meal, there were gulab jamuns from the shop that I was not too fond of.

At the end of the meal, I shuddered as I watched Cookie drink the syrup like it was juice of some sort. She was always opening the fridge after meals asking, "Do you have any ice cream? What about chocolate? Is everything in this house healthy? Don't you ever eat any junk?" Bala and I were always surprised, looking back at her guiltily as if we had done something wrong.

Cookie and her friends went upstairs. I heard faint strains of music, laughter and shrill voices. All through the meal, I had watched that fellow Ravi with Sai Baba or Jimi Hendrix style (as Cookie called the saffron robed Swami) Basket Hair make eyes at her and slyly turn to me to see if I'd caught him doing it. It amazed me to think that generation after generation, it was the same game, no stamp of originality, what a waste of time the whole thing was after all. Conversing about movies, Basket Hair was telling the others about explicit sex in Indian cinema. The bugger wanted to shock an old fart like me. He turned to me and asked what I thought. "That's not for me, " I said. "All that up and down piston engineering business; I'm a humanities chap after all."

Greed and indulgence always leads to trouble. This I knew and yet I fell into the trap from time to time. Too much onion sambhar and snake gourd curry my body said as I belched and tasted what I had consumed earlier. I decided to walk the problem off and went into the garden. Standing under the portico, I looked up at the sky and the stars.

It was not very trendy or fashionable to admit that one was conventional in some ways after all, that one still thought the world had not changed that much. For example, the sounds of thunder and flashes of lightning remained the same. Nature inspired awe and was always seen as God's calling card. If temples spoke to us through a language of symbols, nature too had a parallel—wind, trees, the ocean, mountains. Not to forget things underground—life under the ocean and more that the eye cannot see. So many forms changing and mutating, so many levels of life. I pictured these spreading out like ripples over earth, planets and the stars.

How vast was the universe and how small man.

At the installation ceremonies in Mayapuram, I had closed my eyes in reverie. I was overcome by the beauty of the shiny stone statues that represented the nine planets. My assistants, S.D. and Puncture were there. Priest IQ Senior's voice was clear and strong as he chanted the mantras in praise of the nine planets. I replayed the mantras in my head as I stared that night at the sky. Brahma, Vishnu, and Shiva contemplate the sun, moon, mars, mercury, jupiter, venus, saturn, north node and south node or dragon head and dragon tail, what we Indians called rahu and ketu. May all planets be peaceful, I said to myself. I saw the statues that stood for the nine planets covered in bright silks and closed my eyes at the beauty the image represented to me.

I had carried a big vessel of rice payasam made by Bala to be distributed to all those who attended the special puja at the temple. My thoughts went to the great minds of our Hindu philosophers, also artists, sculptors and craftsmen before us who chose this way to celebrate nature and show their love of the cosmos.

A wave of sourness in my chest reminded me that overindulgence during dinner was the reason I had come out into the garden. I began walking around the perimeter of the house. I was in the front garden where the chikoo and mango trees were. Birds flapped their wings before settling down for the night. I walked past the side of the house where jasmine flowers on the creeper glowed like white stars and perfumed the air.

Then I was in the backyard where coconut fronds swished against a sudden breeze. A radio was playing in one of the shacks behind our house. The woman in the A. R. Rahman song wailed about the usual rubbish, her lost love or some such. There was the smell of smoke and I recalled that the men in the slums huddled around a bonfire some nights, drinking toddy and smoking beedis. Adjacent to Venkat's house, I stopped near the bore well and checked that everything electrical had been turned off. A lizard chirped continuously till I moved again.

I heard the faint but unmistakable sound of the phone in the hall ringing twice. Who could possibly be calling this time of night? I rushed inside.

The line crackled. "Hello, hello," I kept shouting into the phone as if the decibel level of my voice would work some magic. As a citizen of this great city, all I could say was that every single time there was a real crisis in our lives, the phone lines gave trouble. We were turned into quivering putty. Same thing when the summer was at its peak, there was always a power cut. But there was suddenly a voice on the line. "Saar, Sathya, Saar," someone cried. He mentioned the word navagraha and temple. It was the priest, IQ Senior from the Shiva Vishnu temple at Mayapuram. A choked sob and then the words, "I cannot believe people here would do this..." Then the line went dead.

My anger at the poor connection was soon replaced by a sense of something else, a kind of dread at what the priest's voice had left said and unsaid. It was the same feeling I had as a boy when we played a game by piling seven stones that had to be hit by a ball and one team was chased by another till the stones were piled up to be hit again. After I toppled the stones, I ran and ran with my heart thudding, the soles of my feet hurting because of the occasional pebble I stepped on. But I knew the game had to go on so I kept running though a member of the other team was right behind me. I heard him breathing hard behind me and I knew he just had to reach out and touch me with his fingers so I ran and ran with my throat parched and the wind beating against my face.

My mind behaved like a tape recorder and replayed the sounds in the garden from before -- birds settling down for the night, the chirping of lizards, the smell of a bonfire in the air, a woman wailing for her lover over the radio. This was soon replaced by the voice of priest IQ Senior panicking during the telephone call.

***

Venkat drove the car to the bus station where S.D. and Puncture had been summoned. In the darkness of my mood, the sights and sounds outside the car were strange. I barely recognized the fruit carts with hurricane lamps hanging on the sides. The ringing of bicycle bells and honking of horns that seemed benign in the daylight now turned into cacophony and ordinary men and women looked like menacing creatures I was seeing for the first time.

At the temple, the pavilion doors stood ajar. There was a crowd of people, subdued and talking in whispers as if they did not want to disturb the sleep of the idols. As we got down from the car and proceeded to the pavilion, I saw that the big lock that usually hung from these doors was lying broken on the floor. Somebody had had the sense to bring a hurricane lantern and its light showed the idols, cracked, broken, some reduced to bits and pieces, Saturn with his head cut off, Ketu with no body, Venus with no arms. The Shiva Vishnu temple priest I.Q. Senior was standing off to one side, tears pouring from his eyes. Venkat was the only man moving in the dark, the flash of his camera like a bit of moon that shone on and off as he clicked and clicked. S.D. and Puncture too were subdued, their notebooks out, jotting things down. They were talking softly to the group under the neem tree, a couple of yards away from the pavilion.

I recalled how the navagraha idols had appeared during the recent puja after installation of the pavilion. They were shiny and black and decorated with silks. The pillars of the new pavilion were wound with garlands of mango leaves and marigolds; it had all been so beautiful. Sesame seeds had been sprinkled as mantras were said to seek the favor of the gods, of nature, the help of the cosmos. Now everything had been reduced to rubble.

I wanted to get away from here, something I had never felt in a temple, I wanted to be sitting in the easy chair at home where there was order, not chaos. I wanted to be somewhere else, in another country, watching the horseshoe Niagara Falls in Canada or admiring the color of the stones of the Grand Canyon. I wanted to be part of a country like America where things were orderly at least on the surface, never mind that they were so desperate for national treasures that they went begging to other countries for it; at least they knew the value of old things. I did not want to be here, in this country of chaos, where we had so much and tossed it out in disrespect, sulfur fumes yellowing the marble of the Taj Mahal, feces and urine and charred flesh filling the Ganges, so many snot faced big bellied children suffering from malnutrition, beggars whose eyes I could not meet for a sparrow boasted more dignity, corrupt men and women in power whose hearts were dark and slimy and lined with grit.

A voice gripped my arm in the dark so suddenly that I was too startled to react. The man whispered close to my face, "Saar, your trouble has not ended here. It has just begun." By the time I thought of asking him to announce himself, the man had let go of my arm and moved away. In the dark, in the confusion of the moment, I could not think of one distinguishing feature that would help me recognize the man if I saw the chap again.

I felt a wave of nausea spread from my belly to my mouth. It was not a good idea for me to remain here, I knew, because I felt the urge to strike out, to smash his face the way these statues had been destroyed. S.D. and Puncture would make the report and do the needful. I was no use to anyone here. I was no use to myself in this sorry state.

As I walked away from there, O great silent one, it occurred to me that it was not death that one was afraid of but life, the endless repetition of days, one leading into the other, the moments piling up, stacked sky high like toy blocks, all precariously balanced. One was never sure what slight vibration in the air would make it topple, rendering the finely wrought balance useless, making us start all over.

Chapter Four
Lotus of the Heart

My day started with a real estate developer, an oily sounding, stammering Naidu Kerala chap calling and saying he knew my friend Iyer. "So?" I asked, "What do you want me to do about that?"

"No, Saar. I am only saying that you can be sure of my credentials and good intention. I am knowing your friends and neighbors after all. You can ask any of them about me."

"And what do you want me to ask? Please, I'm getting ready to go out, stepping out of the house any minute now. Let's not play games."

"It's not like that, Saar. I am only wanting you to know that your neighbors on Koil street sold their land to me before apartment building was built. You know, Royal Gardens."

"Yes, I know the place and no, I am personally not interested in selling my property. It is a family ancestral home and I am not dead yet. I have to go now."

There was a film of perspiration on my face and my palms had gone cold from a wave of something, a sudden feeling in the pit of my stomach as if I had descended suddenly from the top of the merry go round to the bottom. Vulgarian wheeler-dealer. Do these people think everybody is only interested in money; nobody has any feeling for continuity, respect for family tradition? Chee, chee. I prayed to Ganesha to sweep the rising anger out of my head.

I made use of sick leave to stay home for the day because I needed time to compose myself after the problems in Mayapuram and Periamalai though I had only three working days left before my holiday in the hill stations. A holiday made it easier to sharpen perspective through reflection and goofing off, both essential to ongoing enthusiasm.

When it came to writing, (my plan was to work on the "Temples" book that day) I usually resorted to the following to produce the best results. I cleaned the table where I worked, dusted the lamp and filled my pens with Quink brand Royal Blue ink. I brushed my teeth twice so I would not be writing with a case of bad breath. I bathed and combed my east and west wings of hair and wore freshly ironed cotton clothes that gave me lots of room since I always had the urge to scratch in hard to reach places when I sat down. Then I had to urinate because I drank a couple of glasses of water. One did not want to think with a dehydrated body resembling a prune or some such thing. Then I had to cajole my rascal mind by treating it like a child. It was early in the morning after a night of rest they why this bad behavior, I asked it, you good for nothing rascal? Then I remembered that scolding this swine never got me anywhere. So I said okay okay, let's go out for a walk, indulge in a little chat, stare at the sky, some mindless rubbish or the other and voila! as the French said, the wheels began to creak upstairs, lubrication in the joints was applied. Come, I told this mind of mine, let's go outside and pretend to play, then we can come back inside and pretend to do some work.

Outside, I saw that the sky was quite blue and the clouds cumulus, like cotton balls scattered here and there. Good day to take in some scenery; walk up and down Koil Street. I shut the gate and glanced back at the house. The oleander bushes on either side of the gate were in bloom, clusters of white and pink flowers shining in the sun.

Nagu had hosed the pillar with the marble slab that had the name of the house embedded on it. "Hridaya Kamalam," it said in an old fashioned loopy calligraphic type. The Sanskrit words meant "Lotus of the heart." The name for the house had been chosen by my grandfather, my mother's father, one of the first bankers in this city. The color of the words on the slab was charcoal, a grayish black. Looking at it still gave me a slight thrill. It was as if I was reading it for the first time.

Memories passed through my head as I stared at the pillar: the voice of an aunt, an uncle's gesture, the face of my grandfather, a tune sung by my mother, my father laughing with his head thrown back. The light gray veins visible here and there in the translucent stone resembled someone warm and familiar. It was as if the thing pulsated and came to life.

I continued walking, past Rajan's house which belonged to the Malayali family that owned the cashew plantations in Kottayam and had all those musically inclined female children and grandchildren who practiced singing diligently. Next to this house was the Chettiar family house that now stood sad and empty. It was a huge Chettinad style house with gleaming wooden pillars that had pitted holes like pockmarks. There was a shabby air about the house since it had been neglected for the past two years. The sole heir had left with wife and offspring for Edmonton, Alberta, that awfully frigid place in Canada. Like everybody else in Madras, the owner was scared to rent out the house because one heard stories of terrible tenants. They refused to budge after a couple of years, claiming all sorts of non-existent rights. People were crippled by fear because these rogue tenants threatened landlords with goondas, undesirable muscle men who could beat old fashioned vegetarians into pulp.

The fact that the Chettiar house was empty and their son lived in "America" was common knowledge to all on the street. Canada, England, Australia—everything was America to most people, geography was ultimately of minor importance. I personally did not understand how people gave up their natural home and chose to become immigrants in some cold country. The desire to travel, I understood that, for curiosity and adventure were natural human qualities. But changing passports and following foreign etiquette, all those superficial ways, an upside down life, that was something I could not accept. For example, over there they cannot have farting and belching in public but divorcing and kissing were quite all right. The English turned up their noses saying your country is dirty but when I went there, I held my nose in their subway train tube. All that perfume masking body odor because they were allergic to water. One English family equaled one tubful of water a week. What nonsense idea of cleanliness is that?

**

Walking past the Chettiar house, the smell from the rubbish dump in the corner was strong. I grabbed a corner of my cotton towel slung over my shoulder and covered my nostrils. There were crows, a calf and a cow and a couple of stray dogs competing for banana leaves and god knows what else that had been tossed over all sorts of other rotting stuff. This was what I disliked about our people. They swept their houses twice a day and dumped their trash over the compound fence. There were times I had seen dead rats, even bandicoots lying there along with bloody sanitary napkins.

I did not want to bring out my breakfast so I rushed into the small park adjacent to the U shaped nursing home that joined both sides of Koil street. Mala Nursing Home was a maternity hospital so it was common to see ayahs huddled in the garden while small children squealed and played on the swings, see-saw and slide. Drivers, some in fancy imported cars, gathered and listened to music from the ubiquitous two-in-one, cassette player and transistor. I spotted a lone man doing exercises beside a statue of virgin mother Mary and her smiling child. The doctors and administration in the hospital were a liberal lot so they made sure they catered to all groups—hence the Christian statue in the garden, inside, colorful photographs of Krishna, Guru Nanak and Buddha. I heard there were sayings from the Koran painted on the walls.

"Namaskaram, Saar," the khaki clad security guard said as I approached the corner mansion on the other side of the street. This huge edifice had been built a few years ago after the original inhabitants had sold adjacent bits of land. A couple of times a year, a saffron robed Swami glided in here sitting in a Mercedes-Benz with his entourage of cronies. The gates had grillwork with a surreal touch—a huge eye in the middle. Why a man of the cloth needed such fancy accommodation or such luxurious transportation was beyond me. Most of these characters were frauds making gullible fools part with their money. When the man of the cloth and his gang left, the house lay still and silent like some sleeping giant. Same as the Chettiar house across from it. One owner was freezing his behind in Edmonton, Alberta; the other was busy collecting loot before fleeing to some hill station spot.

The tea stall on Koil Street always did brisk business. The flame of the forest trees in Swami's garden provided colorful shade for customers as they sat on the two or three metal tables wolfing down tiffin. Today, it was onion bhajji, and green chutney along with idlis. One of the servers stood in the corner pouring frothy coffee and tea into glass tumblers. The smokers stood a few feet away, leaning against their bicycles. The fiery red petals from the flame of the forest trees showered the place whenever the wind picked up.

The Aavin milk booth had lines of servants gathered here to collect milk packets for their households morning and evening. The men had large plastic pails tied with rope to the back of their bicycles. These pails were filled with packets for a whole apartment building or a street of houses. I observed the interplay between the men and women here – the sidelong glances, the whispers and giggles. The same game went on and on. First in my house with my niece and Basket Hair, then out here on the road.

I walked past two more houses to the apartments of Royal Gardens. This large lot used to hold three houses along with many trees. These had now been felled. The old bungalows were flattened and box-like flats had risen in their place. There was nothing royal or garden-like about the place. It was all concrete and cement and not a single leaf in sight unless you counted the lined pots of Croton under the edge of the parking lot where children played cricket and hopscotch.

I approached the shrine to the side of the garage. The lingam stood the way it always had, slanted slightly to one side and charcoal black. This shrine was one of three on our Koil street and the most popular. The other two were the Ganesha shrine in front of Misty Glen and the Bhagavati shrine at the back of my neighbor Rajan's house. In the past, we children used to refer to the lingam here as the leaning tower of Pisa but it was not really an apt name, for the stone was too short and squat.

The tiny tailor's shop on the edge of our street faced Fourth Main Road. It was a box-like structure that had the tailor, a fellow always clad in a colorful sarong working the single Singer sewing machine. Behind him and the machine, stuffed into two shelves, were cotton sari blouses and petticoats he had sewn, folded in piles and ready to be picked up by clients. The sarong wearing fellow had a strikingly good looking young wife. She worked as a full time nurse for Venkat's mother.

I opened the gate to the house and behind me was this fut fut noise of a moped. It was Cookie and Basket Hair. She unclasped her hands

71

circled around his waist and adjusted the shoulder straps of her American backpack as she got off. She was wearing a cotton salwar kameez with a pumpkin colored dupatta scarf tied around her waist. "Hi," Basket Hair said to me, waved to Cookie and sped off.

"What happened, you're back?" I asked.

She was blabbering in reply, something about class being cancelled; I did not really listen carefully. The only thing I noticed was that lightning vein running zigzag vertically across her forehead. It throbbed as she spoke. In the past, I noticed this always happened whenever the child was excited.

I recalled the way her hands circled the boy's waist and the way her chin rested on his shoulders when they were on the moped together. It might be time to mention something to Jaya next time she called from Houston. I was too old to be a guardian. This sort of job involved a lot of responsibility and I was not sure I was up to the task at hand. Then I remembered Jaya telling me during the first call that any daily decision her daughter made was fine; I was not to interfere in such things. Jaya assured me Cookie was mature that way; she knew how to make the right friends. Who was I to argue with a confident mother?

***

Cookie and I were in the front verandah.

"Oh, you promised to tell me about the Devi shrine in our neighbor's garden," she reminded me.

"The idol had belonged to a British fellow who had handed it over to Rajan's great grandfather, the new owner of the plantation, before leaving India. The British chap was called E. N. Tully. Everybody called him E.N.T. He said he and the goddess had an agreement. She would remain in India. Some people said the fellow had stripped the idol of the solitary diamond nose stud."

I stopped the narrative to sip my coffee. "This was of course perfectly in keeping with English tradition. They plundered their colonies of art, treasures and jewels before handing over their gifts of bureaucracy and messy multi-party system in return."

"You're right," she enthused. "The Kohinoor diamond, the peacock throne, god knows what else...all of it is now part of the crown jewels. My husband and I enjoy it awfully..." she said, imitating the Queen of England. It was my turn to nod in agreement. I told her she caught on fast, considering she was American.

I cleared my throat and carried on with the story.

E.N.T. was working late one night in his bungalow when a storm broke out. The rain was deafening and there was the sound of a bang and a thud every few minutes, evidence of a neighboring roof or hut wall collapsing and getting washed away in the swirling flood. He looked out the window and saw figures moving and shouting to one another, carrying hurricane lamps.

The front door of his house creaked and suddenly there stood a young girl, tugging at this hand as he threw questions at her, making impatient clucking noises if he lagged behind. He thought she belonged to one of the workers' families, and perhaps a group of them were in trouble, their fragile mud huts washed away or some such thing. He thought of the unstoppable power of nature, its fury unleashed on tarpaulin tents and bamboo poles snapping in the force of the wind. He himself had always felt a surge of impatience at how passive poor people had to be, accepting all that was dealt to them in the name of Indian monsoon season.

Past the enormous garden of the bungalow, palm fronds swishing like windmills in the wind, they were heading towards the temple. Behind him, E.N.T. heard a terrible crash and saw that a portion of the roof on his house had collapsed the very place above his room, his desk. The young girl who had brought him to safety flashed him a stunning smile. Then she was next to him no more. She vanished into the Bhagavati temple as he shouted at her to stop.

Cookie was resting her chin on her hands, her long and slender fingers cupping the sides of her face, reaching almost to the droop of her eyebrows. "Then what happened?" she urged me on.

He rang the temple bell non-stop till the priest and surrounding families rushed to the scene. Hearing his story, the elderly priest wept without shame. "I know where your young girl is," he said to E.N.T. "Tell me if I am right."

The priest went to the inner shrine, the sanctum sanctorum, and performed arati, moving a brass lamp with many wicks all over the form of the deity. Bhagavati's jewels glinted in the light and every crease and fold on her long skirt and sari shone from moisture as if she had just returned from being out in the storm. "It's her," E.N.T. cried; "I've found the girl who saved my life."

The priest sobbed loudly, wailing at the injustice of it all. How many years he had served the goddess and she never bothered to present herself before him all this time. But this Englishman, this meat eating scoundrel was deemed a worthy devotee? Oh Mother! He wailed.

E.N.T. requested a local craftsman to make a copy of the idol and had it affixed with imitation jewels. This he placed in the drawing room in front of the chair where he sat in the evenings practicing silence and meditation while Indians were yakking in the temples.

"The idol at Rajan's is a copy of the one at the temple," I added.

"The rumors about E.N.T. stealing jewels etc. none of that is true?" Cookie asked.

"No. The real idol is still at the Shakti temple, the way it always was... You know our people, how they love to yak," I said.

"And go yodley yodley," she said. We both laughed.

"Is the copy as powerful as the original?"

"It is prayer, our godliness from within that infuses the idol, Cookie. The stone itself is nothing, nothing at all." Cookie and I were silent for a while. Then I saw that she was tapping her foot, her mind traveling elsewhere.

"Have to go wash my hair," she said.

I continued to think of the man, E.N.T., sitting day after day in front of the idol. I remembered reading in the scriptures that he who had disciplined himself to such an extent that the external world of stimuli cannot create in him even a ripple of reaction, he alone knew what peace was. Not the other one, the desirer of desires. Narayana, Krishna, Mahadeva, I prayed, make me unlike the desirer. Let me be the still one. Then I laughed at myself. How we fooled ourselves. The wishful prayer itself was a desire, no doubt about that.

The front gate creaked open and Venkat walked in. He was still in his sarong, a green batik one with a colorful border and an American T-shirt that said Las Vegas in the front. His salt and pepper hair looked uncombed but he seemed rested and relaxed. I was glad to note that the usual packet of Rothman's and lighter was missing in his hands. I asked Bala to bring Venkat a cup of good filter decoction coffee. "Can you make it all frothy like they do in restaurants? I love it like that," Venkat told him. Bala grumbled and said this was no hotel. It took very little to rattle sensitive Mr. Bala.

Venkat had important news for me. He had received a call from S.D. and Puncture who had spent the day taking measurements for new idols at the Mayapuram temple. Things had gone fine and the installation ceremonies would be held in two weeks' time marked by a big puja. The priest had extended an invitation. S.D. and Puncture tried to call and inform me directly but my phone was out of order; it gave the engaged signal. "They said to tell you they may drop by later," Venkat said. "They knew you would be eager to hear all the details of how things went," he added.

I nodded yes.

"By the way, Naidu called me. You know, the developer. He is interested in both our lands. Combined together, it will give him enough room for a double block of apartments and parking garage. He even has a name for the project. "Windy Manor." He said it would show buyers how sea breeze helped make the location more desirable. This was Madras after all and wind flowing through the rooms made a saleable point. Venkat looked at me with a wicked gleam in his eyes. "Oh yes, he hoped I could talk some sense into the old man."

"That rascal," I began.

"Hold it, I'm only teasing, Sathya," he said.

"That oily idiot. If he calls here again, I plan to give him a piece of my mind."

"And where will that get you?" Venkat asked. "Look around you. The city is changing. You've noticed the houses coming down on the streets near by. Do you want to be trapped in between tall structures with hundreds of people looking down at you? You will lose all privacy. With mother so ill, who knows how long.....?" Venkat beseeched me with his face. "I cannot live here permanently, you know that. I have to go where the work is."

So. The fellow was trying to tell me he was considering the offer. I knew the rest. If I went along, the numbers would be fatter; the negotiations would be more in our favor. Last time I broached the subject of the house with Jaya in America and my sisters-in-law in Bombay, they had said they were happy with status quo. Where was the hurry after all? The house was appreciating nicely; what was the big rush? Jaya did not really understand the state of affairs in India. Nephews and sisters-in-law in Bombay were more practical and attuned to things, and they felt it was better to wait till the best offer came along.

"Let us talk about it another time; I have to consult everybody in the family unlike you, " I told Venkat.

Cookie walked in with a towel wrapped around her hair. She and Venkat went to talk to Paru and Nagu who were working in the garden. Paru was sweeping the entrance for the second time that day. She would draw another kolam before the evening prayers. I noticed the swelling in her stomach had become more prominent now. Bala came with coffee and a plate of fresh banana chips. Then he muttered something about monkey trouble and left. Cookie invited Nagu and Paru to come for her dance performance that night. Nagu blocked the end of the hose with his fingers to spray water onto bushes and flowering plants. I breathed in the heady smell of moisture seeping into earth.

Usman was washing the car. He took a cloth from a bucket of soapy water and began wiping the windshield.

"Saar, when you, S.D. Saar, and Puncture Saar, were working on the pavilion for the statues in the temple in Mayapuram, I had the chance to spend a lot of time with the Periamalai locals at lunchtime. That shop owner is known to my wife's family."

"You mean Yusef Ali of Mogul Stores, the one who gives goddess Saraswati calendars to Hindus? I asked.

"Yes, Saar. My in-laws remember his family from childhood. The family is known for stirring up things. They are not liberal minded like city people, Saar."

Usman was a bit of a naive chap, I thought, believing in the goodness of one group over others. I asked him what he had heard in the villages.

After all, he had spent the whole day interacting with people in Periamalai and Mayapuram while S.D., Puncture and I tried to get our work done.

"The villagers in both places complained about the Brahmin priest, I.Q. Senior. After the cyclone last year, they said the children were treated badly, Saar."

"You mean the children who go to school on the Mayapuram temple premises?"

"Yes, Saar." After the winds and rain brought some of the walls and the roof of the village school down, they moved the students to the temple. This was supposed to be a temporary arrangement but the government took a year to give them enough money to repair the school again. Usman was using soap water to wash the front tires now. "The men at the village tea stall told me when we were eating lunch that the priest would not let the non-Brahmin students sit with the others. Because the classes were held inside the temple grounds, the priest said there was a problem with pollution."

"So what happened?"

"They had to sit on the side of the road under the tamarind tree. Lorries and cycles and people were moving through the road, raising dust and making noise and the children had to strain to hear what was being taught."

"Did nobody say anything? Object?" I asked watching Usman pour the last of the water from the bucket on the back tires.

"The priest said it is there in the holy book. What Manu says in the holy books is law. "

"That Manu was a troublemaker all right. But the priest should know not to take such things literally. Everybody, Muslims, Hindus and Christians, we must realize that the time has come not to take the holy books literally. They were written in different times after all. That nincompoop Manu said all sorts of things that deserve no attention."

"Yes, Saar."

I had not observed that Cookie leaned against the door frame between the hall and the verandah sipping a glass of sweet lime juice.

"So what do you think of all this Cookie? Did you understand what we were saying?"

"Of course," she said, offended. "I understand everything perfectly in Tamil. It's just that I can't speak as well myself. Those priests at many of the temples I've seen, they look like lecherous men to me. Have you seen how they look at women? I don't know, Thatha, the whole thing gets to me sometimes. All this giving out of receipts for puja like some commercial business. It's not my idea of simplicity, equality. In the big temples, if you have influence and know how to pull a few strings, you get to the front of the long line."

I kept quiet. What was there to say? The child was right. Usman told her it was that way in the mosque as well.

"Organized religions bore me," she said. "You know what Venkat says about temple priests?" she asked walking towards me and sitting down next to me. I could tell from the expression on her face it was something irreverent. Typical of the atheist Venkat was. "He says they need support bras because their breasts droop from all the ghee they drink and the rich food they eat. He says anytime he sees one flying around town on a moped with their dhotis flapping like sails in the wind and their oily, black topknot kudumis flying, he is tempted to take a photograph and title it Hinduman like Spiderman or Superman."

Ayah opened the gate and smiled her toothless smile. That was when I remembered having sent for her asking for a half massage. I got up and she followed me into my room. A half massage meant she only rubbed oil on my head and neck. Bala handed her the stainless steel cup of warmed oil. Ayah took it from him and made me sit on the stool in the bathroom. My eyes were slits as she came near, her wrinkled pouches of breasts swaying slightly as she increased the pressure of her fingers on my scalp. The scent of her was salty, and her sari rubbed the tip of my nose.

Ayah began telling me again about her older son Siva, the shipbreaker. She said her son and the others had acquired an idol of Lakshmi and installed it in a make-shift temple they had built for themselves. "You have a knot here," Ahah said and proceeded to iron out the vein with the pressure of her thumb. "I pray everyday that Lakshmi, the divine mother, may she look after all those men who are working there without their mothers, sisters, wives. They need some tenderness in their lives."

When she finished, I rang the bell on my desk for Bala to come and pay her. When Bala did not come, I went to the kitchen. Bala was still in the side garden yelling at his monkey. "I don't care how long it takes me, I'm going to get you," he said to the animal sitting on the guava tree. The animal bared its teeth and Bala waved a bamboo pole in its direction. I told him even government offices in New Delhi had this problem according to the papers. They said monkeys had threatened government employees and shredded important documents. Bala gave me a look that said so what? I am more capable than our government. "The monkey might bring its friends here Bala. Do you want to be faced with groups of them, big fellows with pink buttocks sitting in our tree and flashing their teeth?"

Bala muttered under his breath and put away the pole. I saw a cluster of rust colored spots on his dhoti near his backside. I thought it best to not mention anything considering his bad mood.

***

Upstairs of the house used to be a dispensary when father was alive. I remember the compounder who walked with a limp, filling tiny bottles with sugary medicine. My father was a homeopathic doctor, and people came to him in droves. He and Iyer's father were childhood friends, having grown up together in the same village. Iyer's father had a roaring business in town, Durga Silk House, where middle class families went to get saris, dhotis and such. Whenever there was a wedding or special festival, Iyer's father sent over parcels of saris to us tied and protected with gauzy cotton towels. My grandmother, aunts and mother and cousins chose the saris they wanted and sent the rest back. All through my childhood, I don't remember them going to shops. The best selection from Durga Silk House was sent home to us.

I peeked into Cookie's old bedroom. She had moved into the one next door because of a problem with wasps in this one. A pair of wasps had built a tiny ridged and domed nest on top of the window frame in a corner. She was quite agitated when she first noticed the insects and came to me asking did I have a spray or something she could use to kill them.

"They have to live too. You are like a giant to them and they are scared of you. Besides, this is India, not your America. The only thing we spray in this house is water on the plants."

"Never mind, forget it," she had said at the time, shaking her head and moving her things to the room next door where the wasps never went for some reason. "Spray or no spray, I'm killing roaches if I see them," she threatened.

"You can use boric powder; I've no problem with that," I assured her.

From where I stood, Venkat's bedroom across was clearly visible from here. There were no curtains or blinds and he had flung the windows open. The palm fronds of the coconut tree that partially blocked the view swished and sighed in the wind. Their sweeping movement parted the view for me. I saw Venkat and the beauteous woman, the tailor's wife. I had not meant to pry but I stood and stared like an inquisitive old man.

Venkat had his back to me. He sat on the edge of his bed and his head was buried in her chest. Her face had this expression that was a combination of smirk and delicious contempt. She broke away from him as I stood there and watched. Before she left the room she turned towards Venkat again and adjusted what I presumed to be the hooks on her sari blouse that had come undone. She ran her fingers through the top of her head to pat down stray hair. Venkat did not move at all; he sat there on the edge of the bed.

Outside on the terrace, I checked the crevice between the small rocks in the corner garden and the chameleon was there, his globular eyes bulging in every direction as usual. How agile and adaptable they appeared on branches and bushes in the garden, darting from place to place. How awkward they appeared squatting on the ground.

***

Downstairs, Bala informed me he was leaving and that everything was ready for the dinner party that night.

I wanted to surprise Cookie and pulled out her present to me, an American T-shirt. All these months and I had still not worn it. It was soft and butter colored with a penguin embroidered near the pocket. I decided to be thorough and go all the way in my grooming for the evening. I carefully trimmed those annoying little bunches of hair that grew like grass on my ears and inside my nostrils. I spread a layer of Mysore sandalwood talc on my face. Then came the tufts of hair on my head that grew like wings about to open left and right. I combed and tucked them in with coconut oil. The soft cotton cloth of my dhoti I used to wipe the lenses of my spectacles. I surveyed myself in the mirror and reminded myself to tell the child the T-shirt made me feel very posh.

Iyer came into the house bearing gifts—homemade ginger squash, sugarcane syrup from his plantation. Iyer was seventy-five and bald and fair, the color of a pale golden sultana raisin. Though he possessed a pair of false teeth, he claimed they were a nuisance and did not bother wearing them. Because of this, he could only eat soft foods. Iyer had a moderate case of tinnitis. This meant he had some ringing in his ears. He said he felt like he was back in school and all through the day; it was one period ending or the beginning of the next. Since the middle ear was affected, he sometimes lost his balance and crumpled to the floor in a heap. But his two year stint in the U.S. had changed things a bit. His son, Venu, a real doctor in Philadelphia (unlike Iyer who was only a doctor of Philosophy and had taught at Presidency College in Madras) had examined and purchased for his father a hearing aid the size of a tamarind seed. He told Iyer it was called miracle ear because the reception was supposed to be clear. "Doesn't work half the time," Iyer said, shaking his head at me, the first time I saw him when he returned from America.

"So," Iyer asked, "How is the famous American dancer? Marriage has been settled?"

"Cookie is engaged," I clarified. "The chap is doing well in business, Dow Chemicals, I think. But she is waiting for the big thing. You know, the big wait."

"Oho, that one, the big wait of youth. I see. Poor child." Iyer sympathized. "We were all waiting and waiting without giving up. In the end, it became waiting for Godot. Nothing happened. Nobody showed up. Only you sitting there waiting and looking like a fool."

"Yes, yes," I agreed. "That's exactly the way it was."

"Well, what were you waiting for?" Venkat asked.

Iyer asked, "You mean you're not waiting?"

"He is waiting," I replied.

"That is what I thought from the look on his face, his polished style."

I saw that Venkat was getting annoyed; he did not like to be left out. "Waiting, my dear fellow, is the big wait of the young. We were always waiting for something big to happen, the big love, the big job, the big adventure, the big something or other."

Iyer interrupted with a wink. "More big things of course, we need not talk about." I continued with my explanation.

"The funny thing is, we don't know while we are waiting that we are waiting. If we are aware of it, it is too brief to register. All this waiting is slightly embarrassing to admit. In some cases, it is an arrogance problem. Thinking one is different than the rest, but waiting is waiting, no point in denying that."

"So the poor child is waiting?" Iyer asked.

"Yes," I replied.

"What do you expect, Sathya? Does a woman who is in the family way know what it is like to be a mother?" Iyer said.

Venkat looked baffled and shook his head. He had cleaned up nicely, combed his hair and all that, and he was wearing jeans and a T-shirt that said Banff National Park. Iyer appeared Gandhian with his Khadi kurta and sparkling white dhoti with a black pencil width border. Cookie was wearing her embroidered Lucknow kurta and salwar. I guessed her plan was to change into her dance attire later in the evening, closer to her performance. I was too modest to speak for myself in such matters, but the others said I looked dandy in my Yankee duds. That posh feeling I mentioned earlier was dancing madly in my head.

The bar table had gin, Bacardi, Angostura bitters, Scotch and Venkat's Italian wine. Venkat fixed us Scotches and put the bottle down. Iyer saw this and asked why he was not helping himself. "I'm used to Triple xxx rum, Iyer. You both enjoy the scotch. I get to have it all the time," he said. It's part of my regimen. When I'm in India, I drink this."

"Oho," Iyer said. "Going native, huh?"

Mosquito coils were lit by Nagu who placed them on either side of our seating arrangement. Cookie said to Venkat and Iyer, "Thatha uses that sticky ointment stuff; what is it, Odomos? I'm convinced the mosquitos are immune to that. " Iyer had a twinkle in his eyes as he turned towards

Cookie.

"In my childhood, we had to deal with seeing elephants in the village and tigers in the fields. Have you seen dung beetles?" he asked. Cookie wore a look of consternation.

"Forget about dung beetles," I told Iyer. "She sees a single wasp and she is screaming." Iyer and I tsk tsked with our tongues.

"Americans only like animals and insects singing and talking like people Disney style," Iyer said. I saw that Venkat and Cookie rolled their eyes and shook their heads no.

Iyer and I nodded our heads yes.

For hundreds of years," I began, now that I was in the mood, switching to the world arena, "the North Americans lived apart from the rest of the world, is it not? They did not know about other countries or people and others did not know about them. In the case of countries like India and England, we have a played some part in history from the beginning."

Iyer interrupted. "We before the Brits of course. And in a bigger way."

"Our civilization is ancient and it will go on because of what we bring to the table."

"We offer the world things of the spirit. And human spirit will always seek spirituality. As long as people seek, we will be there. What we are offering is eternal wisdom, something that has no beginning or end," Iyer clarified.

"Of course, these days every country has its problems. The Brits are crying over spilt milk, their mighty naval presence is all gone. Now their presence is symbolic and psychological. Now it's all Mr. Bottom Line American," I said.

"Is there anybody you guys like or admire other than yourselves, India?" Cookie asked.

Iyer and I looked at each other and decided we did not.

"But my child," I said, "historical understanding cannot be the same everywhere? What do they teach in schools these days?"

Iyer elaborated, "History is a point of view in the end. I must say our view seems more valid than others."

Iyer and I held hands then slapped our thighs.

"Cookie, you better feed these old men," Venkat said. "I don't want to carry them to their beds."

"Oho, oho, some of the young people are getting a little pompous..." Iyer said.

"Canadians, you know, still following the Queen's ways," I said. "My husband and I..." I began but did not finish.

"So, Sathya, still a member of the Sahib Club in town?" Iyer teased. He explained to Cookie and Venkat. "It's like your American fraternity is it not? Big bulky fellows drinking and what not. Sahib Club. Old British name."

"I've not seen you at the Club in a long time. Nowadays it is filled with all these young big shots. Most of them useless fellows, accepting bribes and what not."

Venkat lit a cigarette and cut in. "It has nothing to do with Sahib Club. It is your stinking city. The inefficiency and corruption is stinking up the place along with horrible pollution. You don't have to smoke to die in this city. You just have to go and stand behind a public transport bus to commit suicide. And forget about decent drinking water. Only brackish brown stuff available everywhere."

"Yes, yes. You are right. What to do my friend? This is India. Not your Canada, America," I said, and Iyer shook his head in agreement.

"That oily Naidu chap, the real estate idiot, he tells me you know him?"

"Yes, yes. He is just doing his job, Sathya. He is making hay while the sun shines. Look around you at what is happening. I am too old to be burdened with running a house. My children are in America; what does the place mean to them?" Iyer was thoughtful. He pulled out his handkerchief from his pockets and dabbed at his mouth. "Once they have tasted that comfort, they are not coming back here. So when Naidu made the offer I thought it was fair. I decided the time has come."

"But where will you go?" I asked.

"I'm not going to live forever. Maybe a little longer at best. I'm tired you know. It's time to prepare."

"Don't talk like that, Iyer."

"What is there? I had a full life. The love of a good woman, children and my work. Now it is time to move on, make space for the new ones."

"You didn't tell me what you're going to do about a place? Where are you going to live?"

"The Theosophical society people have a small house for me, room and kitchen. And I can look at the greenery, be away from the traffic. What more does an old man want?"

"So when is all this happening?"

"Next month. The driver and car I shall have because I am too old to move around on my own."

I saw that everybody was quiet for a few minutes.

"And you Sathya, what are you going to do about the house?" Iyer wanted to know. I saw that Venkat and Cookie had stopped chatting and were listening to us.

"I don't know Iyer. This house is my history. It's part of me. I can't let it go just like that. Maybe I'm not so detached as you."

"You can make the arrangement of asking the builder for a flat you know. Then at least you will have the satisfaction of living on the same land."

"I don't know what to do. I'll talk to the others in the family and find out."

I wanted to change the subject. "Now you see here is the ultimate fence sitter. He has both Canadian and American passports, a house in each country," I said and waved towards Venkat.

"Not a house, man; only an apartment," Venkat said.

"Whatever it is, it is more than the rest of the world has," I said.

"I worked hard for it, do you mind?"

"We don't mind. Do we men look as if we mind?" I asked and turned to Iyer.

Venkat got up to refill his glass and fix us another round. Iyer leaned over to me and whispered, "Does he also have a Canadian and American wife?"

"Currently, no wife in particular," I said.

"Waiting, is it?"

I nodded my head.

"That explains the mood."

Venkat came back with our drinks. "He is very loyal to his mother.

Steadfast in that," I said.

"I'm glad there is some Indian in him left."

Iyer was talking to Cookie. "You are even more beautiful than your mother, child. Now tell me, what are your plans?"

"Well, I'm here to polish and learn some dancing at Kalakshetra."

"And how are you liking it, the dancing and our India?"

"I love it most of the time."

"Excellent. So I hear you are getting married?"

"I'm thinking about it."

"Don't think so much about it. Everything will be all right. The fellow is lucky to get a girl like you. Now my late wife, Kamakshi, was a very thoughtful woman. She did the thinking for both the two of us."

Venkat and the child locked eyes and smiled.

"Come on, Iyer," I said.

"She made everything good for me; she made it all worthwhile. And you know we met each other on our wedding day. No dating or anything like that."

Another small smile from the child.

"Fifty years we were married. What do you Americans say? Soul mates? That's what we were. You know the secret?"

Cookie shook her head.

Iyer leaned towards her. "You don't become instant soul mates. You become one after being together a very long time."

"What are you putting into the child's head?" I asked. I wanted Iyer to spend more time with me.

"Sathya, you mind your business. Old bachelor fellow. What do you know of the finer things in life? Women you are ignorant about."

Iyer always became a bully with a little drink inside.

"I hope you will get your Thatha here to invite me again and I hope you will dance for me a few more times." Cookie smiled and offered him banana chips.

"Cannot eat that stuff, see I'm still softening the same single one," Iyer said.

***

Cookie was wearing a white sari with a blood red border on which was an embossed golden paisley design like a garland of halved mangos. Her inky hair was piled into a bun on the side of her head and circled with jasmine flowers. Mohiniattam, the dance of the enchanted one was what Cookie had chosen to perform. The nightingale of south India, M.S. Subbalakshmi, queen of classical music, sang on the cassette tape. What a voice the woman had. Full of surrender and bhakti and subtleties. It uplifted your spirit to hear just one word.

In the twilight on the terrace with the music and the swaying movements as we watched, Cookie looked like an apsara, a celestial dancer descended from the heavens. Her languorous and lyrical movements beseeched her lover, Krishna, to show himself. The hand movements were circular and graceful, the improvisations dramatic. This was a devotee pining for her lord, waiting for him to romance her soul and spirit. As we watched her dance, the child's skin shone as if lit from within.

I saw that all of us sitting there, Venkat, Iyer and the young couple Nagu and Paru on the floor at the back; we had traveled to a different place because of this child. The feeling at the end of it all was magical, quite magical, I can tell you that. Looking again at the faces around me, I knew the others felt the way I did. They too had experienced beauty, sadness, things that could not be voiced because of their primal nature. Briefly, during the dance performance, we became acutely aware of human limitation, the transience of time, the evanescence of our lives. We did not want to talk and break the spell.

Cookie looked flushed towards the end. Luminous as the moon that night, she made a fine Mohini, one who bagged the heart of her audience.

A minute or so later, because this was India, land of plentiful irony, a donkey brayed loudly on the street and everybody shifted in their seats and laughed.

"Cookie, you reminded me what it was like to feel young. I thank you for that. The founder of Kalakshetra, Rukmini Arundale herself, would have been proud of such a performance. Now an old man like me must go and get his rest," Iyer said.

"Bye." Cookie gave him a hug.

Venkat too, I noticed, had got up to leave. "Nice work, Cookie, so how is Basket Hair?" he asked.

"You mean you told him?" She turned to me.

"What, what are you two talking about?" I feigned surprise. "I am tired, an old man, who needs to get his rest. Cookie, you transported us all tonight. I can see the family genes are still intact."

***

The rest of the night proved restless. This was what alcohol sometimes did to me. Stirred up my thoughts and troubles to make a potent stew. The haunting image of the tailor's wife and Venkat flashed before my eyes. I remembered my own past struggles in this department. In my thirties and forties, I had taken care of physical urges with the same servant woman who was willing and available. Then had begun a period of experimentation after immersing myself in Gandhi's books. I practiced withdrawal at the crucial moment followed by months of lying next to her and doing nothing. That most desirable of women, she had not understood my behavior and stopped coming to see me at night. I planned to discipline myself and conquer the urge so my energies could be devoted to temple work solely. The last ten years, thankfully, the problem had solved itself with old age removing this obstacle for me.

The maid servant woman's face came to me in complete precision after all this time. The doe eyes heavy with desire, the plump and pouting lips waiting for my mouth. Nothing was always as it should be. I felt that old forgotten sensation and saw my fellow coming up like a flag flying at half-mast. Like George scolding his German shepherd Monty, down boy down I said, you old fool, there is nothing for you to do. We are seventy five going on seventy six. Time for a little peace and quiet.

I tossed and turned all night as my dreams mixed up everything. There was my one and only love from all those years ago, Menaka, my own apsara, she danced again and again on the beach beside the shore temples for me. I was next to her as the waves lapped at my feet, a young boy of eighteen with shocking black hair, swallowing the girl in front of me with my eyes. Then as I watched she turned into someone else. She became Cookie, my niece on the terrace, and I changed into the old man that I was. This was all juxtaposed in my mind with shots of Hridaya Kamalam when the oleanders were in bloom and the mangos on the trees ripe and full. The house appeared majestic, alive and whole, then razed, mounds of rubble on the ground. Only the pillar with the marble slab naming the house stood intact like a lone soldier on the battlefield.

Chapter Five
Watergate and Churchgate

The meeting at the museum turned out to be a major affair with almost fifty people there in a big hall. There were long winded speeches and slides. Some idols had been stolen from the field in one of our offices in Shayamalapet. Also, a stone statue of Krishna playing the flute had gone missing from under the noses of museum officials, while it was in their care for stain removal and repair of small chipped areas under the chin. One day it was there as part of the inventory, lying on the floor next to a sitting Hanuman and next morning, it was gone. Rigorous questioning had produced no results, no leads came up. The statue was worth millions of rupees, thousands of dollars in the black market.

The fellow who showed us slides of the Krishna idol turned off the projector and turned on the lights in the room. He moved forward and stood in front of us. "The Indian government does not like mysteries like this. We are given the job of protecting and preserving our culture and if we allow things to vanish from under our noses, how does it look? How does it look to the public and to the world? We have a job to do and let's do it. There are stories of private collectors in Europe, America. There are stories of corruption and bribes. Our own government employees, people like you and me selling out. Let's put a stop to these rumors."

I suspected the above cases were being investigated by the Tamil Nadu Police. No wonder I had seen huddled circles of men in buffalo-horn-like moustaches, men in over-starched khaki shorts that flared out from their bodies. They looked as if they had old-fashioned wooden hoops or stiff canvas bakram under their shorts.

The fellow in front of us making the speech banged the table with a closed fist for emphasis and the laptop jumped slightly and settled.

"Let us do our job as we are supposed to," he whispered and blinked rapidly a few times. Then he narrowed his eyes. Puncture leaned over and said in my ear, "He really means business, Saar, when his eyes do that." Puncture hissed like a balloon letting air out. I felt the hair on my ears tickle me a little as they fanned this way and that. Things came to a close abruptly with all of us signing our names next to our respective projects on several sheets of paper. S.D. and I thought it better we checked on the work being done to the Periamalai stone tablets. We signed our names again on a book and noted the time we entered the restricted area where the inventory was kept.

I saw that the tablets had identification tags. No work had been done; the crack still ran zigzag across the center in one; corner chips and oily stains darkened the lower part of the snakes in the other. There was even some trace of the kumkum and turmeric that had adorned them when we brought them in. The tablets had not even been brushed and cleaned properly. The fellows there claimed they knew nothing. They were door people who worked only on temple doors. "Saar, one people is doing doors, one people is doing idols, one people is doing pillars, Saar. We are being door people."

"And when are the idol people coming?" I asked.

"That I am not knowing, Saar. Idle people are coming when idle people are coming no? You are expecting door people to know about idle people. How can that be no? Are you going to ask me about pillar people also?"

I assured him I would not.

"We are doing specialist work here Saar. Door people not knowing about anything else."

I said I could see that.

***

In the Shiva Vishnu temple in Mayapuram, I saw that three of the nine idols, Rahu, Ketu and Saturn were already in their place. I placed packets of sesame seeds and whole mung beans as auspicious offerings on the edge of the pedestal. The shelter we had built for the old idols held up well under recent trauma—first, the attack and damage and now the construction. The doors to the pavilion remained unlocked since workers needed access to do their job.

I could not help staring at the gaping holes where the old idols had been dug out. Venkat was all over the place clicking his camera. "You could have devised something safer perhaps?" he asked. "Something like this would never have happened anywhere else, in any other country. Things are taken lightly here. These are national treasures, serious measures had to be taken. Why did you not have them also removed and sent to the museum? You did that with the snake tablets in Periamalai."

"That was coming, the next step to be carried out. The tablets in Periamalai were outside the perimeter of the temple. You can see that this is   located inside the temple. This makes things different in our bureaucracy. So we made sure we built something overhead and around to protect these. The instructions we left said clearly that the doors were to remain locked after hours."

"But the thing was manned by people. It was subject to human error."

"Yes, that's true. But you don't understand Venkat; have you taken a look at our budget?"

Venkat shook his head and left. He said he wanted to smoke a cigarette and have a cup of tea.

How could the chap understand the condition under which we worked in this country? Difficult choices had to be made given lack of manpower, financial restrictions etc. This was not Canada or America. We had innumerable temples, art, palaces, documents, all sorts of things of historical value that needed equal protection. And in the meantime, the needs of the people continued to increase in demand also, along with urgent requirements in the area of health, sanitation, education etc. Things were bulging at the seams; it was impossible. How could a fellow like Venkat understand the desperation? He came from a continent where some states or provinces had more sheep or moose or whatever than people. Some of those places remained frozen for most of the year.

The Brahmin priest of the Shiva Vishnu temple, also an artist and painter, the man who had painted the Saraswati calendar that hung in my room, came out to greet me. He was with his oldest son, a carbon copy of the old man. I could see that the priest was on his way out somewhere since he wore an ironed shirt, carried his umbrella and a cloth bag. His name was I.Q. Senior and everybody, even the illiterates in the village, called him I.Q. Saar without knowing that I stood for intelligence and Q for quotient. His son, I.Q. Junior, was the one really responsible for their nicknames since he had undergone a special I.Q. test set up by an uncle when he was six years old. He had come out of the test with flying colors and the father, proud of his child, talked of this family triumph non-stop. So the name had stuck. People began calling the gifted child I.Q. Jr.; and the father who would not shut up about it, I.Q. Sr. The man's religious title assumed secondary importance.

I.Q. Senior said they were going to the city, to Chennai to check out procedures regarding admission to medical colleges for his son, I.Q. Junior. "He is brilliant you know, first rank all the time."

"Very good," I said.

"What a country we live in, you know the problems with reservations, marks don't matter if you're a Brahmin."

Many people resented this reverse discrimination. If their Brahmin ancestors had been unfair, why should children of this generation pay for it with lack of opportunity in education? I.Q. Junior pushed up his specs. "Namaskaram, Saar," he said to me, folding his hands in the usual respectful gesture when I looked at him. "I heard from my friends about the nagapratishta from Periamalai being taken to the museum for the Tamil Nadu temple collection," he said. "They are very valuable pieces, isn't it? " I nodded, surprised that a studious fellow in the sciences would be interested in such a thing. I supposed it was only natural considering his father was a priest. Father and son said goodbye and left, walking towards the bus stop.

S.D. and Puncture inspected the rest of the place carefully and measured the windows surrounding the outer area of the inner shrine. It was best to take no chances and install grillwork there too. On the pedestal in the pavilion, three planets were in place, three being prepared for installation. They would be taken out of gunny sack wrapping and readied in the afternoon. The final three statues had yet to be delivered from Madras. They would be put in place the following few weeks and the whole place readied for the final ceremony. S.D. and Puncture had a note specifying all of this from the idol people back in the department. It was going to be an all-day affair here in the village of Mayapuram.

Standing there and looking at the men working, my mind went back to the night I rushed here after that desperate phone call. The pavilion was a disaster area, the doors gaping open, the big metal lock broken and lying nearby on the floor. The pedestal was all right. It was solid and damage proof but the small idols representing the nine planets were a mess. It was as if they had been attacked with a hammer, some with heads cracked, others broken in the middle, a few chipped all over as if manhandled by a stone eating monster. At least one I could see had been reduced to rubble as if the person had used the hammer to smash the object again and again until the shape of the thing collapsed to a heap of small stones.

Venkat had taken a few quick shots that day but had said nothing all the way back. He had sat in the car next to me, sullen and silent. I did not bother about it at the time because I had been overcome emotionally myself and could hardly think straight that night. Until then, I had worried about omens and Saturn and what not like a good Hindu but this final act put everything over the edge. It was more than ominous. Such an act of desecration involved the worst kind of intolerance and violence. One worried about several things.

Who did this? Why? Did the person/people plan more of the same? Did they have a personal vendetta against the government/department/the three of us --Puncture, S.D. and myself? Would we ever find out what the truth was? If vandals could do this to stone, what could they do to human beings? S.D. and Puncture had been nervous the night of this disaster. The former sputtered unintelligibly and the latter hissed as if a cobra lived in his mouth. The phone call from the priest, I.Q. Senior, had offered me no details that night. All I had gathered was there was an emergency and I needed to be there.

I.Q. Senior had been awakened by a man shouting outside his house which was tucked away behind the temple compound. A man was yelling "Thief! Thief," having seen the broken lock lying on the floor. In the poor light of the evening, it was not possible to take in the damage that had been inflicted. I.Q. Sr. had come rushing out thinking the inner shrine had been ransacked for the diamond and gold jewels there. This was, after all, the usual route of temple robberies. He had come out holding a hurricane lamp. The men hurried to the front of the temple and gasped when the light from the lamp showed the pavilion doors gaping, the idols smashed. A small crowd of street people stood in a crescent shape around the small shrine. Each of them offered an opinion as to what had happened, several versions that only added fuel to the fire. A moment of clarity had managed to pierce through the confusion in I.Q. Sr.'s mind and he had made his phone calls.

How did the priest's family, his wife, and all those healthy and young children, living in the same house, not hear anything of the commotion on the night of the attack? Village nights were so silent, almost eerie, the noise of crickets and chirping lizards, the call of frogs on rainy nights, these were the only sounds that hummed in the background. The surrounding houses on the street, had nobody in them heard anything? Unlike Periamalai's Kali temple, the temple here had the pond across so there was no tea stall or shops nearby which would have been a center of activity. The lack of street lights around the pond made the area pitch black at night. Even a pair of eagle eyes would not have caught much unless he heard some noise that alerted him first.

I decided to conduct a preliminary investigation. First stop was a chat with S. D and Puncture who were busy preparing the holes for installation. "Do either one of you recall if you heard or saw anything unusual that night? No, Saar," began Puncture. "The people say…"

I raised my hand as a signal for him to stop. "Don't tell me anything about that. I am going to talk to I.Q. Sr. next. I want to know if you and S.D. noticed anything?" I lowered my voice as I saw a pair of men approach and stand a few feet away from us. Privacy was not something that was easily achieved in India, certainly not in villages. In cities, at least, there was the comfort of anonymity. S.D. got up from his squatting position and finished wiping his hands on a towel.

"I'll show you something, Saar," he said and suggested we walk towards the road. At the edge of the mud road where the entrance to the temple met the paved main road, there were a few footprints deeply embedded in the soil. A pair of adult size prints and another pair adjacent to it, this pair smaller, almost child-like. The distinguishing feature of this, the second pair, was that at the end of the foot, at the edge of the small fifth toe, was another piggyback toe, same size as the fifth, a sixth toe. I filed this away with an Aha in my mind. Not too many people had six toes. It would be relatively easy to spot this idiot.

S.D. joined us and reminded me about why the soil here was wet and soft. The temple tank overflowed often and made the soil in this area like sculptor's clay. The footprints were clear and fresh.

"But what does this have to do with anything?" I asked. "It has been three weeks since that night."

"No. No. You remember that night? When you were assessing the damage and everything and you were very upset, Saar, I was too, we all were, Saar, only you did not notice or maybe you did I don't know, but (he took a breath here and I felt tired just listening to the trajectory of his rocket-like talk) we were all too upset to take in each other, Saar, but when I came to stand here and contemplate for a minute, I felt the need for a cigarette, Saar, I noticed footprints just like these and one of the villagers told me something strange, Saar; he said they had all rounded up a crowd of people who were here at the time and later most of the men in the village had come to the temple, volunteer basis, Saar, (another breath and I was near collapse myself), and they were going to tell me more, Saar, but I waved them off, told them to leave me alone and stop talking rubbish, but now I am thinking and thinking that we should be finding what exactly happened that is why I am telling you in detail..."

"Why didn't you say something before? Who else knows about this?"

He lifted and dropped his shoulders. Sign language for don't know. I was glad he had decided to not indulge in his verbal acrobatics again. This much going up and down from Sputnik mouth was enough for me. "Let's think about how to find out more about exactly what happened with the footprints," I said. "We'll ask different people then check the results when I come back from the hill stations." He nodded and went back to work. The pair of men who had been watching us all along continued to stand a couple of yards away and stare and stare as if I had sprouted buffalo horns.

I wondered if I was taking my holiday at an inopportune time when so much was waiting to be done.

S.D. was standing before me. Of course, what else can it be, time for tea and lunch and biryani. Always the same with these fellows, minimum work, maximum pleasure. But I am not one to complain so I decided to go and have lunch with Venkat. He had discovered a small hotel which was relatively clean. Serving first class masal dosa and vada along with cold bottles of Mangola. He was waiting for me under the tree in front of the temple, a huge neem tree whose leaves rustled like a silk sari in the sudden breeze. I joined him there in the shade and took a few swallows from my water bottle. As I screwed the cap back on the bottle and wiped my mouth with my handkerchief, my eyes looked down and I saw a sharp stake sticking out of the ground like a stone pencil.

I remembered this instrument of torture was used to impale animals outside temples that had a shrine for Plagueamma like Periamalai. But this was a Brahmin temple housing Shiva Vishnu, and no sacrifice of that kind had been performed here for a long time. Perhaps there was some historical aspect that I had not looked into here, some old struggle between Brahmins and non-Brahmins in this village.

While I was ruminating thus, some slight movement in the wind caught my eyes. It was as if there was a feather on the tip of the stone pencil, a small flutter like butterfly wings. Whatever it was, the pastel colored piece ballooned up and flattened down like a miniscule wind sock.

Venkat had lit a cigarette and squatted down on the mud under the tree, inspecting and cleaning various lenses and organizing his paraphernalia. He had suggested we wait for the driver to return after dropping S.D. and Puncture.

I walked towards the stone pencil sticking out of the ground and grabbed the cloth that was stuck at the tip, a tiny piece that could have come from anything, a shirt, a sarong, a towel, even the border of a sari, some part of female attire–nothing could be ruled out. The material felt soft and cottony and the colors were muted. Stripes of light blue and dark blue. The thing had been washed and worn many times.

So, at this late stage of the game, I had become a South Indian vegetarian sleuth, a dosa-idli eating P.I. with a spiritual bent and no bust and backside endowed woman by his side. I imagined myself as a slightly older version of Peter Sellers, considering my hirsute appearance. But I did not have that silly expression he wore in his pictures, that of a man who has soiled his pants.

The car had arrived. Once inside, I updated Venkat. "I think you should tell the investigating officer in the case about the cloth and the footprints."

"That was my first impulse too. But I cannot help wondering, is that the best course? How do we know that the monster who did this and the inspector, the local police force, are not somehow in cahoots?"

Venkat's eyes widened. "What makes you think that?"

"It has been three weeks since the incident. Has anybody seen a report filed on the case? Has the police inspector conducted interviews with potential witnesses? Where is the data from the authorities on all of this? I've a nagging feeling about all of this. I.Q. Senior tells me he has informed the authorities, but I've seen no evidence of this. "

The smell of uttappam and puris and turmeric and what not was heavy in the air. Waiters were hurrying past our table with small stainless steel buckets of sambhar and rasam. The place was getting crowded as more and more workers arrived for lunch. Venkat whistled. The waiter, a young chap in soiled clothes, plonked down our stainless steel plates with paper dosas jutting out like cones on either side.

I was thinking we should leave as soon as the coffee came when as if to answer my thoughts, the loudspeaker came on.

"I'm a Barbie girl, in a Barbie world
Imagination, life is your creation
Come on Barbie, let's go party…"

***

Venkat made a pained face. "Why is this song so popular in India? I don't get it," he said. I finished the last of the coffee praying that the heat of the liquid had killed off any bacteria that clung to the tumbler. I had made sure I left the cup of chutney untouched in case the idiots in the kitchen diluted the thing with unboiled water. I had a delicate stomach and had to take all kinds of precautions. No safe water for the people and the government wants to blow up bombs in the desert to boost their image and puff up their stunted power. Brainless idiots. As if this was not enough, the country was also crawling with a whole lot of morons who liked bad American music.

Venkat and I agreed that I should visit the police station and meet with I.Q. Senior. I planned to write a detailed report that evening and have it delivered to the office the next day before I left on my holiday to the hill stations. There must be a trail of all that had been done to look into the matter at least on our part, I decided.

Outside the restaurant, we noticed that the car and driver were missing. The foolish fellow had probably gone to eat his lunch without informing us.

Venkat went to an adjacent tea stall where he purchased and lit a cigarette and promptly sat down on a stool outside the shop. A young boy with missing front teeth ran up to me calling, "Thatha, are you Sathya Thatha?" I said yes. He held out a piece of paper. S.D. had scribbled a note for me and Venkat saying the office vehicle had a flat tire, could we please wait for them? They would be here in no time at all. I passed the scrap of paper to Venkat who said "Shit." I suggested to him that we walk back to the temple and visit the temple school and meet with the teacher and students. He had been wanting photographs of a Vedic temple school for inclusion in the book.

***

When we arrived at the side of the temple (a sort of longish verandah with many pillars, a Ficus tree to the west that offered welcome shade) where the children had classes, we noticed it was still lunch time. Many students were screeching and playing some game, kicking up dust with bare feet. Others, especially girls, sat in circles and talked or played with cowrie shells. "Where is your teacher? When does the bell ring?" I asked one of the students. Ten more minutes of lunch recess and it was time for history class, came the answer.

I looked around at these children and tried to picture myself as I had been then, at nine, ten or eleven. I remember dreaming a lot, imagining all sorts of things. There was a book about Europe I read cover to cover that made a deep impression, and I became Dutch or German or French in my dreams, eating cheese and roaming the countryside in a cocked hat. Mostly I liked to think I was English; a large pink man capable of great cruelty; my laughter roared through cold and drafty castles and I slashed off many heads and barked at my many wives, all of them peaches and cream complexioned, innocent maidens who tittered and blushed.

Then I went through a nationalistic period and became an Indian Maharajah, bearded, bejewelled, my father and mother wringing their hands in despair behind me, shocked and proud as they witnessed my burgeoning manhood and bravery. I sent many Englishmen to Indian jails, instructing they be fed the hottest curry possible, breakfast served with plenty of blood red pickles, rice for lunch laced with vettakozhambu, tamarind sauce that acted as a plunger for sinuses, green chili chutney and pepper chapatis that burned holes in their baby bottom English palates.

"Thatha, thatha," one of the small girls was tugging at the edge of my cotton kurta. Her friends and this child pointed to a man at the edge of the temple. He lay in the fetal position under a scrawny tree, in filthy rags. I saw a novice nun (I remembered the uniform from my last visit to George) in her starched uniform, a white sari, feed the man something from a tiffin box and tilt a tumbler to his mouth. Venkat was busy photographing the sweaty and rowdy boys who were now playing cricket in the hot sun. The girls and I walked towards the man though I was not fully willing since I had just had lunch and did not want to witness anything really unpleasant. But how to refuse the charming girls who held my hands so sweetly and drew me there?

"What is the matter with him?" I asked the young nun as she fed the man milk from a stainless steel tumbler. "He came last week from Seshasamudram," she said, "He used to work there as a ship breaker. Thirty of the men there, working on a large American ship, were taken ill. But the local hospital could not do much. They have too many cases to handle. These men are suffering from inhalation of chemical substances. The lungs are badly damaged," she concluded. She watched the man close his eyes and she looked up at me and shook her head. There were stains on his shirt. "He has been bringing out blood," she added softly. "We're trying to keep him as comfortable as possible. What to do? It's a terrible thing. His own family has thrown him out. They don't understand. They're afraid what he has is contagious."

The girls ran away. The novice nun looked at me again. "I know you. Brother and Mrs. George said you might come to the village. You visit them sometimes, don't you? " she asked.

The man opened his eyes and smiled a weak smile at me. "Did you know Siva, brother of Nagu, son of woman called Lakshmi, better known as Ayah? They're from Maramur. The chap has a wife and two children," I said. The sick man looked at me and nodded slightly. He whispered hoarsely, too weak to talk properly.

"He was one of the first to go, few days back. I don't know if anyone has informed the family. They piled them near the ocean and burned the bodies," the man said, his voice cracking.

Poor Ayah. Her son was dead? The whole thing was a miserable business. "Do you have a car?" the nun wanted to know. "We would like to transport him to the church. We have place in the nursing home where he can be given a bath and a change of clothes." Venkat was beside me. He said the car had arrived.

I told the nun she could use the car to take the man back to church. I saw the man cling to her like a child as she wiped his chin. Moments like these confused me. Such suffering. Was there really something like a god? Was there justice? Humanity? Compassion? I gave the nun a hundred rupee note and called for the driver to come and get instructions from me. I did not want to think about Ayah and Nagu, what I'd have to tell them when I got back.

"Venkat," I said, " I think you should go to Seshasamudram and look into what is happening there. This ship breaking business needs exposure. That man has just come from there. Ayah's older son has died there."

"Poor fellow," Venkat said and frowned. "Maybe I'll take Nagu with me? The men might be more willing to talk to him?" I said that was a good idea. Perhaps Nagu would gain some comfort, some closure about his brother's sudden death from seeing the place for himself. I realized that Nagu would now have to provide for his elder brother's wife and children. All that responsibility descending on him before his own firstborn arrived. Such was life in India.

The bell rang and children lined up in rows, getting ready for class.

The teacher arrived and gave the students a writing assignment. He said he wanted to hear no talking from anybody and wagged his finger at the class. Then he approached me and said he wanted to discuss a serious matter. I gestured by showing him the stone bench.

All I knew about the village school teacher was that he was from Benares, everybody called him Guruji -- north Indian style. He spoke Tamil haltingly, with a slight accent. He had settled here for a long time since his wife came from a landowning family from these parts.

"Yes, Guruji?"

"Please call me Sharma, that is quite all right," he implored. He belched heavily and I smelled mango pickle in the air.

I took a good look at the man next to me as he began talking. He wore a dhoti tied the traditional way, a good length of it folded and going down the middle to the back, separating the folds for the legs. He had a sandalwood and vibuti ash mark on his forehead and a Nehru cap on his head. He wore a Lucknow embroidered kurta with the top button missing.

"Sathya saar, you' re coming here for a long time. You are a senior member of the community. So I think I should tell you there has been a problem with the school and the temple. Am I making myself clear?"

"What kind of problem?" I asked.

"You remember the floods after the monsoons last year?" he asked, sending a whiff of sun-dried mango skin in my direction. The whole state had suffered from terrible floods, especially low-lying areas like Periamalai and Mayapuram. So many homeless people and the onset of waterborne diseases as was always the case, as if one misery was not enough that another disaster had to be piled on top to make a misery sandwich."

"Yes, I heard you had trouble with the school building." I said.

"More than trouble Saar, the roof was leaking, practically collapsing onto the students. The whole place was a mess with water damage. So we had to vacate and we moved to the temple grounds, since that had been the traditional solution." He nodded as if to confirm what he had said, and in response, I shook my head also. "Am I making myself clear?" he asked.

Guruji then began telling me about how things had gone smoothly the first two weeks before I.Q. Senior had come by one day and watched the class. He had heard some unsettling rumors about the way things were run in the school. Two templegoers had complained about low caste, meat-eating non-brahmin children being allowed into the temple premises to attend the school. I.Q. Sr. stood there and watched as Guruji taught. Both teacher and students became restless after a while. Guruji asked the children to finish their homework in class and went to I.Q. Sr. saying something about all this watching was making the children and the teacher nervous. I.Q. gave him a long cold stare and said, "Do you realize what you're doing is breaking tradition? You're lucky that too many people have not yet found out."

"Found out what?" Guruji asked.

"That you have some students, at least a dozen or so, from what I can see, who do not belong here? I 'm not even mentioning the Muslim students you have on your roll call that I checked from last week. Since they're not here, there is no need to bring them into the picture. My concern is really the dozen or so low-castes here; do you not realize that your school is within temple grounds?"

"This village temple is for the villagers, right? Do you realize my class has shrunk since I moved here? The few Muslim students you talk about, actually eight of them—they are staying home –on instructions from their frightened parents. They may not catch up with the homework I send home because we are covering a lot of new portion."

I.Q. stood there like a statue. The only movement he made was pushing up his specs. Guruji told me he had stared at I.Q.'s lumpy ear and wondered if there was a hole in there somewhere through which common sense traveled.

"A man like you, a father of so many children, a man who values education, why can you not understand what I say?" Guruji asked.

I.Q. Senior stayed mum on the subject. Perhaps the chap really was as deaf as a temple pillar, Guruji thought. Then he asked, "Who has complained about these students?"

I.Q. Sr. blurted, "Who are you to ask? Is everything based on earthly authorities? Manu has spoken on this many times in our holy books. That no man who is not twice born, one who is without the thread that crosses his chest, may not enter the holy premises."

"Surely, you see that these children here are coming to the temple for classes. They mind their own business, coming here with their books and eager minds."

"Don't be so naïve, Guruji. You're playing with fire here; do you know that? Are you blind, deaf, dumb? Do you not know about the distrust these groups have among themselves? We have the Vanniyars, Dalits, Yadavas, Gaundars, Thevars, Pallars, and Parayars, all sorts of troubling permutations and combinations." Guruji understood that it was a serious warning of some kind.

He turned to me and asked, "Am I making myself clear?"

For the remaining students, Guruji said, there was temptation from other quarters, namely the Christian quarter, because more and more of his students slowly left his temple veranda class. He began telling me about St. Anne's in Periamalai, the school begun by George and Claudia. The school welcomed everybody, giving them free hot lunch and even offering medical services with a nurse there at all times. The only condition was that everybody recite Our Father who Art in heaven first thing in the morning. St. Anne's boasted teachers who had undergone training at the convent headquarters in Calicut, Kerala. Many of the students' families attended open air mass on Sundays.

Next to me on the stone bench, Guruji became the teacher that he was and interrupted himself by asking me, "Am I making myself clear?" He had done this enough times now during our conversation that it began to grate. I wanted to say, "No it is not clear; it is cloudy like a painted window pane, you mango-pickle-smelling-mister, you."

"I remembered these two Thevar children had spent the few days they came to my class sitting outside the temple compound, under the shade of a tree. They had spread their notebooks on the muddy ground and scrawled their lessons there. The other children in the veranda pointed fingers at them and laughed as the two under the tree stood up often straining their ears to hear every word. Men riding bicycles on the road slowed down and stared. Then a lorry came speeding and kicked up a wave of dust and sprayed water from a rain puddle and dirtied the sitting children. That was the last I saw of them."

Guruji and I were silent for a moment, reflecting on childhood cruelty that arose from human insecurity. It was not a place in the past I cared to visit often. I thought of the times I had flung stones at a dog, pretended to step by mistake on a grimy barefooted beggar child, told my mother the servant boy had stolen a new bar of soap because he ran like the wind and was always ahead of me when we raced. The chap had been dismissed on the spot and I had watched him leave from the window, bewildered and amazed by my power.

Guruji coughed then continued with his story again.

"Tales of humiliation inflicted on those two boys grew wild. They said other children had thrown pebbles at the boys and a teacher had laughed along and spat over the compound wall near where the boys sat. At the end of the week, I heard they had gone to the other side -- converted to the cross and gone to St. Anne's."

We walked towards his class. Telling me, he thought, was a way to get some action in the village. But I was unsure. Being a Brahmin, an outsider, an educated, city person at that, what hold did I have over the issue and divisions within the people here? But if I took the attitude that it was not my place, not my business and all that, who would do something? One had to carry a bit of arrogance and idealism combined in oneself to effect change.

Venkat came up to tell me the car and driver had returned and handed me a note from the nun I had seen earlier. The sick man from Seshasamudram would be looked after, she promised in the letter, and thanked me again for the money I had donated. She requested that I drive by the church before leaving the village. Gopal, the leper who lived in the garage of George's house was making trouble, could I come by and help? I recalled the man on his makeshift wooden cart last time I visited George and Claudia, the way he had reached out and touched me when I did not want to be touched. I supposed I had to go and see what it was all about, if only for the sake of my friends. But it was beginning to irritate and tire me the way people took it upon themselves to appoint me caretaker of troubles.

***

The constable was a shifty fellow, his eyes wandering all the time. He pulled out a grimy big book with blackened dog ears and touched his tongue with his finger and turned the pages, the same two or three, over and over as if he hoped to find something that was not already there.

"It was a rainy week that the incident happened, Saar," he said.

"Were there any signs left by the people who did this?" I asked.

"Nothing concrete that can be used as evidence, Saar," he said.

"What about the pair of footprints I heard about?" I asked.

"Oh that. We checked the men out, Saar. Nothing. Just a lot of talk among village folk, you know how it is." The man in front of me shut his book with a bang and said he would let me know if anything new came up. I could tell the fellow had no intention of doing this as he never once met my eyes. Not only did he not take me seriously, he also did not take his job to heart. These useless fellows were meant to safeguard citizens and prevent crime? A toddler would have done better, I thought. No point in speaking too soon and rattling the idiot, I told myself as I got up to leave. I would have to assume the role of private detective on my own when I returned from the hill stations.

S.D. and Puncture had taken a tea break while I was away and they had just begun with the sixth planet installation when I returned to the temple again. There had been a problem with the fifth one; the base hole was too small and the idol stood crooked so they had to redo that one over. I checked that all measurements had been taken and that the placement of the navagraha idols were as they should be, each one looking out at a subtly different angle, according to custom in a Hindu temple.

On the way to Claudia and George's house, I remembered I had forgotten to show the police constable the piece of cloth I found caught in a crack in the metal rod used to impale animals in front of the temple. Perhaps it was just as well. The shifty fellow had not been cooperative after all. He might have dismissed it as inconsequential. I had no way of linking what I had found with any of those who might be involved.

I crossed the road to George and Claudia's house and saw that Gopal, the leper, legless, sat on his wooden contraption with rubber wheels and salaamed me with bandaged fingers. Last time I was here, George had taken Dr. Warrior's name on his behalf. The doctor had a reputation at Vellore hospital as one who offered his fine skill and care to all patients including charity cases like this man.

"Namaskaram, Saar, he said as extended his hands on either side of the cart, moving to keep pace with me.

I suggested we go to the back verandah so we could talk in the shade. The cushioned rattan chairs there were comfortable and the spot had a fine view of the garden. The parijata tree was there, as always, with a carpet of white, star shaped, coral centered flowers all around the trunk. Loud barking announced that George and Claudia's German Shepherd dog Monty was also there, making his presence felt.

"Where is the dog?" I asked Gopal.

"Inside, Saar. He is barking from there." Gopal pointed to one of the rooms. "The servant woman comes and cleans the house daily, Saar, and lets the dog in after his walk. It is too hot for him to stay out all day."

"I hear from Sister Philomena at the nursing home that you have been difficult? Is this any way to behave when Brother George is away? From what I have seen so far, you have a roof over your head, food and clothing and free medical care. What more do you want?"

Gopal said nothing in reply, nodding solemnly at the ground, agreeing with what I said. "What you say, Saar, is correct, true all right. But you do not live here. You visit once in a while only. Remember that. If you lived here like me, you would see that things are not as they should be."

"What do you mean by that?"

"You are told you are a child of Yesu, that you are made in His image, that each and every one is special and unique. Sounds fine in theory but practice is something else."

"Oh?"

"The nuns, both junior and senior ones and all the others in St. Anne's are still the same, high caste in their heart. Inside, here." He pointed to his chest in case I did not know the location of the organ.

"Nobody expects change overnight. These things take time. Everybody knows all this, " I snapped.

"Does everybody know that casteism is still a problem in the church and nursing home, even in the school?" he asked. I threw him a puzzled glance.

He continued, "We are Christians now, all one in the eyes of God, they said before conversion. But after, the same old ways are what we see here again. The low castes commanded by the high castes. Bribing with presents and ordering about. Turning up their noses against some of us, the same old cruel words and generalizations."

"Are you a child, Gopal? First it is only the title of Christian. It takes a long time to become one in the true sense. And a real Hindu does not practice casteism, you know that. It does not matter what religion you are; it is the way we treat one another that makes us who we are."

"All that is easy for you to say, Saar. I am not listening to philosophy. It does not help. I am talking about your friend also being part of this. George Master and wife."

"You mean...?"

"I have proof, Saar. A cell phone recording. Don't worry, I did not steal it from anybody. It was an old one they wanted to throw out. You know how rich people are Saar."

"I don't understand. What are you talking about?"

"I have been with Father George and Doctor madam for over ten months now. They took me in, gave me food and medical care. But I am seeing everything, no? Poor people, sick people like me, we are not blind and stupid."

"Brother George and Claudia Madam are good people. I do not want to hear all this nonsense," I said.

"I am seeing how watchful they are. Always imagining we are stealing, the servants and I. They are flaunting everything they have, but still we are not taking anything because we are hearing what Father is saying during service. That in God's eyes, we are all the same, all one happy family. We are cleaning and cooking for them, doing everything for them, Saar. See all their foreign goods? T.V., transistor, video and all? I am dusting these things everyday for them."

I was getting irritated.

The chap droned on. "Nothing has changed. We are still slaves like before. Dalits and lowcastes had to play servile when we were Hindus and now again when we are Christians. Yes, Saar. They were throwing away this old smart phone that was not working and I told them things are always fixable in India. So they gave it to me and I am using it to record their children from this same place, here in the veranda."

"That is terrible. Invasion of privacy."

The man stared at me as if I were from Mars.

"I took the phone to Guruji, and he is translating some words I did not understand." I felt like a traitor, deceiving my friendship with George and Claudia as I listened to this man. But I must admit I felt a morbid curiosity creeping inside.

The old smart phone hissed for a few seconds as the machine came on.

Gopal told me that George and Claudia's two children, boys who were students at the American school in Kodaikanal had come home for a holiday a few months back. The church construction was in full swing. The workers' children were fascinated by the boys and the attraction seemed to be mutual. I could hear their American accents in the way they spoke Tamil and the raspy voices of the Indian children as they replied.

Indian child 1: "Why did Yesu make me born into a poor family?"

Indian child 2: "It's because of your caste. Don't you know that?"

Indian child 1 (presumably to one of the American children) "But your father said God loves us all equally. Then why did God do that?"

Indian child 2: "No, He does not."

American boy: "The idea is that God does love us all equally. It's just that some people have more things than others but that is not important."

Indian child 2: "Not important? Then why do you have all this? I do not understand what I do not see. That idea is not real to me."

Indian child 1: "My Appa and Amma say your world is like a dreamland we have no ticket to."

The American boys had no response to this final declaration. The empty sound crackled, and the leper banged at the machine with his bandaged hand. We were both silent sitting there and I stared at the Parijata tree and the flowers on the ground. Monty barked from inside breaking into my thoughts. The childish voices in the machine had captured the injustice of life. Why single out George and Claudia's boys for their silence? I too had nothing to say in response.

"I call it a case of Churchgate, Saar. You know how years ago they had the case of Watergate in America?" I nodded wondering where all this was leading to. "I am recording like those people so I am responsible here for

Churchgate case, Saar." The man had a warped sense of humor.

"Be patient and show a little understanding. They are new to our ways," I said to Gopal. He inspected the wheels of his wooden board. "Patience is something we Dalits understand too well."

My heart felt like someone gave it a pinch and I shuddered in the sunlight. This obsession for hierarchy based on caste, occupation, gender, religion—why did we humans do that? What was the point in all that pain when our birth was ultimately a matter of chance, an accident? Why reduce a man to the sum of his skin, his caste, his community? How can a man or woman live like a shell with no spirit inside?

Driving away from the village, as always, S.D. and Puncture were thirsty and wanted to stop at Mogul Stores for a cold drink. Ali was there with his stained teeth, counting grimy rupee notes at the cashier's desk.

My eyes caught a fellow behind him lift up and tie his filthy dhoti above his knees. The movement froze in my mind because of what I saw underneath—a pair of shorts with stripes of light blue and dark blue, the same shades I had seen so recently in that small bit of cloth caught in the crack of the metal rod outside the temple. I pulled out the cloth from my pocket and stared at it. I looked up at the shorts I could still see framing the fellow's dhoti on the bottom. What if there was a tear in it somewhere that I could not see from this distance? The fabric was the same, I saw, looking down at the evidence. I looked up again and saw that the fellow was none other than Thomas, the chap who worked in the shop.

Pillai was pouring rice into a paper cone. He used string to tie the packet and handed it to a woman. Then he turned and moved away. That was when I noticed that he limped slightly. He wore a small bandage on his foot, exposing four toes. I did a double take in my mind as I remembered the footprints outside the temple. That man had six toes and small child size feet. Pillai was a petite chap, and he was hobbling around. I got out of the car.

"What happened to your foot?" I asked.

Thomas appeared behind him like a shadow and answered for him before Pillai could respond. "Oh, he had an abscess of some kind that the doctor said was infected." I was surprised by the quick response that did not match dopey Thomas's vacant eyes.

"Which doctor?" I asked, not willing to be brushed off.

"He went to Erode, Saar. Claudia Amma is not here so he had to go there."

I saw that Pillai and Thomas stole glances at one another as they shuffled to the back of the store. S.D. and Puncture had been listening closely. I shook my head to indicate that the whole business was best left alone at least for now. When I returned from the hills and my holiday, I decided, we would follow up on this suspicious behavior.

***

Back home, I sent for Nagu and told him the bad news. From my experience, it was best to be direct and factual in such matters. I told him what I had heard from the man who worked in Seshasamudram and suggested to Nagu that he take a few days off work before saying anything to his mother. He solemnly nodded his head, and my heart sank as I watched water pool in his eyes.

Cash for the holiday was the first thing I had to cross off my to-do list. I went into the puja room since the big English safe was still there where Patti, grandmother, had left it. Cookie, I noticed, had walked past me into the dining room. The next thing I heard was this bloodcurdling scream. I dropped everything, and in the next room I saw that there was a monkey peering into the fridge as if thinking, hmmm—what shall I have now? Cookie's face was priceless as she looked in my direction. She turned and hurriedly left the room. Bala came running from the garden. I knew monkey business to be his favorite hobby so I told him to handle it sensibly, no violence please, I reminded as I saw him reach for the bamboo pole in the corner. The mess in the kitchen was visible even from this distance -- the plastic onion basket toppled, the bananas, cabbage and tomatoes for dinner, some bitten , no doubt, scattered on the floor.

Before I left, the monkey and I locked eyes for a minute. It felt as if those brown eyes were accusing me of something dire, something important that I had not done. Then I remembered about the vadai malai and the accident on the way to Periamalai. I had meant to tell Bala to take care of this vow, to cook the vadais with fresh pepper and lentils, make a garland of these fritters and take it to the temple as an offering, a favorite of Hanuman. The priest at that temple knew me well. Over the years, I had sent several such garlands each time there had been an inauspicious incident—the time I slipped near the well and fractured my arm; when I fell ill with mumps during final exams, numerous other times I could not recall.

Iyer wished me bon voyage on the phone and promised to come over for dinner again when we got back. I asked him how he was feeling, and he said the tinnitis was threatening to come back. He had fainted in the bathroom and had woken up confused and scared. The migraine problem was surfacing again; he was trying herbal cure, Ayurveda, and massage. I admired his attitude toward illness. He shook his shoulders, creased his nose and made a certain gesture with his right hand that spoke volumes, saying, useless body but what to do, old age is like that, we have no control.

I was rereading my finished notes and report when Bala came into the room with my tumbler of Horlicks. As always, I had arranged for him to sleep in the dining room while Cookie and I were gone. The phone in the hall rang again and I heard him shout hello hello without stopping to take a breath. It was Naidu, the real estate pest informing me not to be alarmed because he was visiting Venkat's house tomorrow and planned to take measurements of our adjoining wall that marked the boundary between our lots.

"Why are you doing this? I don't want you coming over to this side," I said.

"Venkat Saar assured me it would be all right with you provided I asked in advance."

I said nothing in reply.

"There is some confusion about the exact size of the house based on what Venkat Saar told me and what I am seeing in the original plans."

I was curt and said he should do what he needed to do and leave.

"Thank you, Saar, I would like to meet you after your return from Ooty. Venkat Saar told me you were going away. I only wanted to be respectful and let you know what I had planned." I did not realize Venkat was seriously considering this fellow's offer. What did Venkat plan to do with his ailing mother? What a shame to move an old woman out of the house she had known since her youth. History and continuity was sacrificed in favor of convenience these days.

Nagu had ironed and piled the clothes on my bed. He had also done my toiletry shopping for me—shaving cream, coconut oil, new comb, Sandalwood soap, toothpaste, toothbrush and talc.

I finished packing and slid the suitcase under my bed. Then I lay down, exhausted, and went over the events of the day in my head. The power went off and the ceiling fan blades moved in slow motion as a mosquito sang near my ear. Too tired to get up and get the old fashioned bamboo fan from the cupboard, I pulled the sheet over my head like a corpse and prayed the mosquito had not slipped in as well. It was a hot and muggy night. Nothing unusual given Madras was this way most of the time. It helped a little when I reminded myself that as of tomorrow, I would enjoy the cool climes of Little England, Ooty. Eucalyptus trees and a lake with boats. Water rippling in the slight cool breeze. Tea on the lawn. The power was back and the ceiling fan resumed its normal speed. I opened my eyes, pulled the sheet down and turned the light off.

A strange extra-terrestrial face moved towards me in the darkness of the night. The eyes were fiery, the skin yellow, the color of a chrysanthemum bud, not yet open. The mouth formed an O reacting to the fear on my face I supposed, exposing teeth that looked strong, white and sharp enough to tear an old man like me to shreds. The creature switched the light on and I heard myself gasp as body, legs and arms were revealed. It was only Cookie with some rubbish painted on her face. "You gave me a shock child," I said touching my heart with my right palm.

"Sorry, Thatha," she murmured. "There is a flying cockroach in my room. You know how I feel about them. I shut the bedroom door so it's trapped. I'm going to sleep in the living room. Can't talk too much or my mask will crack. It's split pea flour and lemon juice, a little hydrogen peroxide. Am trying to get rid of that terrible tan I got from riding on Ravi's bike. I have a line around here," she said, tracing a finger around her neck. "Good night," she whispered, turned off the light and left the room.

In my dreams that night, there was Menaka, my first and only love, whom I had not thought of in a while, dancing like an apsara. I wanted to hang onto that image, but as I reached out with my mind, pleading with her to stay, she faded away.

At about four o' clock, as the birds in the mango trees outside the windows began to twitter, I got up. In the hall past my bedroom, Cookie was asleep on the floor. Her mouth hung slightly open and her hair spread from her head like a black Japanese paper fan. The colorful concoction I had seen on her face had rubbed off on the pillow and sheet for there was barely any evidence of the stuff on her face. She looked so vulnerable lying there, the beginning of her cleavage exposed by the bundled sheet, her eyelids throbbing as she dreamed something intense. For a moment, I was reminded of Menaka, the way I had seen her the last time, lying there on her bed, sleeping, lost to the world, eyelids fluttering, her virgin body shining and calling out to me. I watched her as she dreamed, hoping her head was full of thoughts and images of me, of us, by the seashore, our hands touching. The memory of the chemistry between us sent a shiver through my body now as I devoured Cookie with my old man eyes.

***

The wind through the open window carried the sound of a wailing child. The cries were insistent. I imagined a shriveled child with a distended belly, ribs sticking out. I remembered how Ayah would wrap used things from our house with her sari. A bit of food, an old shirt, a worn sheet or blanket. These were treasures for her sons. There was that humid afternoon when she caught me doing something cruel. I had seen a group of ants in the garden, took one out and wondered if it would die of loneliness. I squashed it dead and felt energized. She had caught me then and later again, as I watched, fascinated; when lizards ate flies, birds dug out worms and I asked her if that was that way with human beings too. As a child, I had a difficult time watching animals being killed to be eaten though I had been a killer myself. I asked her "Is there one group of predators for one group of victims?"

I wondered about the link between the so-called first and third-world. Developed countries and developing countries. Was this the relationship? One exploiting the other in the name of all sorts of help, using fancy politics to dress down real intention?

I thought of Nagu's face when I told him what I heard about his brother Siva.

Chapter Six
Blue Hills of Ootacamaund

I had finished my ablutions, shaving and what not, when Cookie came down in her towelly bathrobe to ask me how much money she would need since she had forgotten to go to the bank. I could not help but smile inside. She thought plastic cards contained the magic words open sesame and every place in the world cracked wide open like a cave if she carried these in her pocket. I suppose it was true these days but there were some exceptions. "No need for your money child," I said. " We will manage nicely with the money that we will get from Chinnakolam."

She stared at me incomprehendingly. "Remember I told you we will take lunch with the tenant farmer there? He will give me the income for the month from both the sugarcane and coconut plantations. So we will pay cash for everything during our holiday. Maybe I will buy you a present if you behave yourself," I said.

"Ha ha," she said and ran to the phone. Probably Basket Hair, I surmised, as I heard her voice rise uncharacteristically in answering long distance, Indian style. You had to shout whether you liked it or not because the lines were most often bad. This was the way neighbors and relatives found out many delicious secrets.

Then Cookie was back in my room, complaining, "What kind of weather is this?" I come out of the bath and I'm covered in sweat. My eyes are on fire, my mouth always parched. How do people touch each other in this city? I'm surprised couples reproduce. I don't even want to think about that. And everybody's acting like it's normal, saying yes, it's hotting up a little like they're English or something. Pity, it's hotting up a little when we're turning into toast."

"Okay, okay you cowgirl you, I remember it being very hot in Texas is it not?"

"Yes, it is. But we have, as you say Thatha, your language, not mine, bloody airconditioning."

"Aha. You Yankees are the ones screwing up the environment. We are putting up with it smiling. We are having oil bath and what not. Spend your energy on that instead of whining like a child. In India, people are grown up not stuck in childhood shouting and throwing tantrums. This is like a rodeo, this life, you have to stay put on it, however hard it rides."

"All this sun is giving me a headache."

"So carry an umbrella, wear a hat, scarf, anything. I suggest you stop drinking all that fridge water. Everything in moderation."

"This moderation, having to be sensible all the time—it's driving me crazy. India is not for everybody."

"Yes, true. And America is not for everybody, not for me."

"Why not?"

"Too much maya, illusion. It is like one big Hollywood movie, the whole country. Oversized people, all that merchandise piled up in glittering malls, all those sparkling fruits stacked like pyramids in supermarkets. Excess multiplied several times. The whole world suffers and you people carry on this way. All that materialism, isolation, aggression, competition. These are things I cannot understand."

"You don't let up on this self-righteous bit, do you?"

"Who, me? I'm self-righteous? Little old me, Ma'm?" I made a gesture as if I was tipping my unseen hat.

Cookie shook her head and we both laughed.

***

An hour later, after Usman finished checking everything under the bonnet, we were on our way, driving out of Hridaya Kamalam, the wheels blurring the lines of Paru's artistic project of the morning. The air turned cleaner as we drove farther out. There was the first monkey crossing the road with its long tail curled like a question mark. I wondered if Bala had taken care of the vadai malai at Hanuman temple after the catastrophe on the way to Periamalai. A corner of my mind continued to worry about Nagu and Venkat and what they would find in Seshasamudram though I knew such thinking was not productive and useless at best. I tried to bring my concentration back to the fact that I had at least managed to finish a good portion of the text for "Temples." I hoped Doc was faring well also, the tinnitis under control.

I mumbled Gayatri mantra into the warm wind that blew at my face. S.D. and Puncture had given their word to continue with all the work necessary to keep up with the cleaning and restoration of old nagapratishtas before they went to the Museum of Art.

I was glad to look out the window and see the comforting and familiar stretch of land, the family plantations of Chinnakolam. In spite of its name, Chinnakolam, which meant small pond, there was no such pond. It had dried up long ago during one of the severe droughts. The tenant of our land who supervised fifty or so laborers in the farm was called Chinnaiah by everybody. The name meant small master. But Chinnaiah was not small. He was a huge, hulking fellow with inky black skin and very white teeth. It was said that when he made a surprise sprint towards you at night, small children urinated on the spot.

Chinnaiah's father, Periaiah, Big Master, had been the tenant of these lands during my father's time.

After our meal, the young girls in the large family invited Cookie to join them in Kolattam, the energetic dance that was done while holding wooden sticks in their hands. Chinnaiah offered me the easy chair on the balcony. I saw Usman eating his lunch near the car, his stainless steel tiffin container shining as the rays of the sun hit metal. Farther out, the coconut trees swished and whispered in the breeze. There was that unmistakable earthy, farm smell about the place -- a mixture of standing water, soil, vegetation, along with the strong scent of molasses and ripe and rotting sugarcane.

"Ayyah, Saar," Chinnaiah began. " There are many like you who have sold their lands to the tenant families in Chinnakolam and neighboring villages." I was not surprised to hear him broach the subject as I myself, after consultation with siblings' families, had decided the time had come to let the place go. This decision had been made in spite of the wrenching emotion I felt because of my childhood bond to Chinnakolam. Problem with the current arrangement was evident by the bundles of rupees that Chinnaiah pulled out as income from the cloth bag. The amount he quoted was not what I expected.

"Is that all?" I asked. "I thought we made more than that last year."

"Don't forget the purchase of the new tractor, Saar. There is also the rising cost of fertilizers to contend with."

I sighed and shook my head. What he said maybe true but I knew there was also some pilfering of funds going on. I had no proof of course, only gut-level suspicion.

"There is trouble brewing among the workers, Sathya Saar. The Pallars, some of them are members of the Dalit Panther group wanting justice for the past. Our own community of Mudaliars too are restless because of what some of the Brahmin landlords did to them. Using their women, paying them less than half of what they deserved..."

I did not want to hear details of these old stories now. "What is the trouble here in Chinnakolam?" I asked. "Is it your son Murugesan?"

He nodded sheepishly keeping his eyes on the ground. Chinnaiah's wife had produced only daughters and he had taken a feisty Pallar woman as a mistress who gave him two strapping sons. One was a carpenter in the Gulf, funding the covert movements of the other, a leader for the farm labor in the village, inciting rebellion, laughing in his father's face, demanding equal rights for all heirs, legitimate and otherwise. He called himself a Dalit Panther, so called after the Panther party of black Americans in America. He abhorred the feudal system his father was part of.

Chinnaiah's voice had grown feminine when he said," My son and his generation, they do not understand loyalty. How we have grown accustomed to our landlords. They think we are weak like women under attack. Just last month he traveled to Kerala to hear the leader who spoke there. My son says that we, our people, we came from Africa. We were some of the first people on earth, in Africa and in India. These two countries were one land mass before it split. I don't know what to say to him. This fury of his, this talk, this is not the way, Saar."

I nodded. As a child, I remembered Chinnaiah standing outside the local temple in the village, hands clasped and eyes closed as he stood on the street, unable to visit inside. A small part of my heart lurched towards my belly like an American yo yo, making me suddenly uneasy. Authority was a fickle master, our forefathers failed to realize. So now we were on a see-saw from childhood -- power had shifted to the other camp.

' "The black people of America and the Dalits of India, we are like brothers,' " my son says. " 'We do not look for saviors outside ourselves. There are no answers in political parties. The power is within us.' Do you understand?" he asks. Two laborers were filling the boot of the car with a bunch of tender coconuts, a container of sugarcane juice and the usual jute bag filled with small blocks of fresh brown jaggery.

"Let me think about final numbers and I will send word to you about the sale, all right? You know how I feel, Chinnaiah. I would rather you have the farm than anybody else."

"Yes, Saar. I am most grateful to you for saying that." He did namaskaram and bowed his head.

I thought that just once, I would like to ride here again from the city the way it used to be when I was a boy, my eyes closing in spite of the excitement of the journey. In the background was the music of the bells on the horns of the bullocks pulling the cart or the clip clop sound of hooves made by the horse drawn carriage.

Those days my brother and I would spend the night sleeping under the stars, out in the carriage on which hay and quilts had been spread. Father slept out in the open a couple of yards away from us, closer, he said, to get a better view of the entrance to the fields, in case tigers or elephants or local village bandits had any ideas. My brother and I said nothing. We were young but we were not stupid. Truth was, Periaiah, Big Master, sent a woman to him at night. We could hear them whispering and laughing as they shifted around on the rope cot. Once I sat up and saw that he was on top of her, their thighs gleaming like marble, temple sculptures in the moonlight.

***

All the way to Ooty, a hundred miles away, Cookie and I slept on and off in the backseat of the car. When I opened my eyes, I looked out the window and saw the hill train from Mettupalayam to Ooty wind itself around the mountain like a toy choker on a giant goiter neck.

When we pulled into the majestic semi-circular driveway, the comforting and familiar scent of eucalyptus trees greeted my nostrils. Essex House was still the same—that faded splendor of the Raj in its architecture-many pillars, verandas circling the structure like a collar, beds of dahlias, a lush lawn, old English style furniture, the sound of a mellow grandfather clock as we entered, the dingy smell of mosquito netting hanging like shrouds around the beds.

The next two days were a blur. I was determined to finish the chapter as planned. Cookie was working diligently as well, preparing for her dance performance in the neighboring hill station of Kodai in front of George and Claudia. She had chosen a new and rather difficult piece, she told me, as I watched her carry a polished brass plate into her room after breakfast.

One evening, Cookie and I were having gin and tonic in the drawing room. The cook had made finger chips for us as snacks. Cookie, of course, called them French fries. We had a second round of drinks. Cookie had her right ankle resting on her left thigh. Her thumbs massaged her heel. "I want to talk to you about something, Thatha," Cookie said, her voice almost a whisper, putting me on alert. I could tell from her body posture that she was feeling less inhibited as she stopped massaging her foot and scratched herself under her arm.

"During my sophomore year at university in California, there was this guy," she began. "Is it okay for me to tell you this? I don't want to make you uncomfortable or anything." Her eyebrows knitted with concern for my old-man sensibilities.

"It is all right, child. I don't know why we think so many demarcations have to be drawn between generations. Perhaps you can teach me a little something and I can do the same for you? How can we do this if we don't talk and find out?" We called the cook and ordered a fresh plate of finger chips.

She smiled. "This guy Brian I was telling you about. He was American, from the mid-west. You know how bland some of them can be." I smiled at her in return. "But the truth was," here her voice became barely audible and I had to listen closely to decipher what she was saying. "There was this thing between us. It was like a subtle current that zigzagged through my body. There were these vibrations, these plunges in the pit of my stomach. I don't know how else to describe it. It was like something moving in my body. All I could do was watch. "

"What was he doing in Los Angeles? A student like you?"

She nodded yes. "Brian was a doctoral student. He chased eclipses. He was collecting data for his thesis. Wherever there was an eclipse, India, Africa, there he was, traveling all the way from America. I invited him home for dinner once. Mom and Dad did not like Brian. They could not understand what he was doing. Chasing an eclipse? What was the point in that? You know how Indian parents are. It's okay, all right for Americans and others to have these adventures, but don't you come near my children and contaminate them with your ideas." She leaned over and continued, "Ambitious young men choose investment banking, go to Wharton or Harvard and do medicine or at the very least, choose to become lawyers if they are lost." She wagged her finger at me. I smiled weakly at the irony in her voice.

"This thing between you, did he feel this way also?" I asked.

"Maybe in the beginning. The short time we knew each other -- it felt natural, not awkward. Then of course, he lost interest because he sensed my holding back." She stopped speaking but shivered slightly as if we were outside, somewhere near the mountain top. I saw that look on her face that told me she was traveling. Goosebumps went down the length of her arms and the fine hair on her skin stood at attention. I had just witnessed a sensual experience of the mind translated into an experience of the body before my old man eyes.

What was there to say? Feelings were not something you debated. They were what they were and it was no use pretending otherwise. Only consolation was that feelings did in most cases, subside and transform into something manageable over time.

"Kumar called me last night," she said.

"Fiancée? Everything all right?"

She nodded. "He is safe, dependable. But it is awkward between us, you understand?" I said nothing for a while. Hasty reactions lacked credibility at such moments. Then slowly, slowly, the words came to me.

"Feelings fail us sometimes. They are not accurate compasses of everything in life. Anyway, you are doing the right thing, giving yourself time."

"Tell me about yourself, Thatha. Have you ever been in love?" Cookie was direct in her manner as usual. I don't know what she saw on my face but she protested charmingly, "Oh, come on. It's not fair. I share things with you. I won't tell anybody, I promise." We poured ourselves another round of drinks.

"It hardly matters, Cookie, whether you tell anybody or not. The person in question is no longer alive." I do not know whether it was the fatigue in my head after all that writing, the evening air of the blue hills or the company of this beautiful young woman, but I felt a rare need to unburden myself.

"Menaka. She had an apsara's name. And like her name, she was a dancer, a celestial dancer." I took a gulp from my glass tumbler. The cook came into the room and said he was locking up for the night. He had prepared mulligatawny soup for me and a cheese and fruit tray for Cookie.

It would have been childish and cruel of me to mention to Cookie how I used to feel physically when I spoke of Menaka after her death. A cramp began somewhere deep within and spread throughout. With the passage of time, things had changed. Now there was a dull heaviness, a tired feeling that replaced years of regret.

"How did you meet her?"

Cookie's voice took me out of myself.

"She lived in the house across the road. You know the building called Royal Gardens? Her house was there. It used to be called Natyalaya, house of dance."

I looked at Cookie's hungry face and the memories came loose.

My hair was abundant and black and wavy those days. After all, I was only eighteen. A slender chap with buck teeth and an earnest heart waiting to be captivated. First time I went to Natyalaya, I had been invited there by my classmate, Menaka's older brother who scored top marks in Biology and Zoology. Non-scientific students like me were always borrowing his notes and peering into them curiously so that some secret we did not possess would come out and hit us in the face. As I sat on a pai, a bamboo mat spread in a corner of their hall, she came in, looked at me and stopped.

There was nothing coy about her. She knelt down not far from me and asked, "Who are you?" She did not bother to wait for an answer but got up and left abruptly as if she had lost interest on close examination.

Her house was so different from ours. A dancers' house. Not much furniture that I could see anywhere. An odd easy chair, a table in the hall, maybe a cot I glimpsed through the crack of an open bedroom door. Mostly open space everywhere. And always, the sound of music in the air. I could hear her mother singing upstairs and the sound of ankle bells as a student danced tentatively. Both her parents were teachers. I remember the many beautiful mirrors in the house. Oval ones. Skinny rectangular ones that gave a full length view from your head to your toes. It was mad, funny, odd visiting there at times. Except for my studious classmate, the family were all dancing most of the time. Menaka and her parents danced inside the house and outside in the garden. They danced around the well. Once I saw the father leap onto the washing stone and the mother jumped from the ledge of the water tank -- an elegant leap -- landing on her toes.

Visitors who came to the house, all we could do was stop and stare. Even the servants had to be prodded to do what they were supposed to do. The thing that struck me most was this thing they had between them, an energy, this unspoken game they practiced, laughing, delighting in life. For example, I remember the time I went to check notes for my final exams and Menaka and her parents were dancing in the hall. They pushed me in the middle and the three of them formed a circle, dancing around me. I was Krishna, the naughty boy lord who had stolen butter and curds from his helpless female devotees.

I was mesmerized by Menaka, this bold beauty who created her own reality with a tilt of her head, the movement of her eyes, the swagger of her walk. I wondered what she thought of me and my parents. There were a few times she came to visit my sister. Everything at home was so traditional, my mother in the kitchen with her hair wet and all that turmeric smeared on her cheeks. My father in his loincloth sitting near the well, being bathed by Ayah and Ayah herself, cackling and showing betel stained teeth, wearing no blouse to speak of. Then there were my two younger brothers with their crooked teeth and stick legs in wide khaki shorts. They wore shirts with missing buttons held together by safety pins. Finally, all those aunts and uncles and cousins -just so many people at Hridaya Kamalam. So many curious faces gawking at her. A glance from her towards me, that tilt of her head like a bird and I melted like butter on hot coals.

One evening her brother had invited us to Natyalaya for a dress rehearsal. You know how it was those days, we were not allowed out after the lamps were lit in the prayer room at seven o' clock. So I had to find a solid excuse to get out of the house. I lied to Amma that I had an exam in two days and had to look over Zoology notes for the next couple of hours. She placed a banana leaf in front of me as I sat cross legged on the floor and made me eat curds and rice with left over curry from lunch saying I had to be back by ten.

In Natyalaya, Menaka was dressed in a spotted animal print sari for adu pambe, the snake dance. You see, it was a very popular dance at the time.

Cookie's face was rigid with attention; she held a few strands of hair that she coiled over and over with the fingers of her right hand.

The snake dance music wailed and hypnotized, Menaka's body swayed to sound. She moved as if she had no bones, curving herself this way and that. I was enchanted by everything, I felt I was with her, inside her, dancing that mad dance of the serpent, slithering, touching the back of my head with the tip of my foot, circling my body into a bangle as if it was the most natural thing in the world. When she finished, I took a deep breath for I had forgotten everything about myself--where I was, what I was doing. I did not realize that it was her and not I that had made the effort required for the challenging dance. I do not know how to explain the mood of the moment. You see, she had liberated me from myself.

"Do you understand what I am saying, Cookie?" I asked as I turned towards the child.

I saw from the expression on her face that she indeed understood. "It is like discovering the universe all over again. Seeing how big things can be. How much room there is to travel. It is like visiting new, adventurous parts of yourself. That is how it was when my friend told me things I did not know existed in the sky. Did you know that moons break, that the rings of Saturn are made up of rocks of ice?" She was transported, I saw plainly. So I let her speak her piece.

"One evening we walked under the night sky and Brian told me he often thought of himself flying out there. Gaseous celestial bodies swirled about him. The suspense and thrill was whether he would get pulled into the gravitational force. Then he would forever be orbiting with the dust and ice of one of those rings, knowing everything, saying nothing, looking down on earth, alive and dead. Then Brian laughed and said he should snap out of it. But I could not speak because he had made me see it all, he made me realize how much more there was."

We were both drained and slightly sloshed so I decided it was best we ate dinner and retired for the evening.

***

Next morning, Venkat had arrived while I was still in my room, going through my yoga asanas. When I came out for breakfast at nine o clock, he was sitting in one of the lawn chairs, drinking coffee and smoking a cigarette.

"How are you?" I asked out of habit though I could see very clearly for myself that he was exhausted, red eyed, face sagging with all he had seen in Seshasamudram.

He knew what I really wanted to ask so he looked at my face and shook his head. Then he made that sad and helpless gesture, pushing his palm through his hair. "It is bad news, Sathya. Siva was cremated with some of the others. Nagu took the bus back to Maramur. The poor fellow had steeled himself. I'm going to sleep till lunch time," Venkat said and got up. "I managed to pick up the chemicals and things I need for the dark room here," he added.

He saw that I looked at him quizzically because I did not understand.

"I can easily make do with my bedroom for a dark room while I am here," he said.

I needed to walk and sort my thoughts out.

***

Next day, I went back to writing and reading though the going was rough. After a simple lunch served in my room, I fell asleep the whole afternoon.

Post at tea-time brought more anxious news. There was a letter from Iyer.

Dear Sathya:

Due to severe nuisance value of tinnitis problem, I have arranged to make the deal with the realtor fellow, Naidu, earlier than planned. I will have moved into the room in the Theosophical Society grounds by the time you come back to the city. Driver and car as planned will be at my disposal. My son Venu calls regularly from Philadelphia but what can he do now? I keep telling him that I am not doing badly for an old man.

Sleep at night is a thing of the past. There is this racket and roar spreading in my head. It is like the Orient Express hissing and going round and round my brain. There are brief intervals that I revel in, spurts of silence that come and go. Then I lie in the dark and try to wipe the slate clean. I can feel death coming at such moments. It is not a bad feeling at all. There have been times when I have left the body momentarily and floated out of myself. From the ceiling of the room, I have watched myself and said to the body, stop the racket, let it go, whenever the time is. Fighting is too much effort.

Do not let this rambling fool you. I am still cheerful and waiting for you to come back. I would like to walk the grounds with you again, maybe meet your grandniece and watch her dance again. That would be very nice.

Till then,

Poochi Iyer

Usman drove Venkat and me back to our British style bungalow where we were staying, Wenlock Downs, famous for its butler pantry now used for storing rice, lentils and pickles. I spread a blanket under eucalyptus and pine trees.

"The last two to three days have been exhausting, terrible in many ways. But I know what my next project will be after "Temples." Photographs I took from Seshasamudram along with others I'd like to take in the future. Workers sorting through metal waste, leaking batteries, who knows what else." Venkat stared at a pine cone on the ground and lit another cigarette. It was as I imagined. He had been moved and impassioned by what he witnessed.

"This is something we need to expose. Your photographs of the suffering will educate the world," I said.

"You really believe that? Do you think we are affected any more by misery? Or are we immune to suffering because it's not happening in front of us?" he asked.

"It's true we are overdosing on this. But suffering must not be ignored whether the public is tired or not."

Venkat did not reply. "You should have seen the place. Corrugated sheets for roof, filthy living conditions. No plumbing, no bathrooms. The risks they take working on taking apart those old ships for a measly plate of rice and dhal -- the pittance they send home to families. Now I'm sure there is no God. Only cruelty, chaos."

"I want to hear about Siva, Nagu's brother. Did you find out how he died?" I asked.

"It was an accident. Two or three of the men were hurt by a falling corroded beam. Poor fellow, the thing landed on his head. It was a bad skull fracture. The ambulance came but he died on the way to the hospital. The men told me such accidents were almost a daily thing. I lost count of the men I saw with missing fingers. Of course, there's no protective gear like gloves and hardhats."

Again there was that gesture of despair, running his palm through his hair, remembering something troubling he had seen. "The air reeked, the shore water was anything but clear," Venkat said. "The men look like ghosts. They have hacking coughs, you can hear them wheezing. Along with the cigarettes, I might have shortened my life because of the few days I spent there." He shrugged.

We sat in silence for a while before Venkat began talking again.

"Four of the men who stripped ships took me to the place where the previous day a man had died. First thing in the morning, they said he coughed up blood and slumped to the floor. He had been ripping apart insulation for months. It was an American naval ship they were working on. The men tried to burn his body on the shore with cooking oil and wood but there had not been enough. Parts of him still lay on the sand. They said it would be high tide that evening." Venkat whispered. "They cremated him not far from where they shat every morning. The stench of life and death is everywhere in that place."

***

We were in the balcony of the bungalow when the cook brought a tray of ice, rum and ginger ale into the drawing room. Both of us sipped our drinks and listened to birds flapping their wings on the trees in the garden, settling down for the night.

"Why can the western countries not strip the ships of toxic stuff before they send them here?" Venkat asked.

"They call it recycling. A whole lot of countries are involved."

"It is Cambodia all over again," Venkat said in a soft voice.

I knew he was referring to the littering of landmines there, something we were all too familiar with during our brief stay in Angkor Wat. This was a dangerous direction considering the tragedy Venkat had experienced there, so I thought I'd shift gears. Venkat had taken to drinking hard again after a short, dry spell. A bit of stress, a few bumps on the road and the man fell off the wagon, time after time. I supposed it was easy for him to get away with his problem since he always kept things under control, working nights and days by himself, shut up in the dark room.

Next morning, I continued with my writing and planned to make a call or send a telegram home to Maramur about releasing money from the bank for Nagu and Ayah. The cook told me Venkat had stayed up all night and was spending the day at the club with an old friend.

A couple of hours later, outside, a gentle rain had begun and I heard the pitter patter of it falling on bushes and trees in the garden. I wanted to go for a little walk but that was out of the question now. I got up and decided to explore the upstairs portion of the bungalow. Venkat had left the door to his room open and I saw that he had instructed the servants not to clear his room. He had piled things everywhere -- on stools, on both sides of the hastily made bed. The photos he developed hung on a clothesline that he had tied from one end of the room to the other. The man did not believe in using a digital camera like everyone else. He felt his way offered more control, more style.

There was a shot of an emaciated man in Seshasamudram ringing a temple bell. It was obviously a makeshift shrine, a statue of Devi, Lakshmi with her many arms, placed on a wooden crate. The bell had been taken from an American naval ship. I could make out the engraving that said Made in the U.S.A. As I walked from left to right, I saw images of men with sunken cheeks and haggard faces and stick bodies staring into the camera, a long shot of the shoreline and a naval ship, piles of debris like precarious triangles rising towards the sky. There was a photograph with the half-burned body of a man tossed like an animal on the shore. Another one showed the men working, carrying pieces of the ship with their bare hands, wearing flip flops, their cotton sarongs lifted and tied above the knees to provide ease of movement.

I stared out the windows at the rain and thought of Venkat drinking away his pain at the Gymkhana Club. He would get abominable and loose-tongued, talk rubbish and do things he would otherwise not have done. As I turned away from the view of the garden, my eyes settled on a small framed photo that stood on the corner of the bedside table next to the lamp. It was a face from the past—a little Cambodian boy, holding his American Frisbee, smiling that trusting childish smile. I walked away. There was too much hanging in the air of that room.

***

Early in the evening, I walked towards the Murugan temple but did not go inside.

Last time I was here, there had been bamboo scaffolding outside the spires of the temple, men painting the exterior. I saw that the beautiful carvings at the entrance had been covered in gaudy colors; the goddesses in eye piercing reds and greens and the limbs of gods wrapped in jaundice yellow, their bodies pink as beetroot mixed with curds, the effect tasteless and overdone, ruining the effect, hiding the grainy texture of stone. I wondered if my fat boss from our office, Subbudu, had been responsible for this. Subramanyam was his real name and he was an overfed, overdressed, jeweled chap, a smooth talker who had managed to overcome politics in Tamil Nadu by marrying a woman of mixed caste and having parents of mixed caste himself. He belonged to all groups and was everybody's darling, doubly so because he knew how to ingratiate himself with a honey tongue and a flash of diamond rings that said authority to most of the idiots in our government office. His idea of temple renovation and preservation involved covering everything in sight with bright colors of blue, pink, red and yellow. This way, nobody could tell if anything was damaged or not. Why waste time in all that effort and heartache and red tape when a few cans of paint did the job of covering it all up? I suspected he was a corrupt rascal who reached out for bribes but he was too smart to get caught. Fools that they were, S.D. and Puncture thought this sub-optimal Subbudu a fine fellow and followed his bidding, no questions asked. Once a sub-optimal you remained that way for life.

***

We drove to Kodaikanal after a breakfast of onion uthapam, bananas and pomegranate juice. We planned to spend two or three days there. Two hours into the drive, we were stuck in a traffic jam. A bullock cart with rubber wheels was immediately ahead of us. One of the bullocks began the dreaded, familiar movement with its tail, swishing away flies first and then lifting the tail while it did its business, messy number two business right in front of our car. "What seems to be the problem, Usman?" I asked.

"Political demonstration, Saar," he said. One of the chaps on the side of the road was holding a placard, walking to join his gang ahead. Usman stuck his head out and chatted with the fellow. At the end of their conversation, Usman made the Muslim gesture of greeting, touching his forehead with his right palm in deference to an elder. "What is it about?" I asked, unable to stand the curiosity.

"The man I spoke to said there had been a clash between some of the protestors and the police. A lot of them deliver bread to the big shops in neighboring cities and towns and have joined other Muslim merchants in the area in a strike," Usman said.

"Don't tell me puny Hindus are involved?" I asked as I spotted such a fellow to the side of the road, his sarong tied above his knees, spitting into the gutter as usual. "They will be made into chutney by mutton-eating Muslims."

Usman and Venkat laughed. "You're right there," Venkat offered while Usman demurred. "No, Saar, where do poor Muslims go for mutton?"

Ahead of us, I saw that the police had managed to break up the crowd and people were retreating from the spot. Usman enthusiastically pressed the horn. "Muslims, I have to say, are always ready to take up their cause. Never mind their women are suffering and their children are malnourished. Somebody does something and they all run out. We Hindus will never have this kind of unity. We are such a disorganized lot with so many opinions -- there is never a consensus of any kind," I said.

Venkat stared at me in surprise. "You don't really mean that, do you? What about the rise of Hindu fundamentalism? They've all got together and agreed that the majority will rule, haven't they?"

"Bah, humbug. That is bamboozling business. Bullshit in your lingo. "

"No Saar," Usman said. "I know of many cases when Muslims were harassed and beaten by Hindus, why I can give you an example…"

I did not want to hear any of it. "Always the same old rubbish. We are better than you attitude. How will this country, the world, progress? It is always history repeating itself. The Muslim period is the bloodiest in India in spite of fellows like Akbar who tried hard to be just. Who is taking up the cause of Hindus in Pakistan? I don't see anybody doing it. Muslims and all that mutton business fogging their minds," I muttered.

"Saar, I'm telling you we poor Muslims cannot afford mutton, Saar."

"You really surprise me sometimes, Sathya. Your insensitivity," Venkat whispered.

I chose to ignore him. I found it a little funny that coming from busybody big bully America like he did, he was trying to lecture me on sensitivity and prejudice. There was no point in denying that NRI's irritated me endlessly, one foot here and one foot there, lacking in commitment, wanting the moneyed soft life. What was the gutter expression I heard for this in Houston? No balls, that's right, such people had no balls, they were women between their thighs. Simple living and high thinking was the answer, nobody these days seemed to understand that.

***

In Kodaikanal the next morning Cookie and I had finished breakfast in the garden. Usman had taken the car to the petrol bunk so we could go to the local temple in half an hour.

"Thatha, I want to hear the rest of the story like you promised. About you and Menaka. I really want to know," she said and looked searchingly at me. Sitting there in the garden, just the two of us, I felt peaceful enough to share details with the child.

This was the story I told that crisp morning in Kodaikanal, the two of us sitting on wicker chairs, the sun gentle and warm.

Close to the ocean, the waves were lapping at our feet. Menaka faced the sun and I stood and watched her profile. She danced a few steps of an invocation and first dance with which she planned to begin her debut performance the following month. Her hands were raised and palms pressed against each other, her head moving bird-like on her neck. She had made me promise that I would not stay and watch so I proceeded to walk along the shoreline though I stopped at intervals and looked back. Last time I saw, she had moved on to the tillana, that wonderful final piece marked by a definite metrical cycle, a tala. What she had introduced in the initial alarippu number, she elaborated on in grand style now.

"You were perfect, no less," I said, walking back towards her.

"No," she laughed. "I made at least two mistakes that I can think of."

"I felt as if I was dancing too. I was ready to stop being myself and turn into you."

"What a thing to say," she said and looked at me dismayed.

I turned around and saw that her parents were seated on the sand far away, I could barely make them out and I was confident they could not see us. My skinny brothers, sister and Menaka's brother were playing badminton not far from where her parents sat. This was my chance, I realized, and grabbed her hand. I was shaking from emotion and my hand was clammy.

"Sathya, I like you too but I cannot be this perfect person you want me

133

to be. I am not her. I love dancing and it's all I want to think about now. I want to be myself. I do not want to turn into this feverish person like you, willing to lose myself. Please, let's walk and enjoy the beach while we're here. No more talk of love, all right?"

It felt like I'd been slapped hard. But I said nothing, falling into step beside her, watching water turn into foam and spread over our feet as we walked.

On the evening of her debut performance, Menaka danced like one possessed. She was the many faces of Devi -Lakshmi, Saraswati, Durga, Mahishasura Mardini as her eyes glowed with anger and she assumed the stance of a warrior. Because of what she had said to me that day at the seashore, we had not spoken of it again. She had said she liked me. That was enough. I had arranged to go over to her place after the performance for I wanted to tell her myself how well she had done. But when I showed up at her front door, I was told she was not feeling well and I should go home. They would not be receiving any guests for a while. When I pressed her brother for details, his lips trembled and his eyes welled up. He shook his head and slammed the door in my face.

Next time I saw him, he had a message for me from Menaka. She had the dreaded pox and wanted me to know that she often thought of me but I should leave her alone now as she prepared to die. I could think of nothing but her lively eyes, the way I saw myself reflected in them and felt more and more alive when she was by my side.

I loved her so much, I could not help myself, I had to see Menaka once more. I waited behind the hibiscus bushes in her garden and when I saw her mother leave the room. I stood there biting my lip, kneading my hands for a while. Next moment, in a flash, I had lifted my limbs and climbed in through the window. It was early in the evening and I could smell the incense in the air and heard the sounds of prayers coming from the puja room. I was familiar with the mantra reputed to be an efficacious plea to the goddess to protect the well being of everyone in the family.

Menaka's body was covered with a thin, cotton, muslin cloth. Her face, that face I knew so well was unrecognizable. She opened her eyes and saw me there. There were whimpering sounds. Then something strange happened. The expression in her eyes by which I recognized her was fading. I checked *again and again but there was nothing there. It was as if she left her body momentarily and it scared me so badly that I climbed out the window and left.*

Back home, I knew what I had done. I had taken this precious thing between us and held it as if it were only mine. Her parents, her brother, they had all pleaded with me to stay away. Not because the house was quarantined and there was fear that smallpox was highly contagious, which it was. My transgression had nothing to do with any of that. She had asked for a little room, some solitary time to die in peace by herself. She loved me in her own way and did not want me to see her that way—her beauty marred, her body tortured. It was a small, simple request. But I had spoiled our last moments with too much of myself. I felt great shame as I meditated on this later, as a grown man. Would Cookie understand what I struggled to say? I had faced the ugliness of my ego, my human limitations, the depth of my desires veiling what I should have done, her wish to be remembered as she was before. Death is a private matter, not a spectacle. We are born alone and we die alone. This was one experience that could not be shared. Love made it no easier. It was a solitary transition, a mystery for the living, a language shrouded in secret, however hard we tried to reach out.

***

The Kurunji Andavar temple in Kodaikanal was also a Murugan temple. Not far from the lake, the place boasted a magnificent view. On one side there was the Palni Hills along with the expanse of the northern plains and on the other, the famous Vaigai dam and surrounding southern plains. It was a simple temple that had several bushes of a blue flower that bloomed only once in fourteen years. Local people said that on this rare occasion, the descendents of the two eagles from Thirukazhikunram appeared there as if by magic, alighting on two nearby rocks and waiting patiently for offerings from the puja, rice and jaggery that was given to them by the priest. A bush blooming once in fourteen years and descendents of legendary eagles appeared at the same time. It was a sign that reminded humans that not everything could be explained away. Man was not the master of the universe.

"You know Cookie, in the west, there is this idea of man and the universe as two separate things. That approach is very different from the way things are seen in India. In America, you think everything is possible. But this everything is nothing, it is illusion, the whole world is illusion, so the idea of man must be defined anew. This obsession for action is not necessarily a good thing, you understand? Here man is part of the universe, acceptance rather than defiance is instilled in him."

"I see that. As long as it does not contribute to people being passive, I guess it's all right. It's another way of looking at things. I don't feel strongly one way or the other Thatha. Is that fickle of me to admit? It's too much for me to think deeply about everything. I have enough difficulty sorting out my own life."

I smiled. She had given away her position without realizing it. She thought of herself as separate and whole, there was her own problem, her own life, her own world. She was young, what did I expect?

"That is the beauty of the animal, the plant, they do what they're supposed to do, while we're going yodley yodley all the time because we are uncomfortable with silence. We want to break the silence and talk talk all the time."

"I want to ask you something. You don't still blame yourself for what you did--I mean about seeing Menaka one last time?" So that was what had been bothering her. She was thinking over what I had said.

"You know, Cookie, what Gandhiji said? He said, "When disappointment stares me in the face and all alone I see not one ray of light, I go back to the Bhagavad Gita. I find a verse here and a verse there, and I immediately begin to smile in the midst of overwhelming tragedies-and my life has been full of external tragedies-and if they have left no visible, no indelible scar on me, I owe it all to the teaching of the Bhagavad Gita." I find consolation when I remember that."

Cookie looked at me with knitted brows and said, "It worked for him maybe. But how did this help you?"

"It helps me because it reminds me to lift myself from the lower levels of human nature. I should try to live in that state where I am without waves inside. Complete calm within me while I go about doing my duty in life. In my case, preserve our temples and attend to my writing so our Hindu heritage is not neglected. You see, this is my goal -- that I achieve without any desire attached to the job."

I saw that she was not taking any of it in, the child was not ready for my explanation and outlook on life. Such was our fate, the old trying to teach the young but knowing the job to be a futile one. Youth cannot understand the full truth of the matter, the pain of life cannot be experienced second hand. So the cycle continues time and again, generation after generation, the old people trying and trying to voice the pitfalls, the young ones wearing blindfolds, walking into danger as they should, for who does not want to believe that they are special, that they will somehow escape the same traps because of who they are?

"But you were young, what you did was natural."

"I knew better than that. I did not want to listen because I was averse to the silence and quiet within myself. The same disease that makes you whistle in the dark. You whistle to escape yourself. The pure part of me was the same as in her so I knew what was happening. But I had this childish desire to see her one more time. I made her suffer more by doing that."

"You've got rid of this child in you? Have you?"

I looked at her face and sighed for what could I say in answer to that? "He is still there cowering and whining all the time. But it's not like before. I know he's there so I keep a watch out for him and smack him if necessary."

We sat there for a while watching the mist being eaten by the sun, tourist buses bringing noisy people with their transistors blaring cinema songs. It was time to leave, these characters pushed my blood pressure up with their stupidity -- throwing Styrofoam cups by the roadside, talking loudly and laughing for nothing, advertising vacancy upstairs.

"Come, let's go back. You have a dance performance to give tonight, is it not?"

***

George and Claudia had arrived at the guest house and we greeted each other warmly. The cook had set the dining table with tea and coffee, vegetable cutlets, chutney and slices of fruitcake.

After tea, we went for a walk. "George, we wanted to share something with Sathya, remember?" Claudia said. I could tell from her gesture, the way she tugged at the sleeve of his shirt, that it was something serious they wanted to talk about. I myself had been wondering how to bring up the topic of Gopal and all that Churchgate/Watergate business. Maybe they could help pave the way for me now.

George began telling me about the day the stone-laying ceremony for the new church was held. The morning of the Sunday ceremony, Claudia went to the market to buy flowers for decoration. Walking back, she had been approached by a gang of three men. "They blocked my way and walked up real close to me," she said. "I could smell toddy liquor on their breath. I couldn't understand everything they said. But I knew they were making threats about the school, the church, the clinic. I was grateful Gopal was waiting in the car at the time. He had wanted a ride to see his family and it turned out to be a lucky thing for me. If he'd not been there, I don't know what I'd have done. It made me real sad. There on the street, all those women and men and children I had treated in the village and not one of them came up to help." The drop in her voice made me turn and look at her. She looked puzzled and hurt like a child. George put his arm protectively around her shoulders. How naïve she was, I thought. Had the church not prepared her for India?

"Sathya, I'm worried," George said. "I thought these people loved us and they almost attacked Claudia. I've been reading the news reports about harassment of Christians in the North but surely, this problem has not spread to the South?"

"What did Gopal say? Did he explain what was bothering those men?" I asked.

"He said it had to do with us trying to change things. Parents did not like it that we made all the children sit and eat together. I think there were nuances there we did not really catch. Right, honey?" Claudia asked George. I saw that she nodded thoughtfully. "I just want to erase it all from my mind," she added.

"It doesn't stop there. There was an incident before mass the same day. I opened the doors and saw that the crucifix had been garlanded with chappals and shoes, the ends of the rope twisted around rusty nails pounded into the wall on either side. What a moment that was. It really broke my heart." It was the ultimate Indian insult, George and I both knew. Footwear, leather etc. were all stigmatized according to Hindu culture and tradition. A source of pollution.

"I told you before, George. You're coming and changing things. Aiming for conversion, your idea of equalization—all this is a difficult thing when habits are ingrained for a long time. You've upset the mango cart, is it not? I told you before, there's bound to be after shocks," I said. "Did you know that after you left, there had been some trouble with Gopal?"

George and Claudia shifted in their chairs and simultaneously shook their heads.

I told them what had happened at the clinic and how I had gone over to their place and heard complaints from Gopal. "To some extent you are being naive and optimistic. These people must be kept at a certain length. You cannot let Gopal spend so much time in the house and compound, watching every move you make. Kindness can backfire in such cases. Treat servants and such people with compassion but not too much—can you both understand that? It is a difficult balance to maintain, I will grant you that. Such people will walk all over you if you let them. They know their limits with Indians but with foreigners this does not seem to work." I thought this much warning was plain and clear, there was no need to go into minute details. Like Claudia, I too felt like erasing my mind of all this unpleasant business.

***

I freshened up for the evening and came out of my room wearing my American T-shirt which I reserved for special occasions. A private dance performance by Cookie was a good qualification for me to wear my nice clothes. On top of my T-shirt, I wore a pullover since it was important for me to protect my chest from chills. George and Claudia had gone back to their cottage and returned suitably decked out -- George in a jacket and tie and Claudia looking very alluring and feminine in an embroidered Kashmiri salwar kameez set. Venkat too appeared downstairs as if on cue, much to my surprise. He looked a little more rested and relaxed, I was glad to note. Since he did not like to dress up, he wore his usual jeans and shirt but he had wetted his hair down and his beard was trimmed and he was in an agreeable mood, so one could not ask for more than that. Cookie was eating dinner since she needed a good amount of time between ingestion and performance.

***

Cookie was draped in an emerald color silk sari with a mustard color border. Her hair had been braided in the traditional manner, the black velvet kunjalam ornament tied to the end, a garland of jasmine wound around her plait. She had used henna on her palms and feet and the color was rich and vibrant—orangey red under the lights. This was a solo number in which the dancer displayed fleet footed movements, quicksilver, alternating soft and sharp beats to add interest and texture to the piece. The dance was quite a balancing feat since she had her feet on the rim of a brass plate and on the top of her head was a small brass pot filled with water.

Cookie's fine abhinaya skills, her expressive face, was ideal for the story telling nature of the dance. She was Rukmini dancing the tale of her Lord and husband, Krishna. She depicted her lover in all his mischievous splendor, his butter stealing antics, the tricks he played on his young female devotees, gopis, the sweet flute music that he used to enchant and call like a Pied Piper. We watched mesmerized, as Cookie threw swift and heart stabbing looks of love, pined when separated from her Lord. Her eyes spoke eloquently like the rest of her. Everything had been achieved without spilling a single drop of water.

After she had been greeted personally by many who were present, she came and stood next to me. "Was I as good as, you know, her?" She asked.

"You were good. And most important, you were yourself. You're best when you're yourself. Besides, she never did kuchupidi," I whispered. Cookie looked at me and smiled, then reached out and pressed my hand.

***

Next morning, I woke to find there had been letters from my brothers' families about the house. My nieces and nephews and sister-in-law felt the time had come to think about settling family matters. Flats in Bombay

140

and Delhi had to be purchased and they heard the real estate market had peaked in Maramur.

I stood before the picture I had placed on the stone shelf above the fireplace in my room. There was Vishnu as he appeared in Tirupati, garlanded and radiant. Four sandalwood incense sticks had been lit and their wooden bases pressed into a banana. The fragrance was familiar and comforting and I closed my eyes and chanted my mantras. Suddenly, a gust of wind entered the room through the windows and the flame of the small brass lamp was snuffed out. As I moved forward to grab the box of matches and light the wick again, another gust of wind hit the room and the photo on the shelf fell forward flat. My breakfast curdled in my stomach. All night long, I'd heard the distant howling of dogs. The chimney howled like an animal in pain as the wind snaked through to the top. I lifted the Vishnu photo gingerly to see the glass cracked in several pieces.

Same evening, the air was cool and fireflies were scattered like stars in the pitch black of the night. Crickets chirped loudly and continuously as I walked in the garden. Silence of the soul, a certain stillness if you like, can only be cultivated in isolation, not in the company of other human beings. I thought of George and Claudia nursing their dilemma of displacement like a cherished possession. Cookie, in her youth and beauty, dreaming of all that was to come. Then there was Venkat carrying the pain of the past. He was a tortured soul who sought justice in the world as if man really was in charge. Then there was me, healer of temples and doer of duty, in the middle of it all.

Far out on the road leading up to the guest house in the compound, I saw the headlights of a car winding its way to the top. It was an unusual sight to see this late at night.

S.D. and Puncture looked excited as soon as they saw me approach them and the office jeep. They made a nervous pair, with S.D. blurting out, "Saar, Saar, sorry to be causing all this botheration, (trajectory of rocket beginning) but Saar, Saar, what to do, (voice gaining ground, taking off, resultant salivary bubbles evidenced at the corner of the mouth) we are not knowing what to do." This confusing pronouncement followed by Puncture saying, " Sathya Saar, we are trying and trying to take care of everything sssssssssssss, not disturbing you sssssssssssss but Krishna

Rama something or the other sssssssssssssss is always happening to make emergency sssssssssssss."

"Calm down, you two," I said. " I cannot follow a thing you chaps are trying to tell me. Let us go inside and sit down and you tell me what the problem is."

I saw that they looked at each other nervously and fidgeted with their hands. The words came out of me as if I had known them all along though it only occurred to me right then and there. "It is something to do with the nagapratishta?"

They mutely nodded their heads and their eyes dilated in anxiety and surprise. "You are having sixth sense, Saar, feeling some problem is there already before we came?" I gestured asking him to stop. Puncture took up the cause. "It is the old nagapratishta, the one with the stains on it, Saar. It is gone from the museum warehouse. It has disappeared, Saar."

"The other one with the jagged line running across the back, that is all right?" They nodded their heads like two Bharath Natyam dolls, their necks lifted high above their bodies and moving left to right.

Chapter Seven
Churning of the Ocean

Usman and I left Kodi early next day for Maramur. S.D. and Puncture had gone back to Madurai. Mr. Sub-Optimal, I was told, would provide me with all the background and details regarding the circumstances surrounding the missing tablet. I pictured him flashing his diamond rings, his Adam's apple going up and down like an elevator, the lines on the skin of his neck dusted with talc, telling me what a shock it had been for him to find out about the piece of missing art. Superficial bastard that he was, I was certain he would use the incident for some political advantage seeing how he was always appearing supplicant, oily and unctuous to those in charge, changing sides like a whore if the situation demanded it. Why, I remembered a time from last year when he had agreed with me about the ceremonies at Purnipakkam village temple, saying let us do what is important and meaningful, mantras and puja as always, none of this garish lights and blaring music business, low class style. Then when the time came and pressure from headquarters and management was applied, the man caved in, all that talk and promises along with his lips going back into his mouth.

We passed the shacks behind Koil Street and I remembered that Ayah, Nagu and Paru were still in their village, settling matters regarding Siva. I hoped to see Ayah again so I could say an official goodbye. I thought of Iyer in his new surroundings amidst the majestic trees of the Theosophical Society and made a mental note to telephone him as soon as possible. A Fiat coming in the opposite direction had a familiar chap sitting in the back seat. I realized it was that real estate Naidu, scouting the area as always, I supposed, on the lookout for new victims to his grandiose flat building schemes.

***

At the government Museum of Art, while I waited for S.D. and Puncture and Sub-Optimal, I spoke to key people who gave me important information regarding the tablet. The pillar people and door people said they had warned the tablet people that they should be very careful, such old things were irreplaceable, these days everything and everybody was suspect, even ants had eyes and accomplished great tasks through collective strength. Throwing about such platitudes usually meant nobody knew what had happened. Another possibility was that they used such statements to obfuscate facts and send the listener's mind reeling back into inertia. I told a worker that I wished to see the other tablet, the one with the zigzag crack running down the middle that had been stored along with the stained missing one. He began with the usual troublesome signs of scratching his neck, rubbing his beard, finally shaking his head saying he did not understand. I had to call another chap and explain all over again what it was that I wanted when I saw that S.D. and Puncture and Sub-Optimal had arrived, all three of them walking in a row, one after another.

Behind them, I saw the fellow who had shown us slides of the missing Krishna idol months back when there were all those long winded speeches. The worker I had spoken to earlier and the supervisor who had shown us all those slides talked rapidly with one firing off a series of questions and the other one saying yes Saar, no Saar. The final result was we were all taken to the spot I had seen originally where I recognized a few familiar faces among the idol, pillar and door people. S.D. and Puncture went looking for the tablet with the crack while Sub-Optimal and I had a cup of tea.

He began telling me the details surrounding the disappearance of the first tablet. It was as S.D. and Puncture had said. It was here one day and gone the next. Nobody had seen anything so there were no clues.

We heard screaming coming from the area where the men had gone and soon S.D. was before us, making desperate hand signals. I saw that he was attempting to talk but the words seemed to be choking his throat as he made a great effort to release them. "Second one gone, Saar. Same like before, Saar." His face was turning red and sweat streamed down the sides. Sub-Optimal and I got up in a hurry and all three of us rushed to the place where the tablets had been left along with other inventory, waiting to be cleaned and repaired. We walked past headless, limbless idols, broken friezes, chipped doors and pillars. The tablets had been left leaning against the wall between an elaborately carved temple door and a dancing Ganesha idol with a broken trunk. Puncture saw us coming and threw up his hands. "What to do, Saars, all people saying it was here yesterday and nobody knows where it went today…" I raised my hand as a signal requesting him to stop.

Watching men around me who were cleaning, polishing, doing maintenance work, I could tell this kind of panicking was a waste of time. I felt a knot in my stomach from knowing that both pieces were gone. If I had not gone to the hills, perhaps I could have somehow prevented this from happening, If, if, if. This was not a constructive way to think, such thoughts led to confusion and doubt when action and clarity was what was sorely needed at such a time. Sub-Optimal, S.D. and Puncture were whispering like women in a circle.

"What is wrong with you three? This is no time for gossip. Let us find out who saw it last and make some inquiries," I said.

"Do we look like women who gossip?" Sub-Optimal asked, planting his palms on his hips, emphasizing his challenging stance.

"You know, Saar, how the navagrahas are damaged, (hiss) then one nagapratishta stolen (hiss) and when we come here today, (hiss,hiss) another nagapratishta stolen, it seems almost like bad luck is following us (hiss,hiss), Saar," Puncture said, as if presenting a great statement of enlightenment. "Maybe the two village temple projects (small hiss) are cursed." Three faces looked at me seeking confirmation. S.D. spoke next.

"I think maybe, Saar, we should not have removed them no? Maybe there is a curse on them because we interfered with their long time home resting place no? I am telling you no, from before itself no, you are not wanting to believe but such old objects of worship have energy of their own no? What if this bad luck follows all of us involved in this job, no?" The three of them gaped at each other in dismay.

"Stop it," I said. "Let us put an end to all this rubbish talk. Are we children or men? Curse indeed. Bad luck indeed. These are all old superstitious ways of thinking, based on total lack of scientific approach. Maybe Saturn is causing a few problems because of bad timing during initiation of the projects. Such things can be overcome if we put our minds to it."

"Sathya, you have your belief and we have ours. Everyone is entitled to his own way of thinking, is it not?" This was a pointed nudge from Sub-Optimal.

"We're not knowing everything about everything to be so definite, no?" This was S.D., buttering up Sub-Optimal. "Bad luck is following us like a shadow," Puncture hissed. One could not expect rational behavior from such idiots so I decided it was best to leave it be and take care of what had to be done.

Sub-Optimal stroked his chin as if he was capable of deep thoughts. He finally suggested that S. D, Puncture and I make trips to both villages in case we came up with anything. "Anyway, there are things to finish there, is it not?" I nodded.

Perhaps I had underestimated the chaps who cleaned and polished and fixed things at the museum. They were well informed about the value of such objects and it was possible that one or two of them had got involved in some shady operation. I expressed the thought to the men sitting around me. S.D. looked at me with googly eyes and Puncture scrunched up his face like a raisin. Sub-Optimal tapped his ringed fingers on the table. "Anything is possible, of course. But we must have faith in our own men. This looks too sophisticated and smooth for our semi-literate chaps." S.D. and Puncture shook their head yes yes like Bharath Natyam dancing dolls.

I saw that Sub-Optimal's eyes were glazed and imagined his heart and mind were already traveling outside India, seeing how he and his wife were due to leave for Singapore next week. He was attending some conference or the other on Asian art. The fellow was devoid of all sensibilities in the artistic direction but thanks to bureaucracy and office politics, he had been chosen to make the official trip. Yes, O great silent one, you may call me jealous and that may even be true to a small extent, but I believe in the cliché, calling a spade a spade. Honesty, these days, was a scarce commodity and therefore labelled un-P.C. "Does what a man have upstairs count anymore?" I asked Cookie and Venkat every time they mentioned this politically correct business.

S.D. and Puncture promised to pick me up on the dot of ten next morning. They reminded me that we had a standing invitation from priest Chandran in Periamalai for the monthly ceremonies. Showing up in the afternoon for belated blessings was considered quite acceptable. Besides, we had promised priest Chandran that we would install protective railing around the inner Kali shrine. This way, I thought, he would not feel that the temple at Mayapuram was given favorable treatment.

***

It gave me a temporary feeling of comfort to see the new tablets under the trees, piled with mounds of yellow petals, conical masses of ashes from stubs of burning incense, bunches of small ripening bananas nestled against the center. The snakes that usually curled behind were nowhere in sight. I saw that the same village crowd was there as always—the ubiquitous old woman and her young daughter in law, circling the shrine in silence with heads bowed in reverence. The busybody old crone—the woman with no teeth and sunken gums and squashed dates for breasts, the same woman was drinking tea at the stall across the road and chatting with a cluster of men who stood not far from her, smoking beedis and staring at me.

Somebody startled me by speaking suddenly, "Namaskaram, Sathya Saar." I turned around and saw that it was Mr. Australia, Leucoderma-map-faced man who leered at me. At the Kali shrine at the back, priest Chandran was doing arati, raising a brass plate of camphor with his right hand and circling it around the image. The bell in his left hand made a racket at the same time. I saw a man dart across to the side following the almond-treed path that led to the back. The fellow turned sideways because a squirrel rushed across suddenly. That was when I saw his face clearly and realized the idiot was none other than Mani, Chandran's son. The young woman I had seen him with last time was still visiting the shrine with a flat stomach. Perhaps the rogue sperm machine had faulty wiring with an empty fuse blowing up.

The old crone came toward me, calling out to the pair of women who had finished circumambulating the shrine. The way the young one walked towards us now, it would have been hard to believe she was capable of such a transgression as I had seen. Her eyes cast downward and her manner so modest, it never ceased to amaze me what hypocrisy human beings were capable of. The two old women cackled and said something to each other and before I knew it, they had turned tables on me and made me the focus of their talk.

"See how this government big shot brings his men and comes here to the temple and pretends to take care of things. All the time he does not understand how we suffer, what we are going through," the old crone said to the mother (the relationship had been finally clarified by my overhearing the conversation between them) of the younger woman. They were joined now by a few more devotees. "City people have no understanding of us," one man said, looking in my direction.

The mother of the younger woman spoke up. "Do you know of the problems young women in our village have since our old nagapratishta were taken away? Do you know how many women have failed to conceive, miscarried? Many are cursed and remain barren because you have taken away the source of our legacy and blessing." Loud murmurs passed among the devotees. The young woman began weeping silently, staring at the ground. S.D. and Puncture had come back from their tea and cigarette break and were standing in the periphery of the circle. I signaled to them to go supervise the laborers who had come to install the railing around the Kali shrine.

One of the male devotees spoke up. "These new tablets do not have the same power as our old ones. They were blessed by several generations in the village. With these new tablets, now, babies are born without limbs. Who gave you authority to tamper with our shrine?" Voices were raised and body language ominous. The circle edged in closer around me. Mob psychology was not my forte and I was grateful to see Chandran come to my rescue. He told them to disperse and took me to his house. Along the way, I saw the chaps from Mogul Stores, Thomas and Pillai, watching the laborers work on the railing around the inner shrine. Beside them stood Mani, leaning against a pillar, watching the women. I prayed that Puncture and S.D. would keep their word as we had agreed earlier and not say anything about the missing tablets. We had enough difficulties on our hands without hysteria brewing while we were there. Our mission today was to dig up what information we could find.

Chandran and I sat on bamboo chairs on his front verandah. "I wanted to talk to you about an important matter, Sathya Saar," he said.

"Yes?"

"I've heard about the terrible thing that has happened in Mayapuram. The destruction to the navagraha statues. I'm glad you're rebuilding the shrine." He was looking at me intently as if to read my mind.

"You know how I feel about the village temples, Chandran. This is my life. I want the old things to be preserved as part of our great Hindu heritage. That is why I applied for permission to have the tablets removed and sent to the museum. Not because I wanted to disrupt the old village ways of prayer." I spoke these words with a lot of discomfort and a heavy heart for I knew the truth of what had happened to the tablets.

He was silent now, staring sideways at the almond trees and the parrots screeching on top.

"What is all this about women here losing children? Surely, this is something that happens all the time?" I asked, as a way of changing the subject.

"Oh that. Women are always conceiving, losing and having babies. The cycle continues same as always. But you know how some of the devotees believe the old tablets influenced every aspect of their reproductive lives. This emotion is all part of that." His words surprised me. I remembered his confusion and worry when I had told him first, all those months ago, of the need for those tablets to go into the museum. He was concerned about the void such an absence would leave in the lives of villagers and yet, here he was, the same doubting man, speaking so rationally, talking about the devotees as if they were a group of nincompoops carrying on in an old fashioned way and he was the modern, scientific, logical man.

"I see that you are surprised to hear me speak this way. Is it not?"

He had read my mind.

"I learned something important after my meeting with Madame Doctor Claudia. One evening I am going for a walk and she is walking also in the same direction. So we are talking and she is telling me how sorry she is to see that lately many women in the village are having difficulty to

149

conceive and miscarrying. Only she called it something else…."

"You mean spontaneous abortion?" I asked.

"Yes, that's it." He was satisfied that I had given him the right words.

"She is telling me that this problem is happening with the wives of the men working in Seshasamudram. Those chemicals—it is getting into the system and causing reproductive failure in men."

"How is the village inoculation program of hers proceeding? Everything all right?"

"That, Saar -- is a success story. Long time since a child contracted polio or whooping cough so something good will be left behind when they leave…"

"What do you mean? Are George and Claudia leaving? I know nothing about this."

"I too know nothing. Only I am saying when they leave…."

"What is the important matter you wanted to talk about?" I asked.

"Yes. It is a small matter needing connections, Saar. You know the city, you have lived there many years."

"Yes?" I did not like the sound of this so far.

"It is my son, Saar. Mani. He is engaged and getting married shortly to a girl in the city. She is working for a company in Parry's corner and having steady job."

"That is reason for congratulations, Chandran," I said, thinking with relief that the rogue would finally be leaving the village.

"He is setting up business with two other people in Thambu Chetty Street Saar. Import Export business."

"Really? I didn't know he was interested in business like that. I thought he worked as a teller in the Mayapuram bank."

"Yes, Saar. He is having BCom degree and all no? Always wanting to be businessman. That is my son."

"And what can I do about all of this?"

"Bride and groom are looking for renting or buying flat, Saar, and needing help in this area. Nowadays, we are needing connections for everything, is it not?"

"I really don't know many people, Chandran. I'll see what I can do. If I hear anything, I'll let you know." The cheekiness of that scoundrel, making his father ask me for help after I had seen what I had seen. Brazen behavior! Thick hides like buffalos, that was what some of these people had.

Puncture came to tell me that the welder had been called on a family emergency. This welder was the only fellow available to us on short notice and now he had to leave after a few hours because his father was having chest pains and wanted his son next to him. That was the end of the working day for us in the village. Puncture reminded me that he and S.D. had not had their second tea and cigarette break so I waved my hand and gestured go, go all right.

***

George and Claudia were back from the hills but had gone to the vegetable market. "How are you feeling these days?" I asked Gopal. I saw that the bandages on his fingers looked clean and recently changed. "Did you see Dr. Warrior in Vellore?" He shrugged his shoulders and appeared distracted. Monty, the German Shepherd, was eating his meal, the pendant of his metal chain clanging against the stainless steel bowl of his food. He finished, lifted his head, licked his lips and panted in my direction.

"I am little better, Saar," Gopal said. "I am having good naturopathic treatment as per Dr. Warrior. Using neem berries is helping little bit."

"Good, good. I'm glad. I've heard that really helps."

Monty wagged his tail and came and stood next to me. George and Claudia's white Fiat turned into the driveway. The driver had a message about the welder from S.D. and Puncture. The chap was not going to be able to make it back that day and they would wait for me by the temple at six in the evening. In the meantime, they planned to take care of finishing touches on a previous job, a small temple and shrine located at a neighboring village. Nothing was finished when it was supposed to be. Postponing and humming and hawing was a national pastime.

"Good, Sathya. Then you can join us for afternoon Mass before you leave."

I saw that George winked at Claudia in satisfaction seeing the surprised expression on my face. All of us laughed at my predicament.

Claudia touched my wrist lightly. "It has been sad here, Sathya. With the women, I mean. Last month alone there were ten abortions that I know of, and at least ten more that I heard of. A few babies born with problems. No rectum in one case, half an arm in another case. Nothing below the elbow, if you know what I mean."

"What do you make of it all? The priest implied there were problems with the men working in Seshasamudram."

Claudia nodded slightly. "That's only part of it. Am not sure what all the effects of that toxic absorption is. I 'm not sure this has been studied properly. Who knows what is going on within their bodies, what cancers lie dormant, what have begun their growth?" Her voice changed to a whisper, as if she was speaking to herself. "I think it has something to do with hormones, the women are affected by this thing as well. It's not only the men."

It was time for mass and Claudia got up and went inside to freshen up. I sat in the veranda with a cup of tea. I told George, "I think it better that I sit right here where I am. My presence in your church may not be the right thing for you or me right now. Besides, you have those loudspeakers I see. I will hear you loud and clear right from where I am."

They looked at each other, then at me. "All right, old chap," George muttered, watching Gopal push his limbless body on his wooden board, and cross the road. He translated the sermons when George stumbled in his Tamil, which he did, I was told, good humouredly, by Claudia, often enough.

***

George spoke in English and he halted briefly after every paragraph so Gopal could convey his message all over again. The first part was all rhetoric, about conversion being a personal affair between God and man and never a forced issue according to the policy of the Church. There was the not so subtle hint that many chose to leave their birth religion because of the treatment it advocated—ranking some below others, dispersing inequality. The men from the Panchayat village council were also standing along the pavement, listening to what was being said. I wondered if Gopal had a hand in that. I had told George and Claudia to keep him at a distance but they did not understand such things about India. They naively believed that like a paper weight of some kind, you could shake up the Indian system a bit and things would settle down as they should. How to explain to them that such things happened only in our heads, in reality, things turned messy and unpredictable?

I did not take in the next part of the sermon for it seemed to be the usual theology stuff with the Holy Ghost and the Father and the Son and such and my mind always wandered when it came to that part of Christianity. I had enough problems remembering Brahma, Vishnu and Shiva and all their families.

My mind traveled to the missing stone tablets. I had to come clean and tell priest Chandran about it. There was no point in waiting for him to find out from some idiot who embellished facts and made it seem worse than it was. I also thought it a good idea that I meet with the police inspector along with S.D. and Puncture on our way out. As I thought out things in this direction, George's voice changed and I straightened my posture, sat more erect. He switched to the favorite Christian topic of original sin and suffering. He was speaking very softly now, as if he was conspiring with his flock.

"A man and a woman united before Jesus Christ and the church, this is the way to begin your married life. Let your children be born again in the eyes of God through baptism, then confirmation." Gopal translated this though I could tell there really was no need. It seemed that a lot of those present had already picked up on what had just been said by the way they whispered to each other. I had a bad feeling, it was a blunder to bring in history, especially familial history, with such people.

After all this time, George was naive, wanting to turn everybody to his way of thinking. This was one of the problems with Christianity as far as I was concerned, never accepting anything different from their own, calling Hinduism all-inclusive as if it was a bad thing, something to be ashamed of if you embraced the rest of humanity and diverse points of view.

I groaned inwardly when I heard George say again that devotees' current marriages were null and void till they retied the knot in the presence of the Father, the Son and the Holy Spirit. One thing I had to say about George, he always reminded me what a liberal and open-minded fellow I was.

***

S.D. and Puncture drove up in the jeep. The police inspector who served the villages of Periamalai and Mayapuram had found out about the missing nagapratishtas and informed Chandran. "How did he find out so soon?" I asked, not wanting to believe the ramifications of what I heard.

"Subbudu Saar must be, you know they are being very close like this," S.D. pressed forefingers together with no gap in between, to supplement the meaning of what he just said. "Damn and bloody damn," I muttered under my breath.

"You see, Saar, that is why I am telling you always, we are not knowing many things about many things there is so much amplification because of implication are you understanding me properly, Saar? They are both being members of same family MGM political party sect and getting together for meetings and all."

"Land your rocket, S.D. Cool down. I'm more worried about the reaction of the villagers. I should have trusted my instincts and told the priest and devotees when we first got here. We'll see how we can patch up things tomorrow."

The MGM sect was the Mangal Gokul Manram, a southern division of the national saffron brigade, Hindu fundamentalists (fundies I called them) who made all sorts of rubbish claims, scheming to build temples where mosques had been. Their hearts and minds were full of cultural narrow mindedness that wasted time on what women wore and what teenagers did on Valentine's day. Like gossiping women, they were always looking out the windows of their fundie little hearts, shaking their rudraksham bead necks, making googly marble eyes. They fanned trouble like colonial Whities who divided and conquered, drawing imaginary boundaries across the continent based on nonsense.

***

When Chandran and I were alone, things were detailed to him objectively and I assured him that we would do our best to see the treasures returned to the museum where they belonged. "I'm sure you appreciate

154

how much all of this has upset me personally, Chandran. Working with temples has been my whole life. But you know times are different, these days one is up against all sorts of unforeseen obstacles…"

He placed a hand on me in a gesture of sympathy. I told him he would be informed of all progress in the case and could he cooperate also by passing on any information he garnered locally? He nodded his head and blinked his eyes, flashing a stupid, nothing registered face at me. Idiot that he was, I was not sure of any observation powers in the man.

Outside the Kali shrine, there was Mr. Australia, the ever present young and old woman, the mother and daughter combination who seemed to spend their days in the premises of the temple trying to expand the size of the family. There were also some new people I did not recognize. One of the newcomers fuelled the tension in the air by saying, "We have heard from the Police, Saar, what has happened. Such a misfortune would not have taken place if the tablets had not been moved from here."

"God is looking down on us and giving us penance for what we have allowed to be done. Our women are becoming barren, we will die without sons." This from another devotee.

It was Mr. Australia's turn. "The terrible thing is that we had to find out about all this in a roundabout way, from the police. If you really meant to be straightforward, why not come out and tell us about it yourself?"

My stomach churned and I felt my temper rise but I also knew this to be a fair question. I believed when things leaked out, better to open the dams and let the full force out. "The truth is that both tablets have gone missing in similar ways while under the care of government officials. We cannot deny that. I can assure you that hiding the truth from you is not my intention. I'm as shocked and upset as you are. We will do our best to find the pieces." S.D. and Puncture were standing to either side of me and they too, hissed and sputtered complementary sentences.

I got into the office jeep and when the old crone with no blouse came up to my window. She said, "Don't worry, Saar. If you cannot find our nagapratishtas, we have others to help. We are not without supporters, you see. Even little people have friends in big places."

"What are you talking about?" I snapped.

"At one point I thought perhaps you were learned and protective of us devotees. But I see my instincts about you were right. You're just like the others, old man."

***

I went to visit Iyer at the Theosophical Society in Adyar. He looked more shrunken, shoulders hunched as he leaned against his walking stick and waved to me from under the mango tree. He looked at me intently and said, "So, the problems at the village continue, I see, from the preoccupation on your face."

I brought him up to date with recent events and when I told him about the missing tablets, he reminded me about a similar problem that had occurred a few years ago at the Srirangam temple. The place was a favorite of Iyer's since he hailed from the area and went there all the time as a boy.

"We're living in strange times Sathya. It is the age of confusion, all sorts of unnatural things happening around us. Look at what has been happening in Kerala." He was referring to the strange and bizarre phenomenon of red rains there, blood red water leaking from the clouds.

I looked at Iyer and saw his face twitch. "How are you feeling, health-wise?"

"Ah, the same old problems you know. I don't belong here anymore, the soul tells me this, but the body wants to cling on. It is a matter of letting go slowly but the feeling comes and goes. One day I'm all right, the next day is bad."

"What does the doctor say?"

"Doctors! They are like old women, poking around here and there. Useless as far as I am concerned, at this stage of my life. What can they do to help me prepare for death?"

We were both quiet for a while.

"Cookie told me on the telephone that she was planning to perform in Chidambaram. You're going to see her dance?"

"That is the plan."

"You must tell me how she performs."

"But why not tell her yourself? You're coming for our evening terrace session this Saturday night, is it not? The child is preparing a dance and

156

some special comedy routine she says she wants to show us. Thinks we need a taste of our own medicine, I guess."

"Oho, I look forward to that."

Following afternoon, two people arrived at more or less the same time in front of the gate to our house. First one was Basket Hair who was picking up Cookie since they planned to go to the cinema. To my surprise, the second visitor was Sub-Optimal, Singapore-returned as evidenced by his foreign looking sunglasses worn even in the shade, Tamil film-star style. He picked up the edge of his towel on his shoulder with the gold peacock border and patted the sweat on his nose gently, pat pat like a woman, making my blood pressure rise.

He drank a whole tumbler of Peaberry coffee made by Bala before saying what he had obviously come to share.

"It is out of my control, Sathya Saar, he began." Then he began twirling the rings on his fingers as if they were tuning knobs.

"Subbudu, I am an old man and I don't have a lot of patience with all this beating around the bush. Why not come out with it ?"

"It is instructions, orders you might say, from the higher ups in head office. They are discussing ways to defuse the problem at Periamalai by temporary withdrawal of usual staff and management on the job. The villagers are spreading all sorts of things, saying…"

"I see. Then it is a good thing that I am neither staff nor management, is it not?"

"Head office also referring, I think, to consultants like yourself. As far as I am concerned, it is not personal issue, Sathya Saar. You know I have great respect for your experience and integrity. Now it is a question of calming things down. They're afraid of inside jobs." He looked at my face and raised his hand in a defensive gesture. "I know, I know. We are not implicated in any of this rubbish but how to convince people in head office? They're making emergency call to me, giving orders. Only temporary basis, Saar. Maybe this week only, then I will call you to come back. These caste issues are sensitive as you know."

"What has caste got to do with it?"

"They feel a high-caste consultant for village projects is not always the best solution, Saar. All this is based on reports they had from other offices with similar cases in the past. Things ended badly, violence and all…"

He looked at my face and continued. "Of course, in some cases, it has worked out, no doubt. But sensitivity has to be there no, this is what my party MGM…"

"Enough said, Subbudu. I've understood your point. I will continue with my casual leave for the whole week and wait for your call."

"I am appreciating that, Saar." He did namaskaram like a politician, smiling that fake smile.

"S.D. and Puncture will be all right?" I asked. It was as I suspected when he nodded yes. They belonged to the lower castes that deserved more representation in government whether or not they were honest. Useless fellows, corrupt system. What did I expect from such a job?

"I like the name of your house, Hridaya Kamalam," he said as if offering a consolation prize on his way out.

"It has nothing to do with your party symbol. Everything old and Hindu and meaningful cannot be stolen by you MGM fellows after all."

"No Saar, don't think like that. If good people like you are thinking like that, who can we turn to for support?"

I hoped Sub-Optimal would step on goat shit outside the gate on the way to his Contessa car. Government offices were like pits with snakes and scorpions. Once you fell into them, you did not know what kind of poison got into your system.

As I walked past the oval mirror in the hall, I remembered something Iyer said. My face in the mirror that looked back was startled, amazed even. Iyer said that the riddle of life was vastly complex and simple, the strategy easy and difficult at the same time. You lay back and let life happen to you. Other times you slipped on the gloves of the pugilist and went at it, full force. You took yourself seriously and then laughed uproariously at yourself. Life was both a mystery and a simple minded joke. No wonder children and old people lived it best.

Reflecting on the day, standing on the terrace, I thought it was time to shift some energy to writing and revising the remaining text of the book.

I saw the fiery tip of a glowing cigarette next door and knew that Venkat was also outside. The beauteous woman, the tailor's wife who nursed his mother walked towards him and whispered in his ear. I felt sorry for him just then, his youth, his NRI status. Mingling with servant women, if one did not know how it was done, was a dangerous business. They could bring you down to their level if you did not maintain a certain aloofness. It was all right in my youth when the whole sordid business was common enough but these days, with all this political upheaval and tug of war between backward and forward classes, it was best to curb such impulses.

An hour or so later, he invited me over for a gin and tonic.

***

In Venkat's bedroom, I recognized a rare photo I had taken using his camera. The Cambodian child from Angkor Wat stood holding his American Frisbee and Venkat had his arm protectively around the child like a proud father. We used to call the boy Raja. In Cambodia, those days, wherever we went, poverty made its presence felt. He was from the slums, befriended by Venkat. The background in the photograph was the most dazzling frieze from the temple complex that depicted the churning of the ocean legend.

Venkat came in and stood behind me. "There is not a day I don't remember, Sathya. He won't leave me alone, he comes daily in my dreams." I did not know what to say, except reach out and pat his back. Guilt and grief are such terrible things to overcome that you cannot dictate a pace towards healing.

***

Saturday afternoon of the dinner party, the chairs and tables had been arranged in the terrace. Temple bells clanged somewhere and I thought I saw small spirals of white smoke rise in the distance, near the crematorium. The neighbor's children were singing sa sa ri ri ga ga ma ma and there was the smell of roasting groundnuts from the slums at the back. Looking down from the terrace, I saw that Nagu and Paru stood in the garden near the oleander bushes. He was bending towards her, his palm on her stomach. I coughed involuntarily and they parted and looked up.

"You will make a fine mother, you will make a fine father," I said to them both. It was good to see Nagu's teeth gleam in the twilight, forget his worries for a while. He was a proud sort and had not confided any more about the family situation to me but I knew things weighed heavily in his head and heart. I too had lost brothers, in different circumstances, of course, and understood the pain it brought.

I looked into the small enclosure between stones in the rock garden and my old friend the chameleon was there, unblinking, unmoving. Seeing him there, the moon full and luminous in the sky, the stars and planets all up there, some shining, some moving as always, things hurtling towards self-destruction that my eyes could not see and that I was ignorant of, tree bark brown and leaves still green, it was as I had known it all my life. All was right with the world and I had to cling to that. A simplistic view was best for the time being. My mind was too tired for anything else.

***

Iyer looked like Rajaji, famous independence leader with his khadi dhoti and kurta and tortoise shell spectacles and cane. Not to forget the other common factor—both men had no hair. Today he had worn his false teeth which sat like a row of flattened rice in his mouth. "What is it, Sathya? Why the long face?"

I could never fool Iyer about anything for long. It had only taken a few minutes for him to ask. I told him about Sub-Optimal's visit. "So what does the fellow want you to do? Stay out of sight for a while?"

I nodded. "You see where the country is heading. Honesty and hard-working nature is not valued these days. But you must not let it get you down. This is all maya, illusion, this work, this success and all of that. You know that. You must be detached. After all, you are not in this for the rewards but because you are a karma yogi, a servant of the people, is it not? You always told me you wanted to preserve things for future generations. If people like us do not make our countrymen realize the riches in our own backyard, who will? We don't want some Whities telling us that, no thank you sir." We absorbed this for a while as we sat in my room, listening to a noisy mynah make a racket from the chikoo tree outside.

"Any sign of the missing tablets?"

"No. Nothing yet. There have been cases in other temples also. Only in one or two cases the objects have been recovered, in a sorry state at that."

"What a mess. It is Kaliyuga, a bad time, Sathya, it is not in your hands. Try to remember you are working for character formation at this stage of your life. Every experience teaches us, does it not? It is education making us evolve."

"You're right. I remind myself that action should be done in a detached fashion."

"Good, good. Go to that part of yourself where you are aware and still, do this often and it will help you maintain your balance."

"I'm trying but I don't always succeed."

"When the ocean was churned because poison from the giant serpent Vasuki threatened the world, Shiva rescued us by swallowing the toxic substance himself. This is why he is called Neelakantan, the blue throated one. I see Shiva wearing a necklace of Vasuki, circling the serpent around his neck and trapping the poison in his throat forever. Shiva is the benevolent force of destruction. He faces aggression with the most powerful weapon available to all of us—through meditation."

I stared at Iyer.

"You must be Shiva in your current situation. Corruption, greed, chaos, this is the poison of our times. You must not allow it to enter your system. You're objecting, telling me you're only a man. This is the problem, everybody is thinking this way. Goodness has gone out of style."

We joined Cookie and Venkat, who were on their way upstairs. As we walked onto the terrace, there was a sudden croaking sound.

"What was that?" Cookie asked, with big eyes.

Doc winked at me and said to Cookie, "Ah. That is the emerald-sided gobblydonk."

"You mean like the pobblewonk?" she said.

"Yes, yes. That's it. Same family. Cousin on the maternal side. Terrible thing though. Poisonous gene is coming through, passing down generation after generation. What to do? Case of recessive gene turning active or something like that. Is it not Sathya?"

"What do I know of science? I'm a humanitites chap after all. Only thing I understand is that meanness sometimes skips generations and then comes back full force. I've watched the expression of one of those things as it hissed and spurt deadly liquid on its prey, a large earthworm of some kind. The toxic substance attacks the nervous system and renders the victim immoveable. The creature then goes about the business of killing in a systematic way. It's something to watch."

"How terrible. Gobblydonk you say? Remind me never to go near one of those."

"You cannot go near one of those, Cookie, because no such thing exists," Venkat revealed.

"Aiyyo, aiyyo. These NRI's have no sense of humor, I tell you, spoiling all the fun."

"I think these old men are getting sloshed, Cookie, let's eat some dinner," Venkat said in his most playful voice.

Doc too was quick. "Oho, Oho, We're getting Canadian again I see, trying to be proper." Only I needed a drink badly to lift the mood I was in, still dwelling on the conversation we had in my room downstairs.

Doc was telling Venkat and Cookie about his cousin from America who was now a proud grandfather.

"You see this is a big achievement. You want to know why? You see, when he was newly married, he and she and not sleeping together in small Bombay flat. Bride and mother-in-law in kitchen, groom and father in other room. Later when there were complaints about no issues coming forward, then it was found that Raman, he didn't know how to do sex, poor fellow. We were so innocent those days," he added as an afterthought.

I saw that Venkat and Cookie were suppressing smiles. She bit her lower lip, he turned the other away and stared at the rock garden and chameleon.

Cookie was telling Iyer what Awesome Mami said when she met the American neighbor of her daughter's in "Cheekago -- Poor wretched woman," Awesome Mami said, "How many strikes against her! So many handicaps, having blue eyes, blond hair, cannot speak Tamil, what a stupid person she was!"

"Ah, travel, it opens up everything," I said.

"You are a petit bourgeoisie, is he not?" Iyer winked at Cookie and

Venkat.

"I have seen in America, they are still saying Hindi for Hindu and asking me why our women are wearing tents with mesh screen strip over eyes. These people do not know the difference between Hindu and Muslim, I have a big problem with that. And always that damn question, what does the dot on the women stand for? Finally, I told this fellow, hey, you know us Hindu men taking knife every morning and drawing coin of blood to show who is boss. No, he said, shocked."

"Now look at the Japanese. Their collective behavior is excellent -- all that bowing and putting heads together. We Indians are useless at that. Not one decision can be reached. Seeking consensus is major problem with us," Venkat said.

"Too much population—that is the problem with India," Iyer said..

"Compulsory one child policy like China is the only answer," I offered.

"It will never work in India. You need discipline to enforce that," Venkat countered.

"India is a gone case. Nothing will work so easily here. But she will continue and go on, like always, surrounded by confusion. That is the history and that is her future. This country is an enigma. The indefinable Hindu Atman you see?"

"What rubbish Iyer," Venkat said, "Are you getting a little tipsy? You're talking like a Hindu fundamentalist, a fundie, a saffron kesar halvah man."

Iyer's tone pacified, "All of you, one thing I am telling you, you will never be unemployed if you become an official complainer. The world has no shortage of problems, after all."

Cookie walked in dressed for her performance, in a beautiful gold colored kanjeevuram sari. She danced the dance of Mahishasura Mardhini, the goddess in her many forms—as a warrior in battlefield, displaying valor as she sliced off the head of a demon. Then the demure and graceful walk of a young a maiden as she settled into her benign feminine aspect. Cookie's head moved in the traditional Bharath Natyam manner, east and west and north and south, her eyes eloquent, articulating all that could not be said. For a brief minute, Menaka flashed before my eyes but her image was vague and fuzzy, it seemed that I was losing her form somehow. Only the idea of her, of us in the past, remained alive in my head. My heart was not in the performance that evening.

***

After dinner, at Cookie's prompting, Iyer began the game thus: "You see that East West Fusion Swami from America, always saying how Hinduism predicted so many things, there is quantum physics in Vedas, flying saucers and technology, all this already in our old texts. But he is not realizing, silly fellow, that this all knowing aspect annoying Christian Fundies, is it not?"

Venkat continued: "No wonder there is that big case out in California—Hinduhood vs. Hollywood."

I could not help myself, I blurted out, "Really? What is this?"

Iyer: "In children's cartoon movie showing Lakshmi, Mistress of the Universe, holding skulls and dancing near mountain Hollywood sign. She is riding eagle (the kid who made the movie was born in America not knowing proper vehicle—which is for which god)."

Cookie jumping in: "Anyway, she's wearing blue sari with big slit running down thigh. She's flying on American Bald eagle causing much confusion because Hindus putting big red dot on bird forehead Hare Krishna style…"

I could not help myself, I had to add, "Fundies giving eagle Vishnu coin hanging from sacred thread around neck and red shawl across chest so CIA getting involved thinking threat of communism fusion Hinduism who knows what this strange curry mix business is all about! They're asking could they be feeding eagle spicy lentils giving him diarrhea annihilating species further?"

Cookie: "These sprout eating vegetarians were suspicious creatures after all—who knew what any religion with chignon wearing priest called Velayathur Venkatraman Sathyamurthiramarajan was capable of?"

Iyer: "On eagle's legs, all sorts of shiny gold bangles, said they were from India but…"

Cookie: "…looked suspiciously like it was bought from the Avon lady in Waco, Texas. Hindis (as the Americans say) having horrible taste you see how they are decorating coat closets with Christmas bulbs pretending they are shrines and temples and all?"

Venkat: "All the gods painted with bubble gum color faces, Jai Shree Ganesha with bubble gum color snout...."

Cookie interrupting with excitement, "Jai Shree Hanuman wearing lots of blush...."

Venkat: "Lakshmi and Saraswati having pointy mountain chests like pillim stars or Madonna singing under waterfall. Anyway, going back to eagle, Americans not being masters of understatement, it's Mission Eagle America or in more colloquial terms, Hindis or Bust, Get dose (those) damn dots. So before Mistress of the Universe cartoon movie trailer showing bird cage. There is gun salute by Tweety bird, mini-flags with stars and stripes unfurling down."

Cookie: "Everything organized by the Bald Eagle Brotherhood. Picture gospel singing types saying praise the lord he is free at last flying at last thanks sweet Jesus red white and blue eagle again at last."

I'm trying to conclude the game, getting little thirsty for brandy and hot water to cap the evening, saying, "Excuse me, in our religion anything can be adjusted, no?"

Iyer: "Ayyo, wait, wait, let me complete. I say you big shot, Peria Pistha Sathya, why all this hurry burry interrupting all the time?"

After the others had left, I checked the space between the rocks to see the chameleon had vanished.

***

Following week one morning, Subbudu called and I was back on the job. Puncture, S.D. and I, along with Venkat, proceeded to Periamalai temple to check whether the welder had finished the job properly. The temple bell rang continuously announcing the finale of the evening puja. Under the banyan tree, I noticed immediately, one tablet was gone. Stones were piled where the new tablet had been, the cement base broken and jagged. I felt an involuntary shiver as I noticed the serpents had returned and coiled themselves like before behind the pile of stones.

S.D. and Puncture had also seen the same thing. Puncture hissed in my ear. The ubiquitous pair of women appeared, old woman and young woman, this time accompanied by a young man. I noticed the young woman's belly bulged, she was obviously carrying. The mother was soon joined by the crone and they pointed to the young woman and related the good news I had deduced for myself. "Not only this one," the crone continued, flashing me a tamarind colored breast, "many others also, now that our stone is back."

After the puja, the three of us immediately confirmed that the pile of broken bits under the three appeared to be one of the missing tablets. "It is just like the temple in Mayapuram, no? Same type of instrument was used here looks like," S.D. said. The zigzag line was there like a spine cut up into pieces, and one of the pieces even had the tag from the museum half burned by the bunch of incense sticks at the base that made a hole on the side of the tag. How negligent and brazen were the people involved that they had not bothered to remove the official tag that declared the age and authenticity of the piece. Devotees had bound the pile of broken bits with rope and covered the sides with flower petals.

The three of us scouted around the village, asking for information to find out if anybody knew how the pieces came to be there, in that state. As we drove away from the village, I tried hard to focus on the mantra in my mind but it did not work. I could not grasp the words, the meaning. It was time to let the dark mood enter me fully, fighting it was too much.

Tell me, O great silent one, when we had a staring contest as children, why was there that urge to blink and look away, what is it that prevents us from looking deep within each other? Were we afraid of something we might find in the other person that we did not have? The other person was more than a mirror image, for we knew instinctively then of the vastness of the universe, the possibilities and dangers that lurked within and you were scared of what you saw there. And because the other person was also like you, this meant you were also scared of yourself. I've already said this before to you, have I not? The old man has been caught repeating himself.

***

I stopped by the office and met with Sub-Optimal. The thing I noticed first at the entrance beyond the corridor was a big poster on the notice board announcing that information was needed in the case of a precious missing idol of goddess Meenakshi from Purnipakkam temple. Those having any knowledge about the missing idol were urged to contact the superintendent of police. A similar poster featuring the nagapratishtas was pinned next to this giving the address and number of the police station that served the villages of Periamalai and Mayapuram. The reproduction of Venkat's photograph was grainy, but the stone tablets looked magnificent. The text under the photo said that the theft had been undetected by museum officials and it was a puzzle indeed as the tablets were quite heavy and easily recognized, one with a zigzag lightning crack down the center and the other stained heavily from oil. The central bureau of investigation was looking into both cases and closely working to enforce new, stiffer archeological laws.

All this action came about after the fact—the lack of procedure for proper cataloguing of artifacts and inadequate budget that provided insecure storage. All this time, these had not been addressed. Then there was the issue of rampant corruption inside and out, hiring all kinds of riff raff for manual labor by museum and government authorities. Behind me stood two armpit scratching chaps who chatted about a new Tamil film and laughed. I shuddered at the thought that such was the quality of personnel who guarded national treasures. They did not seem to give a hoot about the tragic notices on the notice board. It was as if the news did not concern them at all.

Chapter Eight
The Conch and the Discus

It was bad news, I could tell from their facial expressions, with George scowling at the ground, and Claudia looking grim, her face puffed up. "What is it?" I asked, "Are you two feeling all right?"

"No," said George, in a most uncharacteristic direct manner. "We are not all right. We have had a terrible time of it, Sathya. They threatened us and tried to burn our car. We have the boys staying with us at the Madras Club (I called it Sahib Club). We pulled them out of school and will probably move them somewhere up north."

I was speechless.

Claudia continued, "We're packing up and hope to leave the village in two weeks after installation ceremony for the crucifix. Our school shut down and the temple school has taken back a few of the kids. The church has granted us a transfer to Bihar where they need us badly."

"We will continue our good work there by the grace of God," George said softly and rested his hand on Claudia's shoulder for a brief second. "He saved our lives for a good purpose. We must continue with our work."

She looked at him with a strained expression and smiled a little. It sounded as if George was saying this more to reassure himself and Claudia than to convince me.

"Well, old chap," George asked, "you are unusually quiet."

"I don't know what to say. It's all a bit of a shock. What happened?"

Bala interrupted with Tiffin and it was only after we had eaten our dosas, as we imbibed Peaberry coffee, that the full story came out.

After I had attended Mass last month, matters turned difficult. St. Anne's school was slowly emptied of students, the teachers became resigned. Luckily, the nursing home across the school had more than its share of patients as word spread of the man from Seshasamudram who recovered well enough to take up a part time job at Mogul Stores with Yusef Ali and his gang. Then one day, at the Panchayat village council weekly meeting, a scuffle broke out, George and Claudia heard from Gopal.

"How can you be sure of anything that fellow says? I 'm surprised to hear you let him stay on."

"Gopal is a mixed up fellow but benign at heart. He always treated us with affection. Only pitied us our non-Hindu ways, which he felt were improper."

I saw that Claudia looked at George and smiled encouragingly. These two, husband and wife, I could not always understand. Just when I thought that's it, they are going to argue and fight now, they flashed lovesick faces at one another and talked of divine design and became faithful servants of God, doing his work, minding his lamb. Such devotion to another human being dumbfounded me, and I held a little bit of suspicion about its genuine nature, I confessed secretly to myself.

At the Panchayat village council meeting, Gopal informed them, one of the peons who served the men tea, a recent convert to Christianity, heard the members badmouth and swear at George and Claudia. They were livid because of what had been said at mass about Hindu marriages not being legitimate. It had been said that they were not married in the eyes of the church, in the presence of Christ. This had been repeated over and over by one Hindu to another and it had spread all over the village. The implication made their wives whores and their sons and daughters bastards and bitches.

"You know that is not at all what I was tying to say? I was only referring to total commitment and their own personal worth and dignity. This was what the peon tried to convey also but things had gone too far," George clarified. Soon the children and women who went to Claudia for their vaccinations and various female ailments dwindled down to half the original number. Men swore and spat in front of George and Claudia's house and church and the cruel ones tossed sharp pebbles at Monty when they watched him urinate under the parijata tree.

O great silent one, you know I did not mind criticizing my inept countrymen for their idiocies. But it was a different matter when comments flowed out from foreign mouths. After all, there were nuances they did not understand. I pointed this out to them.

"You have both lived in this country long enough to know that hygiene is an impossible battle with illiterate people. Spitting is the way these people gesture: to show aversion, to clear their system literally sometimes and figuratively—to address their helplessness, to spark a reaction from another human being. They are tired of being absent in the eyes of the world. You understand what I am saying? I am not defending this disgusting behavior though, please know that."

"Maybe you are right, Sathya. I don't like to say we understand because recent events have shown we do not understand everything. Deep down I know it is only a few undesirable elements that have created this gulf between the people of the village and ourselves. That much I do understand."

"Same thing about throwing stones at the dog. A dumb animal that cannot speak is mistreated so these fools feel that temporary sense of power over something. They have been treated cruelly, so who do they strike back at? A dumb, helpless animal. Also, did you know that the parijata tree is revered by Hindus and Muslims alike?"

George and Claudia sighed and looked at Misty Glen and the Radha Krishna statue shining in the sun across the road.

The superiors of the church said George had not shown enough sensitivity in handling the issue and suggested he go to Bihar where he would be guided by another senior, more experienced priest there. From what I gathered, this was always the solution of the church management, if there was a problem, move it around from parish to parish. Lack of sensitivity was at the bottom of proselytization, the superior attitude of playing the savior, was it not? So how could management blame labor for the philosophy it espoused? Surely, the church did not recommend deception by its men?

"The scuffle at the Panchayat village council turned into a fight and Gopal was knocked off his wooden wagon trying to defend us. Imagine that! Picking on a legless leper. I don't understand what to think anymore. The world is getting uglier all the time. I sometimes feel as if I was born at the wrong time. You know what I mean, Sathya?"

"Come on, George. The world is the world. It has always been contaminated. I too feel the way you describe sometimes. When I am calm, I realize the imbalance of the world is the imbalance we have inside us. So many things tugging us in different directions."

I could not help notice that George and Claudia exchanged glances that translated into, 'you do not understand old man.' Missionaries could not be balanced in their thinking, they carried too much agenda. Of course, I did not tell them that.

"We thought that we would take back the crucifix with us and go through with the installation ceremony next week. Claudia had a wonderful idea about it. She thinks we should make the whole thing more Indian, give out leaf packets of sweet pongal rice. By the time I conduct the final Mass before we leave, things would have settled down I feel."

"Yes, yes of course. It's worth a try. There are many there you have helped over the years and I'm sure they would like to give you a suitable send-off." They seemed pleased with my response.

"The fire in the car--none of you were injured, I hope?"

"It was a frightening thing, Sathya. I am grateful none of us was inside. We had gone to the market with the boys. I parked in one of the side streets and when we returned there was a crowd around the car, two fellows throwing sand into the engine that had caught fire. They claim it was nobody's fault, that it was some electrical thing, but how can that be when the ignition was off?" There was the distinct smell of kerosene."

"Let's not talk about this anymore. I've gone over and over the scene so many times in my mind," Claudia said.

We were all silent for a few minutes.

"All those years we spent in Penang, maybe we became complacent, I don't know. India is more difficult, unpredictable. You think you've figured out things more or less and then boom something impossible happens. What to think anymore, I don't know." This was George, in a reflective tone.

***

I was surprised to see Iyer sitting up in a cane chair, waiting for me.

The nurse hovered nearby, fussing with the remains of a tray. "You may walk the grounds," Iyer told him, dismissing him because for the two small rooms did not offer much privacy. We watched the fellow leave and his figure receded in the early evening twilight as he walked farther away into the distance.

"How are you feeling? You look tired," I began. I noticed again, as if for the first time, that milky veil over his eyes, giving him a wise and slightly unfocused look. The skin of his arms was crinkled like tissue paper, so many fine lines running amok north to south, east to west. I saw that Iyer had developed that quintessential old sick man habit of moving his mouth slightly as if chewing something, movement meant to soothe and pacify the nerves, a fish like thing to do that translated into a slightly dopey human expression, especially so in a man of Iyer's stature. But then, nature was cruel and spared none in her touch, these were the small indignities of old age, a goofy countenance from time to time along with frequent passing of wind and constant bladder emptying.

"No sleep, all the racket in my ears you know. But today seems better. Sathya, I need you to do something for me," Iyer said.

"Yes, what is it?"

"You know how I have told you about the temple in Srirangam, my faith in the power of Vishnu there, how every time I have been there and made a vow, my tinnitis and health problems have diminished? The bad energy sent out by my body is sucked in by the divine conch. I believe the idol there radiates pure goodness. This enters my body fortifying it with health."

I nodded my head and sighed. I secretly wanted to rubbish this claim but who understood everything about the nature of faith? The suggestion of the mind to the body? After all, even Harvard educated doctors did not understand everything about the power of placebos in the process of healing in the body.

"I see that you are doubtful about the efficacy of my claim. Let me tell you, Sathya, you will see for yourself. Then come back and tell me what it was like. I want you to go there and bring me back some prasadham, kumkum and vibhuti. I know it will help me, Vishnu's blessing, touching my body with the power of that temple, that energy. This is the only way remaining now to better my health."

"I will go there on one condition. That you call the doctor tomorrow and ask him to check you out. Perhaps it is time to phone your son in Philadelphia and have him visit you?" I asked.

"Sathya, seeing you once in a while is good enough distraction for me these days. As for medical science, I think I'm beyond all that now. I'm now what they call a pain management case. That means they ease you towards death. And I don't need anybody's help for that."

Iyer wanted two more things. He wanted me to accompany Cookie to Chidambaram temple and report on her dance performance, and he wanted me to bring him sweet and succulent sunset colored jilebis from Grand Sweets in Adyar when I came to see him next. I promised to do both.

"You know that song, Sathya, the one that M.S. Subbalakshmi sings about us coming into the world on our own and that is the only way we also leave--alone, with no assistance from anybody else? It is only now I understand the full import of those words."

I did not know what to say in response.

"You see, Sathya, it is difficult to treat the slow attrition of the soul by the passage of time, by the passage of life being what it is. I can feel doubts creeping in ..." Iyer leaned forward and looked directly into my eyes to clarify, "doubts about how I will handle the final moments. I don't like that, I have always sought dignity for the end and I will have it I know, only I have to make myself ready for it, you understand?"

"You will call your son?" I asked again.

"All right. If you feel that way. You know, Sathya, his happiness is what is important but I miss him. So far away. America. But this is the new order of things. You reap what you sow, the proverb says, is it not?"

He saw my puzzled expression and went on to explain. "We gave them conflicting signals, keep your Indianness and your Hindu way of life but have a flashy career in terms of material success. We put them on the path towards westernization because we had begun it ourselves. Adopting the English language, British civil service and what not. We thought don't get too close to the white man but only be like him in the educational, practical sense but these days, you cannot compartmentalize like that."

"Can I get you anything before I leave?" I wanted desperately to change the subject for I saw Iyer's eyes were misting and I felt uncomfortable in the face of such turbulent emotions.

"Don't be in such a rush all the time. I'm not going to embarrass you by howling like a baby, I promise you that." He always saw through me, I could never hide. "I want to tell you what I'm feeling, thinking. You may need all this sooner than you think. We are all going there, same journey, same destination, is it not?"

I sighed. "This neurotic preoccupation that you have about controlling things..."

I stared at him and shook my head.

"Oh don't object like you don't know what I am talking about. What does Cookie call you playfully, that Americanism, "control freak?" Let's face it, there is that little bit of a bully in most of us. In your case, you want to leave a legacy for the younger generation. You want to reach this goal by your work, managing people, take charge of life, plan the future, all of that. You see yourself as a savior of some sort. Problem is life is like a garden, you cannot always weed this or that out. You cannot control human nature."

"But I am not a bully, I am only trying...."

"I know, I know. You just want your moment of attention, that fleeting sense of something bigger than you really are. It is a false sense, an illusion. I understand only too well because I have wanted it sometimes. I too have led a conflicted life. I belittled money, success -- what I could not have. But I wanted it all sometimes, things I pretended not to care about."

"What are you saying?"

"Think of all that energy we spend practicing control all our lives! It seems silly because in the end you have to let go, surrender. You get what I am saying, no?"

"I don't know what you are saying, am not sure I understand."

"I am saying that you have to accept your contradictions, your weakness, unlearn control. You have to approach death like a child, full of innocence and openness. It is watching yourself watch yourself. The force of nature, the beauty, the newness. I am trying to get a sense of that."

He turned away towards the wall and closed his eyes.

On my way out, I told the nurse to keep a close eye on him and call me the minute there was any change.

***

We were sitting on the verandah having beer and peanuts. Venkat was telling Cookie about his servant, Anwar Khan, who had brought his wives and children to see his mother and in the process, get some "baksheesh" from Venkat since the family had recently acquired another addition.

As I had mentioned before, O great silent one, such characters were always procreating so they could fill India with Muslim children. Their religion allowed more than one wife, so they multiplied faster due to the extra wombs available to their men. Anyway, as we discussed before, Muslim men were heavily sexed from birth to death. I did not say any of this out loud because political correctness was a serious affliction with both these young people.

From where I sat in the verandah, I could see servant women with plastic kodams on their head, bringing water from the water lorry that came to the street adjacent to Koil Street this time of evening. Our water lorry came bright and early in the morning. All this water business was tiresome all right but you see, water was to the Madras resident what weather was to the Englishman.

"Hello? Are you there?" It was Cookie, tilting her head and smiling at me. Venkat hushed her and they stared out at Misty Glen. We heard Awesome Mami complaining to Awesome Mama as they walked up and down their driveway. She was speaking in that loud, quarrelsome voice of hers that meant trouble was brewing. Awesome Mama saw the light in our verandah and waved to me. "Sowkyama?" he shouted and I waved back. They crossed the road and entered my garden, much to my dismay. Awesome Mami sat demurely on the cement bench near the oleander bushes when she saw Venkat holding his beer glass. I had instinctively put my glass under my table as I always did by force of habit.

"We have brackish water in our well," Awesome Mama began.

"That milkman thinks I'm an idiot?" began Awesome Mami, "he uses

175

it to dilute the milk and it curdled today." She would not let her husband slip in more than one sentence per conversation. "I know all his tricks, slipping in blotting paper pretending it is cream, adding water, Chee, Chee! He is a useless fellow."

Venkat and Cookie, I noticed, were trying hard to keep themselves from laughing.

"It is all because of Kannagi's curse," Awesome Mami continued.

Cookie was getting into the game now. "Yes, I heard about that during lunch at Kalakeshtra," she replied in an encouraging tone.

"See, see. What did I tell you? You never believe me," she said and shook her head at her husband. "The whole city knows it except for you. You live like an ostrich in that cloth shop of yours, sticking your head into towels and sheets. All of Madras knows about the angry woman on the marina holding up an anklet, pointing towards the city. I heard on the news that we have to turn her towards the sea so she will become harmless."

Venkat coughed into a cupped fist and Cookie gulped from her glass.

"Who told that group of men?" Awesome Mami asked, "morons that they are, to bring the statue here from Thanjavur and install her in Madras? Is it not inviting trouble?"

I reminded Venkat that Kannagi was a character from the Tamil epic of Cilapaddikaram who avenged the death of her husband by tearing off a breast and hurled it at the town of Madurai. Cookie nodded her head solemnly as if she saw the connection between the story and the water problem in Madras.

"Wow. The power of women. Even a statue. It's astounding really," said Venkat.

"Ha!" said Awesome Mami. "That is all in stories concerning mythical women only. Don't worry, we are nicely still maintaining our good old Indian chauvinistic attitudes right into Y2K time and beyond."

All of us laughed. Suddenly there was a gust of wind and I smelled rain in the air. Everybody got up to leave. I had a long and early day tomorrow with trips to Mayapuram and Periamalai.

***

Usman drove with his usual enthusiasm, as if handling a rocket, zooming past the street and lanes of the crowded city. Venkat tossed his cigarette out the window and said, "I have been wanting to talk to you something. My insomnia is getting worse, the doctor feels maybe it will help me to unburden myself. You are the only one I can talk to about this."

"I have been waiting for you to come to me, Venkat. How long are you going to suffer this way? It's not human, what you are putting yourself through."

He nodded his head and sighed.

"When I left the U.S. for India, everything seemed so logical. I would work on the book, maybe line up a few more projects, which I have managed to do by the way. The Seshasamudram thing, for one, it's a big issue the world needs to know about."

Our eyes met and I said, "I'm glad you're here to record these things. Few people read these days, maybe your pictures will show how urgent the suffering is."

"The boy's face comes to me in my dreams every night. Raja is playing in the paddy fields in Angkor Wat. I have tried and tried, I cannot get him out of my head." Venkat's face was scrunched up.

"This is foolish, my dear chap." I took a deep breath before I proceeded. This was risky business. I was no expert on such matters and I had to weigh things carefully before voicing them out loud. I thought the best thing was to let him talk, get it all out of his system.

"I remember how he loved to look through all my camera equipment. He and I had planned that one day, he too would be a photographer like me. It was all agreed upon--he had made me talk to his mother about my paying for his school and then college. I had promised him. He was the first person who really loved me as I was. His face lit up when he saw me. I can never forget that."

I did not have to look at Venkat's face, I knew from the slight change of tenor in his voice that the emotion was thick in the words that followed. "Then that terrible day…"

"Try not to think of it, Venkat. There are so many things you can do. Why not set up a fund with your award money for children in the hospital in Angkor Wat?

"Maybe. I'll think about it," he said.

I was glad I had offered help, however transient it was. Soon Usman turned into the main road and there was Mogul Stores, Yusef Ali with his dirty cap. We stopped for our usual Frooti mango drink and a bit of stretching, emptying bladder business behind trees before proceeding to Periamalai.

Ironic as it was, I was actually looking forward to meeting Puncture and S.D. and perhaps even Sub-Optimal who I knew would be there to join me for the investigation regarding the tablets. Iyer had spoken to the right person in headquarters, in Delhi, regarding my personal situation, and things had been ironed out, at least temporarily, about my consulting job. When I told Venkat about it last evening, he shook my hand enthusiastically. After all, he and I both understood that work gave us identity, defining who we were.

***

I spotted the old crone, the ubiquitous pair of women, mother and pregnant daughter making their offerings, reliable Mr. Australia and his surly cronies. I felt excited and alert, it was good to be back on the job.

Villagers were staring at us as Venkat gathered his bulky metallic paraphernalia from the boot of the car and I wiped my spectacles standing there on the road.

The first odd thing I noticed as I gazed at the new tablet and the pile of broken stones that made up the second tablet was that the snakes were still there. Coiled, they dozed amongst the flower petals and small mounds of ashes caused by constant burning of incense. Soon the old crone with her earrings grazing her shoulder blades was next to me asking, "Enna Saar, Sowkyama? How have you been?"

She pointed to the mother and daughter prostrating in front of the tree and said, "You see, it is like I told you last time. Things are as they should be, brides are becoming mothers in the village now that at least one of our tablets is back."

Chandran walked towards me and greeted me with folded hands.

"We are very grateful to have our stone back, Saar. I want to tell you that I understood about your wish to preserve these antiques in the museum. But you know how it is. Devotees are not understanding this. After all, our idols in our temples are living, breathing things." Slit eyed and slouching, Mani, Mr. Population himself, stood next to his father, a toothpick dangling out the corner of his mouth. "I'm going to Mayapuram," he said to his father, threw me a knowing smile, and left.

I noticed that across the road, Pillai and Thomas were waiting for him, leaning against an old car.

"I see that your son and his friends are traveling together?" I asked as the whole disreputable gang got into an old Ambassador with Mani at the wheel.

"Ah, but you are going there too this afternoon, is it not, to Mayapuram, I mean? I.Q. Senior Saar told me he has invited you and Venkat Saar to the graduation party for I.Q. Junior this afternoon. I.Q. Junior is also having engagement done same time, double ceremony, you know. I am always saying how clever thinking Brahmin families are, finishing off so many birds with same stone."

I walked over to Venkat who was photographing a new and strange spectacle at the shrine. A two headed baby snake had joined the adults. I walked closer and stood in front of the broken and piled nagapratishta. The zigzag line on top was still there, as it had been in the original, the same oily stain where it had been before. Priest Chandran was behind, watching every move I made.

"Yes, Saar, I know what you are thinking. I too am thinking the same. It is a great loss, the damage to such a fine piece. The inspector was here also, saying the same thing."

"Have there been any leads to this thing? Any clue of who did this, where is the other missing one?" Priest Chandran scowled and shook his head. I saw Puncture and S.D. arrive in the office jeep and park next to my car.

"Did you see the protective railing, Saar? The Kali shrine at the back?" Puncture hissed.

There was a slight smugness in Puncture's voice, an edge to it, as if he were telling me that I was dispensable after all. I could not help but notice that S.D.'s and his eyes locked briefly, they turned away with knowing expressions. Later, Venkat was at the shrine, taking photographs of Chandran doing arati, the flame dancing wildly on the camphor bits in the middle of a brass plate. Mr. Australia was looking pious as he stood there surrounded by the usual gang. "Subbudu Saar is here," Puncture and S.D. said almost simultaneously, fanning my suspicions.

As you knew, O great Silent One, I was not a paranoid sort, but I had a feeling that was spreading from the middle of my body to the bottom and top. This feeling was like water, it shook and waves spread rapidly pouring into my brain. I was the fool in the horror movie who entered forbidden rooms and ventured out where he should not have.

Sub-Optimal and his hypocritical smile was next to me in no time. He folded his palms to say namaskaram as I checked his fingers closely to see if he had acquired any new Singapore returned rings. Around his neck a new chain shone in twenty four carat manner, gleaming and winking in the sun.

"Some information that we were not aware of has come to light," he said, puffing and raising his chest like an orangutan about to beat his chest in the manly manner. He snapped his fingers and asked the driver to bring the brown file. We walked towards a cement bench to the side of the temple. There was a report of an interview with the inspector for Periamalai and Mayapuram that he had conducted during my recent absence.

Sub-Optimal showed me a copy of an article that the inspector had passed on to him. It had to do with a small statue of Krishna that had disappeared from the Purnipakkam temple years ago. The item had been discovered a year later, the statue resting against one of the stone footrests that jutted out on the inside wall of the temple well.

"What is this information you are talking about?" I asked as I closed the file.

"The piece was smuggled out of the south to Mumbai and from the port there to Singapore or some such place and onward to the west. Who knows, maybe America, Europe, some such thing. From there some collector is bidding on the item and then finished, we cannot trace it -- partly like the piece from Srirangam that made half the trip--up to Mumbai, then some fellows got scared, felt guilty or something and returned it with all packaging, address to Greece intact on the corrugated paper wrapper."

"How is the art smuggling connection to our tablets made on the basis of what you have said?"

"You will keep what I am about to tell you to yourself?" he asked and looked around, as if villagers praying at the temple cared what he, a bureaucrat, carried in his head.

"Of course. When have you ever had to worry about my lack of professionalism in such matters?"

He nodded his head as if he recognized only at that moment that I had proven to be a reliable chap all these years.

"The inspector has a young wife who is enamored of all things foreign and goes often to the city to look through the journals at the American library."

"You mean the USIS library on Mount Road?"

"Yes, yes, the same one."

"What did she see? Out with it, man!"

"Wait, Saar, I am telling you only. You're getting so impatient all of a sudden." He inhaled and puffed his cheeks like a middle aged Hanuman. "She thinks she saw one of the tablets in a full color photograph. One of those fancy decorating magazines. It had the nagapratishta sitting in some New York drawing room."

"She could have been mistaken, did you check it out?"

"No need, Saar. I am hearing double confirmation of this fact from the husband, Mr. Inspector himself, who as you know, is my brother-in-law's second cousin. He saw same thing on internet. Have you doubted the word of your close relation, tell me Saar?"

I had no intention of answering his question. Sub-Optimal wiped his beaded brow with a cotton handkerchief and flared his nostrils at me like a Japanese umbrella opening and closing in a hurry.

Then he walked over to Puncture and S.D. and they were huddled in a tight circle, whispering something. This was the way it was with these fellows, maximum gossip and garbage talk, minimum work. They saw me approach, Sub-Optimal assuming that oily expression, the smile not traveling to his eyes as he said, "I had very delicate and tough call from headquarters Rao Saar. I think your friend Iyer Saar is speaking to him about recent events in department, no? You see, this kind of thing is not nice, Sathya Saar. We are all here, together, doing same job with same goal of saving our culture, is it not?"

I saw every need to address this complaint of his immediately, nip his surly arrogance in the bud. "I did not know Iyer Saar would talk to Rao. People are doing things all the time independent of me. Let us not talk about this anymore, all right? Let us concentrate on what has to be done. I will go talk to the inspector myself even if he is your very close relation. You are not having objections?" I was touched that Iyer had spoken to his old friend Rao. A little string pulling was necessary from time to time if one wanted to continue work under such conditions and show subordinates what was what.

"None at all," Sub-Optimal said through stiffened lips. Puncture and S.D. were up to their servile tricks, I saw, one hissing and one sputtering, to a higher degree than normal. My thoughts at the time, if I tried to explain to you, O great silent one, would be that I clammed up on seeing this behavior, my brain traveled back in time to generations before, grandfathers and fathers who taught that one did not associate too closely with certain types, certain classes of peoples who were not as developed mentally.

Venkat and I were on our way to my meeting with the police inspector when I passed George and Claudia's house and church. The place looked deserted and sad and I missed my friends. I asked Usman to slow down and found out from Gopal that the Indianized version of the crucifix installation ceremony had gone well and the goodbye function for my friends had been full of pomp and grandeur and affection. Even the Panchayat village council fellows had gone to see them carrying large watermelons in their hands. Gopal was on his way to Dr. Warrior's clinic in Vellore where he had also been offered a job in the hospital. I asked about my furry friend, Monty. He had been taken to the cool climes of Kodai by a family friend. I was happy to hear this. Any level of life is life, important and valuable after all. Besides Monty always laughed at my jokes and agreed with everything I said. Like me, he too laughed at life and everybody else also, espousing my personal philosophy. Final common point between us was like him, I too felt like barking at the whole world sometimes.

As I feared, no luck at the inspector's office. I knew that there was the danger that he might not open up to me, but I had not expected the fool to choose this inopportune time to go on holiday to attend a wedding. I supposed that Sub-Optimal had known this all along and thought it highly amusing that old man Sathya be sent on a wild goose chase.

***

Mayapuram temple was deserted since it was well past noon and people here adhered to the rule that only mad dogs and Englishmen went out in the afternoon sun. Venkat was taking photographs of the navagraha pavilion and the small icons nestled in alcoves along the side of the temple.

All of a sudden, I had a bad case of pins and needles on my left side and I decided to rest a bit on the bench under the neem tree. Puncture and S.D. had finished their beedis and chai so they came and stood next to me. Puncture was fidgeting with the coins in his pocket and S.D began cracking his knuckles one by one.

"What is bothering you both? Why not come out and tell me whatever it is?" I asked them.

"Nothing, Saar. Only like that." This was Puncture.

"What?" I said.

"He is only trying to say we are having suspicion about missing stained nagapratishta. Only theory stage, that's all. That's why we are not telling anything even to Subbudu Saar," S.D. added. I don't know why, but I believed them.

"What's your theory?" I asked.

"We're hearing rumor from villagers, Saar. They're hearing that Thomas and Pillai from Yusef Ali's Mogul Stores, those loafers are talking and laughing about navagraha damage near the tea stall," S.D. said.

"The police inspector's peon, Saar, he is hearing everything going on in the office no?" Puncture asked, looking at me intently for confirmation of this fact. "He is saying that I.Q. Junior Saar and Mani Saar, sons of priests, those chaps are knowing many things and ganging up with Thomas and Pillai, those loafers," he said, jingling coins in his pocket as if this was a signal of some sort.

"That Pillai chap having toe removed in Chingelpet hospital and you know the footprint near the…"

"I know, I know," I said, lifting my palm and slicing the air, a sign for S.D. to come to a stop.

"They are talking about children being harassed in temple school. One of the Muslim children harassed is that Yusef Ali's relation, Saar. They are asking devotees about navagraha damage and saying did your government temple people catch the fellows responsible for this?" Puncture said, looking crestfallen.

"Without proof we cannot do anything…" I mumbled.

"Yes, Saar, that is what we are also knowing. But now Subbudu Saar is saying that we people, all of us working on this project, we are all getting affected by this problem. This is not right, Saar." This final trajectory came from S.D.

We heard a sudden surge of music and I.Q. Senior appeared before us, asking, "Why are you waiting here? The festivities have begun, come and join us. We are waiting for your honored presence, Sathya Saar."

In his garden, several cane and metal chairs had been placed in circles with all the men sitting on them while squealing children and women squatted on the ground where a colorful, striped carpet had been spread. I.Q. Junior was being taken around and introduced by his father along with a reed-like girl who looked as if she had not been fed in months.

"My daughter-in-law to be, Saar," I.Q. Senior said sheepishly, as the emaciated child stood in front of me. "She is getting centum marks in Maths since she was a child. Horoscope is matching in every way. After all, intellectual matching is also very important Saar, is it not? This genetics business, we Indians are knowing more about this from long ago, is it not?"

Venkat had walked over to the women's side and was chatting with a woman gesticulating wildly. He saw me and winked, before ambling over with a glass of mango squash in one hand and a half eaten capsicum bhajji in the other. "Looks like I.Q. Senior and Junior have outdone themselves this time. The woman you saw me talking to says that all dowry arrangements have been finalized. The father-in-law to be will pay for most of the capitation fees, provide new Bajaj scooter, Godrej cupboard and blue Rexine vinyl sofa. Of course, all this on top of the usual elaborate wedding, gold jewels, saris and all," he said, imitating the woman's rolling eyes and impressed tone of voice.

"I thought this party was mainly for the fellow's admission into medical school or some such thing," I said to Venkat.

"Ah. But you are not having all the details Saar." This was from one of the garrulous men sitting behind me, one of whom claimed to be the I.Q. Jr.'s uncle. "Centum girl's family is having lot of influence in Chennai. They are already booking flat in Kotturpuram--very fancy building with lift and what not." The chap sitting next to him had red teeth from chewing betel nuts. He laughed and asked, "Why not arranging marriage with that green card girl from Niagara Falls?"

"Aiyyo. Don't you understand anything?" Uncle said and hit his forehead. "That girl from Ste. Catharines, Canada no? They are not having green card. You are not knowing anything about abroad peoples. Anyway, I.Q. Junior boy is liking our culture, not wanting to contribute to brain drain, no? Besides, he is having big tonsils getting fever with ice cream how can he survive in that igloo country it is too much."

I.Q. Senior and Junior came towards me again with Centum girl bowing her head like a broken stalk. They did namaskaram, seeking my blessings.

"My son is already making money, you know. He is doing import export business with that shrewd fellow Mani, from Periamalai, you know."

"Oh?"

"You don't know about Mani Saar, Poor Chandran paying for son's B.Com degree, four years college and still no proper job. What to do? Our country is like that only, no? That is why I am telling my son from the time he was crawling, medicine, medicine, no dearth of sick people anywhere-- market is always there, right?"

Puncture, S.D. and Venkat were beside me. "What kind of business is this your son and Mani are involved in?" I asked.

"Oh you know, I am not a worldly man. You should ask Mani all the details."

S.D. was shaking his head. "Office is in Thambu Chetty Street. We are knowing this much already," said Puncture, aiming a big piece of bhajji from waist level to his open mouth.

Venkat caught my eye and tilted his head to the right. I saw the whole gang of idiots there in the distance—Thomas, Pillai and Mani, laughing under the neem tree, holding Gold Spot bottles and flashing orange teeth.

***

The next day, Chinniah, Small Master, came to see me from Chinnkolam with samples from the recent harvest. We had finally come to an agreement about the price and the bank, accountant and lawyers had all done their bit to make the deal pucca. I tried not to think about my brother and myself spending nights under the stars in the ancestral farm. No point in such attachments now, not these days, especially, as I continued to get pleading letters from my sisters-in-law and nephew regarding preparations for the sale of the house.

I called Iyer to find out how he was doing and was relieved to hear him talk and laugh as he usually did. He was eagerly waiting for the arrival of his son and daughter-in- law from America. "Whatever you say, Sathya, blood is thicker than water after all, a son is a son. But how would you know about such things?" I told him about the rumor and my suspicions regarding the theft of nagapratishtas and damage to the navagrahas being an inside job done by villagers themselves.

Iyer was saying something about flowering mango trees in the Theosophical Society compound but I was already thinking about what I had to do next. "Don't let your ego interfere with your work, Sathya," Iyer said. "That Rao fellow hummed and hawed like a woman before he agreed to let you in again."

"Thank you for your kindness, Iyer. I can always count on your support."

"No, not always. I am not planning to be here always."

"I understand." It was best to agree with the aging and slightly senile. Why create discord over trivial matters?

I went to see Venkat's mother before Naidu's men came to pull down their house the following week. When I peeped in her room, I saw that the woman was not awake and the beauteous nurse, the tailor's wife, was sitting on a rocking chair, sewing something that hung from her hand. I went upstairs.

Venkat was preparing for his award show in France. He was in a room adjacent to his bedroom and dark room. The walls had been embedded with several nails and from them hung garlands of photos, still glistening from the developing liquid. "I am making a fresh set as you can see. I just got some of the negatives from the States yesterday."

We sat out on the terrace. He poured gin into his glass. "Last night was terrible again, Sathya." He dragged on his cigarette and looked in the distance.

"Why? What happened?" I prodded, gently.

"The whole terrible scene played over and over in my head. It was Raja and I in Angkor Wat. I had gone to his hut and tempted him out of there with my Toblerone bar and shiny Frisbee. You take a fancy to a kid you see in a poor country…" Venkat buried his face in his palms in a gesture of despair.

"Come on Venkat, don't belittle your feelings. You loved the boy. We all loved the boy. That pure energy for life, all sweetness and laughter. It was easy to love him." Venkat's lip quivered as he struggled to compose himself. I knew the story already but if it helped him to tell it again, I had no problems listening.

"That day I had woken up with thoughts of him." Venkat looked me squarely in the eyes. "If I had had a child, I supposed I would have felt a little of all that love burbling up inside me daily. I don't know how any one bears it. It is hard to bear."

I said nothing. Love and pain came mingled, this much I knew from my own experience with Menaka. I supposed it felt the same way with children.

"We went to the usual place where we played. You remember it, don't you?" he asked.

I nodded unable to wipe the ensuing image in my head of the child's bloody body before Venkat 's narrative took me there. "How could I have done it? I don't understand. I knew there were landmines all over the place

187

and yet I chose to believe him and gave myself up to the childish enjoyment of the moment. I can still hear the whiz off the Frisbee as it sliced through the air. And then Raja steps back and there is this fountain of fire that comes up from the ground…" Venkat's face was in his hands again. Then he sat down and lit another cigarette.

Both of us said nothing for a few minutes. It was too much. The memories of the panic, the screams, the image of Venkat running, carrying the boy's body to the hospital, the shattered limbs and torn flesh, bones jutting out. Grief and despair sometimes were successfully diluted with practical instructions. I decided to try such a route. "Have you thought of what we talked about before? You know, making a donation in his name to the hospital?"

"I wrote to his parents. They have not responded. Not that I expected to hear anything. That would be too much." His voice had dropped to a hoarse whisper. I will stop there on my way to Paris."

We went through the photographs he would take to France and I could not help noticing the boy in several of them, his face captured in its openness, thoughtful or smiling as if he had lived all his life in front of a camera. That image of the child in Venkat's arms, all bloodied and torn up by the accident, the wail of his parents when they came to the hospital, the frozen look of shock and disbelief on Venkat's face all of the following week as he kept saying, "Why did I bring the Frisbee? Why did we go there? If only I had not….."The words still rang in my mind.

Downstairs, on my way out, I took another peep into Venkat's mother's room and saw that she was moving. She had spotted me and waved for me to go inside. I moved closer and she stroked the skin on my hand as if I were a helpless pet. "I came here as a young bride and learned all about the struggles of life as I walked through the rooms of this house. Everything I know about life I learned here in this house," she said.

***

At home, Cookie was in the front verandah with Basket Hair. His moped was parked in the portico. They were chatting with Nagu and

Paru who had returned from a trip to the Murugan temple. The festival of Thaipusam was coming up and the neighborhood temple sent invitations to all of us. Cookie told us she wanted to see the gypsy korathi dance.

Paru's stomach was enormous now, as if she was carrying a basketball. Nagu and Paru had rented Ayah's hut in the slum tenements to the tailor and his beauteous wife. This provided an additional source of income, they reasoned, since Nagu now had a bigger family support with Siva's wife and children living with Ayah in their ancestral village.

There was a terrible stench in the air and we heard a lot of shouting from the side of the garden. I went to investigate and looked up at the drumstick tree to see several branches swinging as a monkey jumped from branch to branch. A huge brown cannonball had fallen on the ground from the neighbor's tree. Bala was a warrior standing there with the bamboo pole in his hand. "It did not fall down naturally, Saar. The monkey did it, I saw it, I tell you. "

"All right, all right, calm down Bala. It is nothing to get excited about."

"You don't understand, Saar. That rascal deliberately aimed the thing at me. I might be seriously injured if I had not prayed at the Hanuman temple last week. Now this mother monkey has a little one hanging on to the stomach so the population keeps on growing," he wailed.

I pressed the edge of my towel to the lower half of my face and told him to go back to the kitchen. "It is a sign, I tell you," Bala said and glared at me, muttering something intelligible, retreating into the house.

Cookie and Basket Hair were busy shutting all the windows and doors. "God, it's just like a skunk sprayed the house," Cookie proclaimed, scrunching up her nose. She was telling me about the dance they hoped to perform at the Chidambaram temple. "I wish Iyer could have been there," she sighed. "Is he feeling better?" I told her he was, I had spoken to him early that morning.

Bala came in with steaming tumblers of coffee and Britannia biscuits. "I have to leave early today, Saar. I am going to Grand Sweets with my wife. She is taking up part-time job there."

"Anything else you want to tell me, Bala?" I asked.

"This Grand Sweets owner, Saar, he is also calling me for their catering unit. They are delivering meals to many houses and they want a good cook.

Part-time only. They are offering medical allowance and all but I am saying wait, wait, I have to find somebody suitable for Sathya Saar. Doctor says I should work less, I'm getting old."

"Is this a prison? Does this house look like a place where people are forced to stay? You can do what you like. One fellow like me, how much food do I need?"

I left the hotel for a walk. The famous and ancient temple of dancing Siva, Nataraja, was a glorious and majestic structure, an example of stunning Chola architecture. Situated in the heart of Chidambaram, the main deity here was represented in a most unusual fashion. Instead of the usual pillar-like lingam, you had the akasha lingam, representing air, one of the five elements of the universe. This meant you saw nothing.

On my return to the hotel lobby, I sat at a small table in the bar. That was when I heard the distinct voices of Basket Hair and Cookie. A plant obscured my presence and they had not seen me but I could hear them clearly all right. Eavesdropping was one of my weaknesses and I strained to hear what they were saying.

"Do you think he has seen it?" Basket Hair asked.

"I don't think so. Poor Thatha. He thinks so much of himself and his work and now this awful thing. I wonder what it means for the future."

I had heard enough and thought I should get up and make my presence felt. They were both surprised to see me emerge so suddenly and exchanged startled glances.

"What is it that you're talking about? Best to tell me, no point in hiding things from me," I said. Authority was one of the few things at my disposal these days, at least with people outside of work.

My hands shook as I looked at the evening paper she handed me. To the right hand corner of the front page was an article with the headline, "Temple projects aid loss of artifacts." The piece went on to say that two small temple restoration projects, in Periamalai and Mayapuram, originally meant to save ancient art, had in fact, achieved the reverse. Navagraha idols were damaged in Mayapuram and irreplaceable stone tablets had disappeared from under the noses of museum guards, one of them turning up in pieces under the tree shrine of the temple after a few weeks. The other tablet remained missing and the journalist speculated that it was probably another victim of art smuggling like so many pieces of antique temple art. The journalist said the people concerned in these two projects could not be held personally responsible (he had at least had the sense to fathom that and say so). The article ended with a quote from Sub-Optimal who had agreed to orders from head office that people involved in the projects would be sent home on extended leave. He had gone on to name names including mine, Puncture and S.D.

Basket Hair excused himself and said he wanted to retire for the night. It was obvious that he was uncomfortable with the direction of the conversation and wanted to leave Cookie and me alone so as not to embarrass me in my plight.

"Are you all right?" the child asked in a concerned voice.

"I don't know," I said. "I don't know what to think, how to feel about this. This is the first time I have been in the paper for the wrong reasons."

We were both silent for a while. "It is only an evening paper, not many people would have seen it. Besides, look at the crowd here for the festival. Everybody is thinking about tomorrow."

I nodded weakly. What was the point in going over the pain I felt with Cookie? Was I a child to seek words of comfort from another child? The sensation of having swallowed a flame traveled from my mouth to my insides as I sipped beer and ate masala peanuts.

"Tell me about the secret of Chidambaram."

The child was trying to distract me. It was not as if I had not related the story of the drum and the flame to Cookie before. She wanted to hear it again, I surmised, because she and Basket Hair were performing the famous tandavam dance tomorrow.

"To the right of the silver icon of Nataraja dancing his cosmic dance is the chidambara rahasyam, the secret of secrets. All you see is a garland of leaves. You look at the statue to the left and you see God externally and to the right, when you glimpse the secret, you see him internally. He is doing the cosmic dance within you. The whole universe is within you. "

"I'm not sure I understand."

"You see the world around you is the external world, the illusory version. Our job is to find release from all this, to go to a level where we are not trapped by time and space. Siva's being signifies the universe, he is total equilibrium and he is in the temple of your mind, he is dancing inside you and me. We only have to look within. This is the secret, the nothing represented here."

***

The Natyanjali dance festival opened on the day of Sivarathri, at dusk, when Siva did his famous dance. Basket Hair and Cookie made a fine pair, emulating Siva and the goddess. Basket Hair was all fire and muscle, his body powerful in its movements as he danced. The elemental chaos of the world, the fury of Siva was displayed brilliantly by the young man. Cookie, on the other hand, was equally good, a softer version, rising up to the challenge of the task at hand.

That night, I tossed restlessly as I thought of the newspaper article and what lay ahead. I would talk to Iyer, I told myself. He was one person I could turn to in times of trouble. He would show me the way back to myself.

***

During the drive back to the city, Cookie told me she had made the decision to go ahead with her marriage to Kumar. "He is kind and considerate and a good man. What more is there, Thatha? I'm such a dreamy type, always looking for things that may or may not be there in real life."

"You should do what you like. That is best," I said, surprised she had undergone the transformation from illusion to reality with such speed and finality. That was the unique strength of youth, rushing headlong into things without thinking too much. Analysis and weighing the pros and cons sometimes only furthered confusion and contributed to nothing much in particular in terms of action. How many marriages were based on rational thought? My own heart and head were full of ebbing and rising waves.

"You have thought this through then?" I could not help ask.

She shook her head yes. "This love thing...it's scary. I don't think I could handle failure, a divorce. I guess it's true what my parents say, this way I feel more secure. That's not a bad thing, is it?"

I did not know what to say.

Cookie continued, "My parents think I'm not Indian enough. They don't realize how Indian I really am. Very practical about important matters, you know." Her laugh had a cynical tinge to it.

" With us Indians, you know, marriage is a life long affair."

"I can be practical all my life. I sometimes want things that are not there and I fail to see the things that are there. Do you have that problem? Not knowing what is real and not real? I don't want to be confused by abstract things like love. Life is specific after all, one day after another. Today I am single, soon I will be married, I feel resilient enough. I don't want to suffer from paralysis through analysis," she said, turning to look out the window.

I did not know what to say in response. Perhaps she would make it all work. Women were an enigma to me, and marriage too was an arrangement I had only observed second hand. Basket Hair was riding behind us and now he was adjacent to us. The black windcheater he wore ballooned up on his back like a huge boil as he overtook us.

"What about him?" It slipped out of my mouth as I looked at Basket Hair. Perhaps I should have edited myself, I thought as I caught the amused expression on her face.

"What about him? You didn't think there was anything between us? We're just friends. He's a super practical guy. His family has arranged for him to marry a girl in IT who works for Wipro. She will be making a good and solid salary and he will continue to dance."

"Oh." How earthbound these youngsters were. The idealism of my youth and adulthood stretching into old age, my ideas of clinging onto intangibles as a way to better my soul, all of that seemed quaint and outdated somehow.

I thought of the telephone call earlier from Puncture and S.D. "Saar, Saar, what will we do now? Subbudu Saar says they may not be able to give us pay after two weeks. What kind of fate has befallen us that we should suffer in this manner?" S.D. spluttered and passed the phone to Puncture who inflated and deflated in his usual style. We would talk again soon, I promised, telling them of my plans to visit Srirangam.

***

At home, there was another frantic letter from my nephew in Bombay, followed by a phone call from my sister-in-law. They had contacted all the concerned parties who had a share in the ancestral property and taken a consensus. There was no point in postponing the sale of the house anymore. My sister-in-law had tracked down Naidu and the oily fellow was before me, wiping his neck and face with a blue and white checked handkerchief.

"The papers are all fine and in ready form, Saar. The final okay is yours," he said, bringing his palms together. There was nothing to decide, we both knew, the numbers had been agreed upon through negotiation between Cigarette Chellappa, his boss in Bombay and my relatives. Signatures were there in black and white. I scribbled my signature and told him to come back after a month. "We will then decide on the nitty gritty stuff," I said. My sister-in-law and nephew had organized through a friend for me to occupy a one bedroom flat in Royal Gardens, the apartment building on Koil Street, during the interim period. Even this small detail had been engineered for me. The letter Naidu showed me said that they all felt I should be compensated for the sudden uprooting and inconvenience with a rental flat nearby while I waited for more permanent lodging.

"No problem with anything, Sathya Saar. I have piece of good news for you. My boss Cigarette Chellappa says we can arrange for you to have small flat on top floor of building we will build here. Bottom rate, reduced price. Nobody else need be knowing this, confidential matter between us three parties."

"Let's talk about all of this another time," I said and the chap nodded violently. The compound gate creaked in protest as he let himself out. I resisted the urge to howl along with it as I watched it swing shut.

I wondered if I would hear from Sub-Optimal next morning as I prepared to leave for Srirangam. Men were already hard at work next door, at Venkat's house, dismantling all sorts of things. Cookie reminded me that Venkat would be back for the Thaipusam festival at the local temple to photograph the firewalkers before his departure. She was leaving on her sari shopping trip to Kanchipuram with Mrs. Awesome in a few hours.

I watched Paru and Nagu doing their usual duties in the garden, she plucking flowers for the morning puja and he watering the oleander and gardenia bushes before he left for work. Paru's child was due in a week's time. I called out to them and told her to go home.

Early that evening, I was at Theosophical Society to see Iyer. His son and daughter-in-law from America had arrived. They were staying at the Adyar Gate, the nearest five star hotel. We made some small talk for a few minutes and they left to go shopping. Iyer's face looked sunken, cheeks caved in, two hollows on either side. His eyes were misty as he began telling me about all his plans. His pen and walking stick he wanted me to have, he said. "Please Iyer, " I said. "Don't talk like that. The children are here, your nurse tells me you are doing better, we should be making plans for something else, not all this inauspicious talk."

"Now what is all this I hear about this newspaper article business?"

"It is all rubbish Iyer. I feel as if I have been used like a pawn of some kind. You know my feeling, this is my dharma, my duty, my work. I want to do my best and leave something behind. And they turn around and blame me for other people's stupidity and inefficiency? The whole system is going to the dogs."

Iyer's face assumed a grave expression and he said, "I say, listen to me, Sathya. What is all this business of looking like you have lost everything? A little newspaper article business and you are falling apart. Just simply retire and reflect, Sathya. We cannot take ourselves too seriously in this life. Running after so much job satisfaction like an American, then wanting honor on top of it like a good Indian, accolades for your efforts from people. This is all rubbish, man, you know that."

I stared at Iyer and my expression of hurt and surprise must have been plain for his eyes softened and he reached out and took my hand.

"Our time is over, Sathya. I am trying to tell you that the time for us is gone. What we want and what we worked towards, that's all in the past. This new time is different. We do not understand its rhythms; we are misfits now. The people now, they're dancing to a different tune. It's money, corruption, all kinds of underhanded business. My old contacts except Rao are dead and so are yours. How do you want to leave the work you have done? Willingly, based on your decision or theirs? Retire and reflect. The time has come. I do not know what else to tell you. It is unfair, what they are doing. Old Brahmins like us who cherish the old values, our time is gone."

I was taken aback.

"And now it is time for me to rest. Come back from Srirangam with my prasadham. Now go home and let me sleep. All these emotions are exhausting for me. The noise in my head wants precedence. Go home and leave me alone."

When I glanced briefly again at Iyer's face as I left, I shuddered slightly and touched the gold Ganesha pendant that hung from the key chain I held in my hand. Iyer had given it to me as a good luck omen before I began working on the book and before I began my first day of work on the Periamalai and Mayapuram projects. Now the book was done, the village projects were close to completion in spite of the mess. I wanted all the luck in the world to cap things.

I left for Srirangam following morning.

The famous temple of Ranganatha was undergoing renovation, the team led by a garrulous chap called Sunder. He was not a chap I knew well. His reputation preceded him and the only thing I was sure of was that he was a lackadaisical sort and not given to caring deeply about his work. Like Sub-Optimal, this fellow also favored the gaudy multi-color approach for the carved towers so they looked like pillars of candy, their awe-inspiring beauty relegated to pink and blue and yellow and green as if the carved stones came from a child's coloring box.

I stared at the image of Vishnu as Ranganatha. He rested so elegantly on the coiled form of Aadi Sesha, the giant serpent. I prayed that Iyer would find relief from his illness, that my own problems with the project would diminish to a negligible level. Then I prayed again so that God would forgive me for it was indeed childish to pray for things that only related to one's own benefit.

After circumambulation, I brought my hands close to the flame on the brass plate the priest offered me and brushed the warmth of the fire to my face and eyes. I drank thirtham, holy water, that he poured into my cupped hands and tucked a wet jasmine flower from the liquid behind my right ear. The priest blessed me with the silver crown he placed on my head and gave me packets of red kumkum and vibhuti to take to Iyer.

I walked away from the center of the temple and went to a spot which presented an ample view of the street and goings on. In the distance, there was a lorry and I saw men carrying large doors towards the vehicle. Two other chaps were heaving and pushing in elaborately carved statues.

Sunder walked towards me at that moment and I grabbed the binoculars from around his neck and looked at the lorry and men. My stomach lurched as I saw what I had felt instinctively. The men were none other than Mani, Thomas and Pillai. I.Q. Junior emerged from behind a door, pushed up his specs on his nose, looked furtively around.

"Do you know those men? Why are they taking those things from here? Do they have your permission?"

"Please, Sathya. No need to burst a blood vessel. It is only our usual gang, they are in import export business. We are only giving very badly damaged and useless items to them."

"And who is certifying these items to be useless and not valuable?"

"Are you questioning my honesty?"

"Maybe I am. I find this strange, I have not heard of anybody giving damaged items away."

"Look, Sathya. You are having big, impractical ideas. We are having huge temple here, costs are rising all the time We have creative ways of raising funds. You need not get involved in everything. Subbudu is knowing everything going on here, all right?"

"Ah yes, of course. That makes it all all right. I should have known."

Sunder glared at me. "Look, what you do here is your business but these items are priceless, so many of them irreplaceable, is it not?" I asked.

I was getting ready to leave when something slipped out from my right hand and I heard a crunch as I stepped on it. The gold plated Ganesha pendant that Iyer had given me had slipped out of my key chain and now the plastic covering was hopelessly cracked.

***

Bala was nervously wringing his hands as if he was thinking about a particularly sticky problem. "What is it?" I asked as he brought me my Tiffin of dosa and chutney and buttermilk. Instead of replying, he walked away fast muttering something. I was not in the frame of mind to handle one of his menopausal moods or hear about his monkey business so I ignored the man. Cookie's face looked swollen and her eyes were red. "What is it? Everything all right between the lovebirds, you and Kumar?"

"It's Iyer, Thatha. His son Venu called this morning. It's bad." I stared at her as tears fell from her eyes. "You should go now, they're waiting for you. Venkat and I were there earlier." I continued to stare at her though I understood every word and it occurred to me that I had failed my dear friend in delivering the prasadham he so badly wanted. I remembered that churning feeling in my stomach when the pendant broke in Srirangam. The same sensation returned, only now it stayed longer, coming in waves as I thought of Iyer's face, his manner of speaking, his wisdom, our relationship over the years. I could not think of what to do next. Everything seemed a little unreal, as if I was watching myself feel what I was feeling, watching myself get up and prepare. I stared at my face in the mirror and wanted to ask who was that? I did not know that man.

Iyer's body lay on the bed dressed in white cotton dhoti and kurta. Venu came to meet me and took my hands. "He went peacefully in his sleep. Thank God he did not suffer." I nodded and patted his back. Words of condolence did not come to me easily as I stood there watching my dear friend's face. A thin muslin towel was wound around the chin and sides of his face to hold his jaw shut. His eyes were closed; I did not know how they had done that. Incense sticks burned nearby and the atmosphere was serene and peaceful. I brushed the vibhuti and kumkum from Srirangam on Iyer's forehead.

The cremation was to take place in a few hours. They were waiting for more relatives and friends who wanted to visit and say goodbye. I took Iyer's hand and it was cold as I knew it would be. Naturally, the fingers did not curl around my hand or exert any pressure in response. On his desk, I saw his spectacles, a glass tumbler with his dentures floating in water. A garlanded picture of Hanuman stood next to a pile of Iyer's books. I remembered that the monkey god was one of his favorites for Hanuman was a great devotee of Lord Rama as was Iyer.

I could hear car doors closing as a group of people arrived. I took in my friend's face one last time.

On the drive back home, I could not stop thinking about the photo of Hanuman on Iyer's desk.

Hanuman was always the one who came to your aid in times of trouble. Taking the shape of a monkey disabled that terrible thing, the ego. This way, he became free from desires and moved smoothly towards the path of true service. None of the usual crippling obstacles that fell in the way of progress of human beings. How often it was that I dwelt on myself as myself and forgot that I was merely an implement of something else. Was that the final message from my friend? I wondered.

Life without Iyer was strange to think about. He had always been a part of my life, infusing my days with his wisdom and elastic humor. When there was a problem and I could not find a way to address it, I could always take it to him. Mind you, I did not want to put the man on a pedestal or anything like that. Iyer thought long and hard deeply about how to live life. He thought about things like love and God and work and death. These were not issues one wanted to delve in deeply on a daily basis for they irritated like cactus needles embedded in the skin. Yes, yes, we knew these things were somewhere out there but please, we said, leave it alone for now, let us think of the moment and our enjoyment. Anyway, O great silent one, as you and I knew, old men made people uncomfortable. You wished to look away from the struggle of their bodies and their minds to escape the decay, the end.

While I had been away at Srirangam, more of Venkat's house was gone. The view was eerie, concrete beams broken in an uneven manner with metal rods sticking out like antennae. Thick columns from the ground rose like fingers in the dark. I looked behind the two rocks in the rock garden. The space was empty. The skin the chameleon shed lay there like a hollow tube with jagged edges. Crawling ants were carrying away bits of it. Life after death, the cycle continued as always. Iyer was looking for his next body, the clock was ticking for me.

Chapter Nine
Auspicious Beginnings

Ayah came carrying raisins and sugar candy, looking more coffee colored than usual because of her outdoor life in the country. "Auspicious beginning today," she said smiling and showing her gums. Paru had given birth early in the morning to a child, a boy at that. Nagu entered the hall, his face radiant as well. Mother and son were on their way to the Ganesha shrine in front of Misty Glen, to offer fruits and flowers and mark the start of a new life. Ayah was staying on for the Thaipusam celebrations before she went back to the village.

Cookie joined me in the verandah and Bala came with coffee and tea for the two of us. "So how was your shopping trip to Kanchipuram?" I asked.

"Mrs. Awesome is something else, Thatha. She made the poor salesman take out so many saris from the shelves. It took her hours to buy one." She giggled at the recollection.

"The men would unfold the saris, one vibrant color after another and she would shake her head unimpressed. Finally she chose the gaudiest of the lot. Orange with magenta border! I got all my saris in the first hour. Now there's only the jewelry shopping in Bombay. But I must tell you, she told me the saddest thing about the beginning of her hysteria."

"What did she say?" I asked.

Venkat joined us in the verandah. He was staying these days at the Sahib Club. Bala came with another tumbler of coffee and made noises about Grand Sweets again, saying he would arrange to have food delivered for me in the new apartment, something I did not care to think about. I dismissed him with a wave of my hand. "Later, let us talk about this some other time," I said. Naidu's oily face had faded from my mind, and I wanted to keep it that way at least for a few more days.

Cookie continued her story about Mrs. Awesome. Going home for her first confinement, as was the custom those days, Mrs. Awesome had watched elders in the family tuck a tiny grain of raw rice into a newborn's velvety mouth, her cousin sister's fourth girl child. The child had gasped and choked to death. That night, Mrs. Awesome experienced her first bout of hysteria when she circled her own cot a hundred times as the girl child's image followed her round and round. Of course, things had turned out all right when Mrs. Awesome gave birth to a boy. But the hysteria persisted and she had never been the same since then.

***

We were all silent for a few minutes, overwhelmed by the sadness of the story.

Usman wanted to talk to me. He was twisting his hands in that nervous way of his, rubbing his fingers together as if he had arthritis. "What is it?" I asked.

Venkat answered for him. "He came to me last month for a company job. Seems his family is growing and he needs a bigger salary. I have managed to connect him with one of the fellows at Amalgamations through a friend and they have made him an offer. He is wondering how to tell you, right, old chap?"

Usman nodded his head like a woman, moving slightly north, south, east and west as if he could not make up his mind which direction to choose. "I have told all you fellows, you, Bala, Nagu, all of you, this man does not need a staff. This house is not a prison, all right? Anybody is free to leave and do as they wish. Forget the old man, how does it matter? I myself am looking for a way to leave this planet, make room for another body and soul. Is this not what we must all do?"

I watched Usman still doing making that nervous movement with his hands. "You can leave this evening, no problem. I will ask Bala to have your money ready at the end of the day." Usman went to wash the car telling me he would come back and visit me in the new flat.

***

The day of Thaipusam festival dawned bright and clear and the whole lot of us walked to the temple together. There was Nagu and Ayah, Cookie, Venkat and myself. I knew that Puncture and S.D. and Sub-Optimal would also be there, since we had worked on a small renovation project at the temple ten months back. This was the first major festival after that job and they would be arriving to take credit at the appointed hour.

As usual, the holy day had fallen on the day of the full moon, on the day of the star pusam. Ardent male devotees carried kavadis, bow-like contraptions on their shoulders, loaded with milk pots as an offering for Lord Subramanya. There was a story associated with this celebration. During the wedding between Siva and Parvati, at Kailas, the north side of planet earth tilted because of the collective weight of those gathered for the grand occasion. Conversely, the southern part of the planet rose like a see-saw since the other side tipped downwards. Siva requested sage Agasthya to move south to achieve balance, promising him that he would indeed see the ceremony again.

The temple was decorated gaily with garlands of leaves and flowers and there was the smell of incense and overripe bananas along with human sweat. I was surprised to see a larger crowd than normal that had gathered outside with vendors hustling all sorts of cheap trinkets and beggar children offering to mind footwear for a few coins. Venkat had pulled out his camera and vanished into the thickest part of the crowd. The gypsy korathi dance was taking place to the side of the temple and Cookie moved away in that direction. Firewalkers were preparing to walk over coals and there were men and boys carrying kavadis on their shoulders in front of the temple. Ayah found old acquaintances to greet so she joined them. Only Nagu stayed by my side like a shadow.

A lean young man, his skin gray with the smearing of large quantities of vibhuti, swayed as if to some internal mantra. He had pierced his cheek from one side to the other with a trident so his mouth hung open. There was not a single drop of blood on him anywhere. His eyes were glassy and elsewhere, it indicated that he had transferred himself spiritually to a different plane, he was certainly not on the grounds of Maramur,

Madras, India, or even on the slowly rolling blue planet where human beings belonged. The effort of transcendence must involve supreme effort, I surmised, for on his back was a map from body sweat wiping out the superficial layer of ash. Several near him had long needles pierced through their tongues, their mouths hanging open too as if they panted for the Lord. My mind leapt to an image of self-flagellation I had witnessed in Manila during a Lent procession and I realized this is was a universal impulse. We inflicted suffering on ourselves in the name of faith and religion. I wondered if one ascribed the impulse to low class beings who could not think and reflect?

There were firewalkers walking on live coals to the east of the temple. As I observed the men smear their feet with ashes and work themselves into a frenzy before stepping on the coals, I thought it was paradoxical, like a sexual experience where all control was abandoned and given up to some primitive force. I watched again and again as one firewalker after another spoke and yelled things to himself, addressing some self that lurked within, working up the outside self, hypnotizing both the inner and outer parts within himself, making them both move, one superimposed over the other. I had a natural resistance to this basically mumbo-jumbo stuff. Yes, yes, I saw the principle of the thing, I could even somewhat accept this more or less on one level but the real thinking level said no no, all this was rubbish.

One of the firewalkers came and stood by my side. He lifted one foot and checked it. There were few red marks, maybe a blister or two. Our eyes met and I had the feeling he was not there, that I was looking into something vacant. I shuddered at the idea of a man erasing himself so completely, killing his own identity so he could move somewhere else. It was an abnormal thing. True devotees claimed they erased themselves completely so they could experience nothingness. I did not like the thought of not being myself, submerging my ego and identity so completely that I was unrecognizable from the rest—the thought frightened me.

Venkat was with Cookie, I could tell, by the way the flash went off every now and then in the northwest corner, where the gypsy dancers performed. Ayah and Nagu were still watching the firewalkers. I moved on ahead. A mango tree with a circular seat at the base was only twenty feet or so away so I decided to sit down for a bit. It was only nine thirty and there was still plenty of time for puja and arati at eleven o' clock. Sub-Optimal, Puncture and S.D. joined me under the tree. They did their usual namaskaram Saar business and pointed out key people in the crowd to me.

"See, Sathya Saar," Puncture hissed, "Thomas and Pillai are here. See them there? What are those Christian fellows doing here?"

"I see I.Q. Junior and that skinny wife-to-be of his, Centum girl you are calling her no?" This was S.D.

Sub-Optimal was twirling the rings on his finger like a nervous bride. I saw that he walked towards the firewalkers to view the spectacle. Then he came back. "How long before they are doing what they are supposed to so people like us who have to work can go back to the office?" He put on his businesslike, self-important face and pushed his head up like a giraffe. Puncture and S.D. elbowed each other and giggled. When they saw that I was looking at them, they assumed serious expressions.

"So what are you both doing these days?" I could not help asking.

"Working, Sathya Saar. Subbudu Saar is being very helpful no, finding us temporary things to do. We are traveling to Coimbatore and doing big repair work on Hanuman temple, building compound wall and adding doors and gates." This was S.D.

"Yes and now museum people also behaving nicely, simbly listening to everything, no trouble making or anything like that. We have to show them who is boss -- not like before," Puncture added with obvious satisfaction.

"I thought you two had also been asked to take leave like me, what happened to change all that?"

Sub-Optimal came closer to us and sat under the tree. He answered my question. "They are being poor, Sathya Saar. They need their jobs to survive. They are having wives and families to support. Besides, they are not being held so responsible for what has happened, people losing their treasures because of mismanagement." Uttering this false and rotten pronouncement, he got up and said he would see about the priest starting the puja, he had no time to waste in this manner. My blood pressure was moving up, I could feel it surging in my ears.

I saw that Puncture and S.D. watched me carefully. "What do you two have to say about all of this?"

"We are agreeing, Saar. They are old village treasures, no? Priceless and all. If we had left them there only, none of this would have happened. We should have checked with the villagers before embarking on such a project." S.D. built a strong trajectory.

"Who are we to say anything, Saar? We have not studied so much like you but we are respecting tradition of all peoples whether Brahmin or not. We are believing all are same and giving them respect." I noticed that Puncture puffed up his cheeks after hissing, as if he was Hanuman. He and S.D. looked at each other and their eyes met. In that fleeting moment, I knew they had sold me out completely. All these years we had worked together and they let me down, just like that. What did I expect from these low class illiterates who only took orders and could not think for themselves? Loyalty? This was my mistake, expecting too much from people who were unable to deliver. Also, I often forgot that most people worked because they had to, not because they wanted to. I did my job with dharma, duty to future generations in mind. The legacy of our religion and culture was something I did not want to see die. This yearning of mine was top priority always, I hoped to experience the satisfaction of having left this much to the world when I died. But of course, most people live on a superficial level and rarely think long enough to delve into the kind of insight I am talking about. The kind of reflective power it takes to see through the outer layers and get to the core of the matter. From the rind to the core was a long journey indeed.

"Of course, you two realize," I added with a touch of irony in my voice, "since the article appeared in the paper, your names are indelibly associated with the Periamalai and Mayapuram projects so you are equally responsible in the eyes of the public."

Their eyes narrowed and Puncture coughed nervously into his cupped fist while S.D. spat on the ground, something I had never seen him do in the vicinity of a temple. Then he said, "You may be saying so and all, but we are knowing the reality, no?"

Puncture clarified what he meant. "You are being leader and boss and all. Blame only falling on your head since you are claiming always to be expert at everything and having so many years of experience."

I could feel the heat rising from the base of my spine, traveling all the way to my head like a tree of anger that rose up to my full height and breadth. Before I could respond, Sub-Optimal was rushing towards us saying, "the priest is in the inner shrine. Arati will be in a few minutes." I observed from the corner of my eye that Nagu was moving towards me pushing himself through the crowd that was thickening around us as we moved towards the incantations and singing. Drums were beating loudly, the bells ringing and there was the slightly rancid smell of coconut oil from the many flaming brass lamps.

Venkat was perched on one of the lower limbs of the mango tree, a spot which gave him the best view. Cookie, I saw, was standing not far from the tree with Awesome Mami and Mama. The three of them had trouble being in the middle of crowds and preferred to watch things from a distance. I too was not very fond of crowds since I hated the assault of offensive smells from sweat and body odor and what not. But today I decided to make an exception and show that I too was capable when it came to being part of things like everybody else.

There was that dirty Indian habit spreading through the rows, men and women elbowing and pushing to move themselves up front as if a first row view meant certain exemption from reincarnation. I turned around and saw that Nagu was right behind me, his palms together in reverence, his eyes closed. I felt guilty that I was not so easily transported. Before I turned back towards the music and the shining face of Lord Murugan, I thought I saw two men that resembled those swines from Periamalai, Thomas and Pillai, edging their way to the front of the crowd. Then I met the dark, icy eyes of Mani. Centum girl smiled shyly at me.

My attention was drawn to the front, the inner shrine of the temple which appeared like a cave with no natural light. The many temple bells clanged together and the chanting of mantras rose to a fevered pitch. The priest rotated a many wicked lamp around the stone faces of Murugan and the accompanying, smaller idol of his son, Subramanya, leaning against a peacock showing off its fan of feathers and innumerable eyes. All around me, devotees muttered their prayers, slapped their cheeks to ask for penance and pressed their palms together.

The next moment, something flew past me, a blur of brown, an object

I was not familiar with. The fact had barely registered that something had been flung by somebody before I heard the boom of an explosion like rock breaking apart and the commotion of people screaming, faces flying past me, bruised, bloodied. I heard a child wail, each shrill screech drilling into my ears.

"Molotov cocktail," a man yelled. Somebody was pressing himself hard against me, pinning his weight on my body so I gasped for a whole minute and the next thing I felt was sweet relief for the weight had been magically removed from my back and Nagu was asking me if I was all right.

"Yes, yes," I screamed, my throat suddenly dry. " I think it is time for us to leave." All around me, there was confusion and chaos with people jostling and pushing each other as they struggled with the row of people ahead and behind them. The inner shrine in front of me was a pitch black hole.

At the time, it did not occur to me that whoever did this, they had been attempting to get me, that vile rumors had spread about my inflexible attitude when it came to preserving so called national treasures. The objections of such idiots was that the tablets were living and alive and holy in the present, helping devotees reach their goal with their blessing and unseen powers. The faithful did not wish to be disturbed by the likes of me.

When I turned around again in a few minutes to see if Nagu was still behind me, I saw that he was slumping to the ground, holding his chest. He had been stabbed and blood was spurting from the wound, covering his fingers, dripping to the ground. I did not even think about it, I pressed the towel from my shoulder to his chest and applied slight pressure, telling him to be quiet and not talk, not waste his breath. I looked up at the mango tree and Venkat was not there. My eyes searched frantically for a face I could recognize and thankfully, in a few seconds, Venkat was rushing towards me. He must have noticed immediately what had happened. I was grateful that he too was keeping an eye on me in the crowd.

"Somebody has called for an ambulance but let's not wait for them. Who knows how long they'll take? They can take the injured priest. You and Nagu get in here, I have a car and driver waiting, come on, come on. Help us," he was yelling to chaps gawking nearby, so Nagu could be lifted and helped onto the back seat.

I got into the front seat with Venkat. Centum girl and Mani gawked at us as we drove away.

All I remember of that lightning ride was the driver used the horn non-stop like a siren and I could smell that overripe, sticky-sweet smell of blood leaking from Nagu's body at the back.

The driver halted at VHS, the city charity hospital, and I remember seeing men in white open the doors quickly and remove Nagu from the car.

"Look after him and make him well soon. He is a new father," I said to one of the men.

"Yes, Saar," the man replied. Venkat put his arm around me though we were already seated in a fairly snug manner, the two of us and the driver in the front vinyl seat of the Ambassador.

"Relax, Sathya. Don't talk, we'll take you to Wellingdon and make sure you are all right." His voice was the last thing I remembered before entering darkness, my consciousness obliterated temporarily from recent events and reality.

***

The next morning, Bala came to see me with a meal in a Tiffin carrier. There was papad and pickle, snake gourd curry with coconut, rice, drumstick sambhar and tomato rasam, and of course, the ubiquitous curd rice, a must for cooling down the system in a place like Madras.

The doctor informed me that one of my ribs had a hairline crack and it would heal itself over time. This explained the pain on my upper side under my right arm. I was to be discharged the following day since all sorts of tests had shown that everything else was all right. I was worried about Nagu. Paru had just brought a new life into the world and he had additional responsibilities. I wished he had not tried to block my body from the criminal who did this. I was an old chap after all, my time with Yama could not be far away.

I saw that Bala opened a banana leaf packet that held two vadais, the string holding them together still intact. It was part of a vadai malai, a customary offering our family made at the Hanuman temple. "What's all this?" I asked.

"Jaya, Cookie's Amma telephoned to say I must do this, Saar. All the way from America Saar. Cookie talked to her and Jaya Amma was crying on the phone saying I must do this because you and Cookie child are all right." He unfolded another smaller leaf packet that had the bright orange paste prasadham from the Hanuman temple. I automatically put a finger to the paste and smeared a mark on my forehead. We could use blessings from all the gods and temples during these trying Saturn-dominated times.

"How is Nagu, Saar?" Bala asked.

"Relieved to say he is doing better. That is what they tell me. Take some biscuits and bananas when you go to see him at the city hospital. And tell Ayah she must keep up her strength."

"Yes, Saar."

Bala got up to leave and I noticed the usual tell-tale marks on the back of his dhoti. How many times to tell that idiot to change clothes before he left the house? Things don't sink into some people's heads, there was no point in wasting one's efforts.

I was not sure why my mind leapt to the past, it was not something I encouraged. All right, all right, O great silent one, now was the time to be totally frank and honest. I was worrying about Nagu and his injury and some part of me wanted to protect myself from myself.

When I was a boy, during school summer holidays, life in the village with grandfather passed pleasantly enough. I spent my spare time in and around the temple. Everybody who came there patted my head and talked to me. I got all the coconut and jaggery I could eat after morning and evening puja. I played cricket and gilli-danda on the road with other boys. I forgot what my mother and father had done to me, showing favoritism towards my brothers, sending them to English medium school because they were good at math and science while a humanities chap like me went to the Tamil school, saying yum for m and yen for n, as Cookie often pointed out.

I remembered my favorite train ride as a boy from Erode back to Maramur at the end of the holidays. Early in the morning, the air would be cool and crisp even in the summer. When the train jerked and screeched to a stop, I heard the familiar cries of vendors on the platform calling as if from a distant dream. Soon I was awake with excitement and hunger. Outside the window, I saw women holding baskets of flowers; tuberoses clustered like my school drawing of the sun and held together with silver and gold paper discs, garlands of jasmine, bright yellow chrysanthemums, leaves of patchouli and rose petals. I pressed my face against the rusted bars of the window and smelled the cloying sweet fragrance along with the stench of urine, vomit, human and dog feces. It was that time of day when it was standard ritual for people to carry a vessel of water and walk away from their huts. Men and women on the platform brushed their teeth and ate idlis, vadas and chutney from dried leaf plates. Passengers jumped out to fill flasks with water, some bought food bundles tied in banana leaves, curd rice with lime pickle, sambhar rice with onions and drumsticks, tamarind rice with peanuts. Appa got me Glaxo biscuits and two thumb-sized bananas that went down like sugar. I watched for the railway inspector in his starched white uniform, a rotund, self-important man who looked English and out of place amidst the chaos on the platform. As the train hissed and sighed and whistled out of Erode, I stared at the khaki-clad man who waved a flag. A few minutes past the station, rows of adults and children squatted in a line past neighboring tracks, their buttocks and dark heads whizzing by faster and faster as the train sped.

A nurse came to examine me and offered me sweet lime juice and Anacin tablets. I had complained about pain when I coughed or slept on my side. The Anglo-Indian Mrs. Paes said, "You'll be right as rain in no time." She adjusted my hospital gown and fluffed up my pillows. She smelled of 4711 cologne and talcum powder. "You get to go home tomorrow afternoon. Make sure you've arranged for somebody to pick you up and drop you home." I nodded. Venkat and Cookie had already agreed to take me home, a whole twenty four hours before they took the tourist taxi to the airport--Venkat going to Bombay on his way to France and Cookie getting off in Bombay for all that wedding business and jewelry shopping.

***

At home, late next afternoon, I was still in that half-conscious state when I was partly asleep and partly awake, an unusual thing for me. It was an after effect of the valium I took in the middle of the night to calm myself. Bala was making noise in the kitchen. He had dutifully postponed his job at Grand Sweets to look after me till I moved into the small hideous flat at Royal Gardens. A stab of pain accompanied this unsavory thought. I was still debating whether to get up and ask for my customary tumbler of coffee when I heard voices in the adjoining verandah. If you recall, I had mentioned to you during one of our earlier conversations that the window above my bedroom door always remained open. Cookie and Venkat were having coffee I could tell, from the aroma of Peaberry and the smell of a burning cigarette.

"Do you think you'll be able to use all your temple photographs?" Cookie asked.

"Yes. Yes. I never work for nothing. Not like you know who around here. Let's face it, Cookie. The man is a pompous ass. What makes him think he can effect any change in India? That kind of thinking takes a special kind of arrogance. He's just an old busybody thinking he's helping by doing his duty when in fact he's helping screw it up."

"He means well you know. Like Iyer said, he's just an old fart who can't let go. But he has his moments. You know what he said to me at the hospital when I went to see him there?" This was Cookie.

The silence, I imagined, meant Venkat shook his head no. It hurt me that Iyer had betrayed me and said something negative about me to them.

Cookie got momentarily distracted, it was obvious. She suddenly asked Venkat, "By the way, what happened to the car?"

"He finally agreed he had no need for it. With Usman gone, he should not be driving. He is a menace on the road. Anyway, I offered him a good price and engaged a driver for my mother and aunt. You know my mother is going to live with her."

"Good idea. What was I saying before? Oh yes. About our conversation in the hospital. He said the aspects of plot, our external life, the permutations and combinations of this has been worked out. All possible combinations have been done before. There is nothing new left. "The only thing that will give you originality," he said to me, "are your thoughts relating to work and what you do with them. If you want to blend bharath natyam and western dance, then that is what you must do. That is where your originality lies. This is how you make your stamp on the world."

"Did he say what he had done in this respect?"

"He said he tried to do his duty. He had this calling to save ancient temples for future generations and the world, show them the beauty and agelessness of it. This idea of leaving your stamp on the world," he said, "others need not even know about it. It could be some kind of delicious secret. It is enough that you know," he told me. "Are you not living for yourself first?" Cookie imitated the way Sathya spoke, the slight lilt in her voice indicating Indian accent.

"I like that, I must say. Fine intentions. But look at the mess now." This was Venkat.

There was Cookie's audible sigh in response.

The telephone rang and one of them must have answered for after that, their voices turned hushed and distant. I got out of bed with some effort and the room spun slightly before settling down. I clutched the metal headboard to steady myself and looked out. Venkat and Cookie were standing on the street beyond the gate, looking very solemn. Bala walked in with coffee and I returned to bed.

***

After lunch, I heard the bad news about Nagu. Venkat's contact from the hospital had phoned to say he was worse. There was sepsis in the blood and they were trying potent infusion of antibiotics through the intravenous method, hoping this would stabilize things. I prayed he would recover soon.

I gathered from Bala that Venkat had gone to spend time with his mother and aunt and Cookie had run to Basket Hair. As was the case with most international flights, Venkat was leaving after midnight, an ungodly hour, for his trip to France. He had promised to pay me a final flying visit. Cookie was leaving in the morning but spending the night with friends so she too would be saying goodbye.

To distract myself, I looked through my final draft of notes for the book. That feeling of satisfaction and fatigue settled on me as I read the last page and thought it was a job well done. I hoped Venkat would see the thing to fruition. The selling and marketing of it was all up to him now. I shut the file and thought about the conversation I had heard earlier in the day. So they thought I had made a mess of things. That I was an arrogant bastard and fancied myself some kind of agent to effect change in this impossible country. Did it matter what they thought? Was it really important? Did they even know what to think about what had happened given their non-resident status? One must do what one has to do without dwelling on what others thought.

I finished my evening prayers and cultivated some level of peace with great difficulty when I heard a lot of crying and shouting in the front verandah. Bala was outside in a flash, as I was still in the puja room past the hall. I used my cane and went out to see Ayah crying loudly and slumping to the floor.

"What is it? I asked in alarm.

She wailed loudly and I had to calm her down and ask Bala to get her a cup of tea. Finally I got it out of her that Nagu had lapsed into a coma and the people at the hospital had told her to go home, there was no use in so many relatives crowding the place. There was nothing they could do for him there. My stomach somersaulted at the sight of the old woman's pain. To think that I had somehow been responsible for all this. I closed my eyes and muttered a mantra. Then I called, "Bala, get Ayah some food."

I turned my attentions to the moment at hand and told her she had to keep up her strength for the sake of her son. "There is Paru, the baby. You are the rock of your family. Are you not? These young people, you know how they are. It is hard for them to admit how much they need us old folks." Ayah wiped her tears with the edge of her pallu and began to eat the left overs Bala offered her on a freshly washed banana leaf. I asked Bala to give her a hundred rupees before she left. "Don't worry about the cost of anything Ayah. I will take care of everything. You look after your grandchild." She nodded and asked me how I was doing, pointing to my chest. As I watched her leave, I felt fresh the imbalance of the situation, her asking me how I was doing as her only son lay in a coma.

***

213

Later, Cookie and Venkat came over and we sat in the verandah, as was our usual habit. Bala was telling us about the mother and baby monkey from Misty Glen across the road. It seemed that Mrs. Awesome had adopted the baby since the mother had been electrocuted on one of her jaunts on the wires hanging on the main road. The baby now appeared dressed in little boy or little girl clothes depending on the hysterical woman's mood. Venkat and Cookie laughed and said they would miss all the excitement of Koil Street and Maramur.

The tourist taxi arrived and we said goodbye. I needed solitary time to think so I went up to the terrace in spite of the pain while I climbed the stairs. Cookie had left the bedroom door open. The rosewood dresser with the oval mirror was empty except for a bottle of nail polish. I picked it up and saw that it was called Pearly Pink. I would miss the child with her white teeth and shining eyes and piercing questions.

On the terrace, the chameleon skin, I saw, was gone. The washerwomen at the slums were cooking dinner, the smell of kerosene from their stove was strong in the air. A two-in-one transistor was playing Pettai rap loudly so I walked to the other corner of the terrace and stood there facing Misty Glen. The Radha Krishna statue still had the crack at the bottom and pigeons flew out of there with regular frequency. Twigs and hay hung from their beaks as they flew back.

Nagu's face came to me again, his expression haunting. Then he slumped to the ground, holding his bloody chest. The past few days, this had been happening frequently, his face coming to me over and over, my mind thrashing like a fish out of water. I could not believe that I was facing such crises at this, the twilight of my life. Who would have thought that I would be worrying about somebody injuring himself in the process of saving my old and frail body? My mind traveled to times when Nagu had been little and I had insisted that he go to school and get an education and then later, a job. At every stage of life, I had done what I could. I tried hard to fulfill my duty, my dharma when it came to all the important aspects of my life -- work, relationships. Was this not what I should have chosen as the highest principle towards the goal of salvation?

I took a valium to help me sleep that night.

Chapter Ten
Arjuna's Penance

Nagu was dead. The sepsis in his blood turned pervasive, the doctor shook his head and wrung his hands. I felt shattered but could not bring myself to go out of the house and face Paru and Ayah grieving in the garage. I prayed fervently that God would forgive me for I had been the cause of this tragedy. A child would not know his father because of me. That thought would not leave me as I pretended to move about the house and carry on with my day. I was almost grateful later in the morning when Bala told me Ayah and Paru waited for me in the verandah. They were braver than I. All of us wept unashamedly when we saw each other. Ayah held my hands and said it was written on her forehead that she would cremate both her sons within six months, unnatural as it was for a mother to witness such a double tragedy in her lifetime.

She had decided to go back to the village with Paru and her grandson. I arranged for taxis to take them back, one to take Nagu's body accompanied by two of his male relatives, and the second one to take the women and the child. I placed a garland of marigolds on Nagu's body before the vehicles left Koil Street. I was immensely grateful that everything was done in a dignified manner and the women had not wailed and screeched, there was none of that country bumpkin hysterical behavior.

An hour earlier, a crowd of Nagu's colleagues from the post-office and other characters he had known for many years growing up here in "Hridaya Kamalam" in Maramur had shown up. They marched silently to the garage where his body lay and paid their respects, placed garlands of flowers on his body. I watched from the bedroom window and every time a mourner took Ayah's hands and she kissed them from generosity and affection, her body wracked by sobs, I felt the pain anew. Paru was abnormally quiet and withdrawn as if she was merely witnessing the spectacle and all of it was happening to somebody else. The poor child would probably suffer terribly later, after the cremation, when it would finally hit her and the absence of her young husband would introduce itself day after day as she became part of an extended family in the village. Then and there I decided that I would contribute whatever it took, a sum of money to ensure she would have her independence if she desired. A small piece of land for her or her own hut perhaps. Paru had stared at the ground and taken the check and envelope from my hands when I spoke to her about this. It did not matter that she did not reply, I told myself, once the gift was given, it was hers to do with as she pleased.

***

The next morning, I longed for the soothing sound of the sea and the salt air of Mahabalipuram. As you knew, O great silent one, the temples there always comforted me and replenished my spirit. I had to wait for a tourist taxi fellow to come and take me since I was stranded without a car these days.

Naidu called and I wrote down the details he gave me regarding the flat in Royal Gardens. I planned to visit the place next week when my mind was less agitated. I could tell Bala too was upset and restless these days, what with the mother monkey having been electrocuted and the baby monkey coming and sitting on the kitchen window sill looking at him with sad brown eyes. He had finalized his afternoon job at Grand Sweets and had managed to acquire two other clients on Koil Street for whom he would provide daily meals. I gave him his salary and a generous bonus and told him to go begin his small business life.

While I waited for the taxi chap to take me to Mahabalipuram, I decided to take a walk along Koil Street. It had been a long time since I had taken in these familiar sights and once I was ensconced in a flat, who knew how often I could come out. Stuck somewhere on the sixth floor, with the power going off as often as it did and lifts turning into immoveable cages, chances were unlikely that I would descend down speedily and walk like I could do so easily now, just step out of the house and onto the street.

Sandalwood incense lent a perfume to the air near the Ganesha shrine in front of Misty Glen. There were fresh garlands on the Radha Krishna statues telling me it was a special day in the Awesomes' household. The Kottayam family, Rajan and his musically inclined children and grandchildren had gone for a wedding and their house stood strangely silent. The Chettinad house with the pockmarked pillars and the sole heir freezing his buns off in Edmonton, Alberta, was undergoing some kind of facelift. I noticed a construction crew there painting and fixing the place. The "We two, Our two" government advertisement for birth control on the compound wall had been defaced by people spitting betel juice on the couple so the mother and the father looked like some violent confrontation had wounded them terribly. The isthrykaran under the neem tree was missing. Probably he too had gone to some function since it was the season for weddings and such nonsense. The rubbish bin was covered with banana leaves and recently eaten remains of a feast that crows swooshed down and pecked. Mala Nursing Home looked like it always did, fat ayahs tending to overfed toddlers in the park, imported cars dropping off women about to give birth. The Swami's house was desolate and the huge eye painted on the metal gates stared back at me accusingly.

The tea stall chap was frying onion bhajjis while a fellow in a colorful sarong fanned out all sorts of magazines and books on the pavement adjacent to the two metal tables. The Aavin milk booth too was quiet since morning deliveries had been completed and the queues of chatty servant women had dispersed more than a few hours ago. The Royal Gardens apartment building had the usual cluster of drivers gossiping and I walked past the place quickly since I would have plenty of time to examine this all too closely in the near future. The tailor's shop at the street corner was open for business as usual. Venkat's house was unrecognizable because of partial demolition. Naidu was there and he nodded to me and did namaskaram. What little peace had been carefully cultivated by me in the last twenty minutes evaporated immediately when I saw that unctuous face.

Before I turned back towards Hridaya Kamalam, I spotted the usual tender coconut vendor at the end of the street, removing the coconuts jutting out on either side of his bicycle and arranging them on the pavement, pyramid style. I supposed that I would get a view of all these goings on in Koil Street from the balcony of the sixth floor flat. People would look like insects moving about and my vertigo would make me step inside before I felt myself moving towards the ground.

***

In Mahabalipuram, the bas-relief in front of me showed the story of Arjuna's Penance from the famous epic of Mahabharata. There were the mingled elements from the earthly and the heavenly here. For example, you saw a natural cleft from which water poured down to simulate the flowing river Ganga. On either side of the cleft were the swaying hoods and slithering bodies of serpents. To the left was Arjuna, consummate archer, arms raised to the heavens, standing on one leg, a yogic posture of penance, his call for a boon to the almighty Siva. He was praying for a powerful weapon with which to destroy his enemies. Watching him, to the right, were rows and clusters of adult and baby elephants, all sorts of animals and other semi-divine and celestial beings.

Venkat had taken memorable photographs of this piece. He had managed to capture on paper the vivaciousness of the carvings by catching the play of light and shadow that highlighted the skill and depth of detail. The impression of moving sunlight and patches of darkness showed off the texture of stone, the magnificence of the massive job done on two huge boulders. I hoped he would remember to use it for the cover of "Temples" as we had discussed.

That night, I heard a bloodcurdling scream from the slums at the back and a lot of shouting and more screaming as I lay in bed. I must have fallen asleep after that for when I woke up the next day, I was not sure if I had really heard something or it was a nightmare of some sort. Both mind and body were too exhausted for me to investigate the matter at that hour of the morning. I was sure Bala would give me the news. Then I remembered Bala had left.

Mr. Awesome came to visit next morning and it took all my effort to get up and open the door for him. How strange and empty the house was without Nagu, Paru, Usman and Bala, not to mention Cookie and her chatter. Mr. Awesome was celebrating (he offered me a plate of sunset colored jilebis) because a favorite nephew had got into the famous I.I.T. Admission to this institution, for us Indians, was guarantee to a prosperous life. Never mind that the two smelly young fellows I met from I.I.T. spoke in a language I could not fathom; throwing about phrases like Giga bytes making me suspicious of their intelligence.

Mr. Awesome soon confirmed that the scream I heard the previous night had been real. The beauteous woman, the tailor's wife, had been sleeping in her hut when somebody came to her window and tossed acid on her face. She had been rushed to the hospital and the prognosis was that she would live but her face had been marred for life. The people from the slums were telling all sorts of stories, that it was her husband himself who had done it to put an end to her clandestine affairs. He had become enraged on finding out about her dealings with the Brahmin Saar Venkat and the extra money he had given her. I remembered Venkat mentioning to me that he had given her a lump sum as bonus along with her salary for all that she had done for his mother. Good intentions were easily misconstrued, this was the way of the world. Who better than I knew that? Mr. Awesome concluded, "Useless bugger. That tailor fellow has now disappeared. Probably one of his drinking binges. Nobody knows where he is or if he indeed is the culprit. Rotten fellow. You cannot trust this lower class type."

I told Mr. Awesome that I needed to rest and asked him to shut the door on his way out.

"Myself and wife and family are going to a wedding today. We will be back in the evening. You know this is the season for that now. Our Kerala neighbors have also gone to Trivandrum for a relation's wedding. Now Venkat's house is also down. Practically the whole street is becoming empty or changing. What to do? This is life, things are always changing. Nothing is the same like before."

***

As I sat there in the empty house, I heard thunder and soon the smell

219

of rain was in the air. Somewhere, I heard the cry of a monkey or a child. Perhaps it was Nagu's son. Then I remembered they were no longer in the garage. Paru and the child had left for their ancestral village along with Nagu's body. The pain came down like a sharp knife on my left side. How could I forget Ayah's face, that cry that came out of her mouth when she came to see me? Her eyes burned a hole in my soul. My body, my face, turned away from her suffering, but the spirit had seen everything I had caused. A part of me sensed that though I could not hear them, drums were playing in the house and in my head, Siva was doing his dance of destruction, Yama, god of death was waiting impatiently for me.

My mind traveled to the past, to my childhood. I no longer remembered when I made the decision to be an Indologist. I always felt I belonged to the temples, came wholly alive in their setting. Running to Ganesha every morning on the way to school, carrying the slate with sums and slinging the cloth book bag over my left shoulder, I stopped for a few minutes and watched the temple elephant sway his ears. I leaned my slate and bag against the wall behind the nandi and said namaskaram to all the women. Parrots were making a racket in the almond tree to the side of the temple. Shrill cries and *phut phut* of many beating wings made me look up. They rose and vanished like so many green check marks in the bright sky. Now only the structure of the temple loomed up, the slant of the gopuram reaching for the clouds, the ornate carvings depicting scenes from the epics. The priest came out with the arati plate, the flame burning madly. I joined others around me, reaching out for the heat, seeking blessings. Water was poured into my cupped hands. I swallowed some of it and brushed the rest on my head and scalp. It tasted of sweet basil and flower petals and tingled like cool well water.

All these years later, I still never found anything like it in Madras.

I was back in the present, staring at my old man hands. Sometimes, my eyesight became unreliable. Last week, I looked outside the window at the chikoo and mango trees in the garden and saw spirits hanging upside down like bats on the trees. They were so heavy, they made the branches bend. I heard them calling out to me. Later when I looked, there was nothing. Only the brown of the bark and the green of the leaves.

Next day, The Hindu brought a chill to my heart as right there on the second page was an article on two recent temple projects that had disastrous consequences. Below the headline, on the left, was a photograph of Sub-Optimal pointing to the tree shrine in Periamalai and on the right, the photo showed the damaged pavilion in Mayapuram. I stood in the middle of the second photo and Puncture and S.D. were on either side. The whole sorry story had been reported in detail by the paper: the theft of the tablets, the resurrection of a damaged and broken nagapratishta, the late night sabotage of the navagraha planet idols in Mayapuram and the inability of government agencies to do anything about such repeated losses.

Even senior personnel (meaning me, the article specifically referred to me by name to my great shame and dishonor) who had been at the game for decades were proving useless at tackling this new trend of art smuggling to the west. The missing stone tablet had been spotted in some glossy architecture magazine published out of New York. The fancy picture had shown the nagapratishta stone tablet against a background of lilac satin and glowing candles, a "primal and exotic element" in citified American décor.

As I read through the article, I realized that the entire mystery had been solved for everybody by this nosey reporter chap. He had named names, the real people responsible for all this mess. As we suspected, Mani, I.Q. Junior, Thomas and Pillai from Mogul Stores had all been involved in the art smuggling business, having some kind of import export business as their front. The main reason for senseless destruction of the navagraha planet idols at Mayapuram was revenge in the name of Christian and Muslim, non-Hindu students who had been mistreated by the temple school teachers. The suspects were unable to give any more substantial reason than that.

I spent the day in a daze, wondering how I could have been so naive as to have stayed on in the department when things were clearly getting too complex for me to handle. Perhaps this was what Iyer meant, my sense of duty going beyond practicality, staying on at the job when I should have left. I played the events over and over in my head and I could not come up with what I could have done differently. Responsible people had to take on the duty of passing on a legacy to future generations and preserving historical artifacts. With my deep concern, knowledge and honesty, it was only proper that one of these persons should be myself.

***

The same day in the evening, there was a peal of thunder and the lights went out. I rummaged through all the drawers in the house. I could not find candles anywhere and had forgotten where the hurricane lamp was kept. Of course, there were the brass oil wick lamps from the prayer room so I moved one of these to the bedroom. I thought I should check with Mr. and Mrs. Awesome to see if they had a spare torch for mine had died with rusty batteries in its belly. I needed something for the coming night in case I needed to use the bathroom.

Misty Glen was dark and gloomy except for a soft glow coming from two windows upstairs. Their Hong Kong generator was making an awful racket, I could see through the window and hear, as it burped and farted under the stairs. The back door was open but there was nobody to answer my calls. I had no choice but to climb upstairs where the first open window revealed Mrs. Awesome sitting in her pink bathtub wearing a bright silk sari, mumbling rubbish to a pants and T-shirt wearing baby monkey on her lap. No point in approaching her, I decided. What if the woman was deep in one of her hysteria moods and did something unpredictable?

Mr. Awesome was clearly visible through the next window, a few yards past Mrs. Awesome. His two-in-one transistor or boom box, as Cookie called it, was on full blast, playing one of his American rock music songs. The words made little sense to me.

> I'm coming up so you better you better get this party started
> I'm coming up so you better you better get this party started
> Get this party started on a Saturday night
> Everybody's waiting for me to arrive
> Sendin' out the message to all of my friends
> We'll be looking flashy in my Mercedes Benz.

I watched, fascinated as the silly man danced bare bellied, his sacred thread throbbing on his chest, the knot on his head undone, his eyes closed, immersed in the meaningless music. I called out to him four times and when it started to drizzle, I decided the whole business was useless and it was best I returned home at once. How could I have come here for help from these absurd characters? I crossed the street in a hurry and just as I got into the front balcony of Hridaya Kamalam, it began to pour.

Minutes later, when I stepped into the hall, the house felt eerie. It was as if the body of the house sighed and shifted against the wind. Through windows that had been left open, water came in and made the floors wet. A frog had jumped in and croaked from the corner of the room. I saw an earthworm crawling in the middle of a puddle. It occurred to me at that moment that I loved too much and too hard. The house. Menaka. She had felt the rot of my intensity, it had been too much of a good thing. And now the same thing was happening to the house.

Walking towards my room, I slipped and fell. Bits of leaves and twigs from the garden had blown in. It was as if nature was claiming back what belonged to her in the first place. It reminded me of the trees holding the temples in their grip in Angkor Wat, away from the prying eyes of man, the jungle, nature claiming back its own. It was no use, just lying there in the dark on the floor, I got up and decided to have a bath before going to bed.

As I stood there one final moment in the hall, I stared at the family photographs on the wall -- grandfather, grandmother, mother and father, all waiting, silent. They opened their mouths matching the sound of the wind that howled outside. Their joint voices filled the empty house. From my bedroom window, I thought I saw those spirits hanging upside down again like bats on the chikoo tree.

After a comforting bath, half an hour later, I was slumped with pain against the wall of the bathroom, wet, nude, my brown shell of a body shriveled and exposed for all to see. I heard, at regular intervals, the hissing and spluttering of the tap but no water came out. I looked up and met a pair of gentle brown eyes belonging to the baby monkey as it sat there on the window sill tilting its head to one side and staring at me. My image was reflected in the animal's eyes. I felt a sense of surrender, a strange new sensation that I had not known before. The monkey opened its baby mouth and yawned. The universe, the world, everything was there as it had been in Lord Krishna's mouth --the flutter of a moth's wing in the chameleon's mouth, the choke of a snake on a mouse, the way of nature, it was all there.

When Hanuman went searching for Sita in the Ramayana, he carried the ring of Rama in his mouth so that he could cross hurdles with the name of the Lord on his lips. To find the ultimate reality, O silent one, there were so many obstacles. The first was that I had to rise above identifying myself with this self, this chap Sathya, this body. Hanuman encountered the mother of serpents who planned to swallow him. He overcame this cruel plan by shrinking to the tiniest of proportions as she swelled to gigantic proportions to accommodate his normal size. I learned from this that adversity was faced not only with bravery but also with flexibility and humbleness, that most underrated quality. For Hanuman the devotee to reach his Lord Rama, the mind, the body and the intellect, were all in beautiful harmony.

I had been too arrogant, caught up in my own illusion, so sure of things. Now I was filled with all sorts of doubts. Had my life been of any use, how did one measure this? The only thing I had learned was that I had to unlearn everything and begin all over. I had to approach the end in all innocence like a child. This was what Iyer had been talking about. There were so many realities in the same world. Did I stay within mine, the boundaries of my own interpretation, that circle of security that did not let in other views? How could one be afraid of confusion and contradiction when this was the way of the world, of man and human nature?

The pain was sudden and sharp on my side and I thought I should perhaps shout for help or try to get up. I decided on the latter and grabbed the bamboo pole Bala had left in the corner. I clutched it for support and straightened myself. The next moment, a large, adult monkey appeared next to the baby monkey and bared its teeth at me. It was a reflex action on my part, the stupid thing I did next. I lifted the pole and brought it down *thwack* on the creature.

In a flash, monkeys were everywhere in the bathroom, on the commode tank, one dipping a plastic mug into the toilet, another coming close and grabbing the stick from me. Things went blurry and I felt the hairy touch of a paw on my chest and saw fuzzy outlines around me, screeching and jumping all over the place.

I heard the persistent cawing of a crow and thought perhaps my time had come. I traveled towards the ceiling of the room and looked down at the frail brown body, that pathetic shell of a thing and felt nothing for it. It was time to give it back to the earth, like a common bird flying into the glass of a window, breaking its neck and falling on the ground, like a worm that got squashed. I remembered the words of that famous Subbalakhsmi song, you are born alone and you die alone. Nobody could support you at these crucial times.

Somebody was at the gate and I heard a shout near the window. Must be Bala coming to collect his things and check up on me. The monkeys stopped moving and in a minute, as quickly as they had come, the animals left.

The superficial scratch bled red through the gauzy bandage because my hand shook uncontrollably as I splashed Mercurochrome on my chest.

Yet another surprise when I thought I was going to die. I looked at the reflection in the mirror and wondered where was the sense of humor in that chap? Always taking things so seriously, my duty and work and what not, forgetting life had an element of the absurd, the random, it was all a game in the end. See the game of the lizard recently dead there, the game extended by the ant biting him, the spider spinning her cobweb in the corner, the fly trapped in its lacy web. You did not have to go all the way up to Saturn to be swayed by the winds of hope and fear. This was just the way things were in nature, sudden, creative and destructive at the same time. This was the universal presence you felt all the time.

After all these years, I had found no cause bigger than myself. That ego problem had been mine too after all. I had had enough of this tiresome cause. What a joke it had all been. A big laugh.

You see the old man had nursed his sense of drama.

I had hoped Venkat and Cookie would return on hearing the sad news about me. Bala would find me soon and the next morning and Venkat would bathe and dress me in that butter colored American penguin T-shirt and they would scatter my ashes on the seashore. They would toss petals on the water and watch me dance away into the horizon, mutating, assuming another shape for my next life.

I, too, had been like the others, waiting for Godot in the end. Waiting for some kind of enlightenment that would make life bearable. Waiting to be called, chosen above others. Based on my uniqueness, that grandiose obsession of the self. I considered myself a first class sort. So I deserved a seat in the senior special waiting room for divine revelation.

O silent one, you and I both agreed before, did we not, that we did not care for somebody who eavesdropped continuously and did not contribute, had nothing to say for himself? The time has come to go back to your own life. I have nothing to say. Philosophy of Zero. Zilch according to the Americans. Cipher according to the Indians. Don't know what the Canadians are calling this.

Now, go, let me face the night in peace.

None of the usual tricks to fall asleep worked. I tried to travel to the slum dwellers and their transistor radio music at the back of the house, chant Gayatri mantra to calm my mind. The shore temples of Mahabalipuram beckoned and I knew nothing else would do. I had to go there and smell and salt in the sea air, feel the texture of rock against the skin of my palm for comfort.

Of course, I could not drive myself there this time.

I placed my hand on my heart and felt the reassuring, familiar beats. It did not matter that I could not go there, the temples were here, the secret of Chidambaram, the rahasyam, the space you filled with the power of your own mind. There was an echo of my words from my last trip there. "To the right of the silver icon of Nataraja dancing his cosmic dance is the chidambara rahasyam, the secret of secrets. All you see is a garland of leaves. You look at the statue to the left and you see God externally and to the right, when you glimpse the secret, you see him internally. He is doing the cosmic dance within you. The whole universe is within you."

***

Next morning out on Koil Street, the cement fence skirting the Chettiar house had been freshly painted with a garish advertisement. "We two, our two" the slogan said, a popular message from the government for population control. Next to the slogan on the fence was a drawing of a mother and father and two children. They had moon-like round faces and plump bodes, presumably because of better health since the family was small. All four were wearing clothes in white and red as if only a limited palette of colors was allowed in their planned and organized world. They stood there on the wall with cinnamon colored faces and red chili colored lips, their eyes as dark as ripe mangosteens and their hair shiny and sleeked back and on their collective lips, the same hovering smile. It was as if they had a secret they could hardly wait to spill out. If you stared strongly at the mother you could almost say she looked like she had a bun in the oven. The father smiled because he knew. The children smiled because they knew too and the parents did not know that they knew. The children's smile lingered because of their fun filled nature. They planned to torture this poor bun in the oven. A sense of déjà vu as I remembered having seen this before.

The isthrykaran, ironing fellow, parked his mobile cart under the neem tree in front of the Chettiar house. It provided nice shade for the family since they had erected a tarpaulin roofed tent leaning against a portion of the fence. The isthrykaran's wife squatted in front of their make-do shack, a child suckling her breast and a toddler dressed only in a dirty torn shirt running about. She sat there selling a basket of black plums and gooseberries, fruit that had been pinched from the trees in the Chettiar house.

The coal iron hissed as isthrykaran sprinkled water and moved the iron back and forth creasing a pair of trousers. He looked up and flashed a smile at me, his yellow teeth glinting like old harmonium keys in the sun. The toddler finished urinating against a bush in the corner and came running up to me and held out his hand. I'd left the house without any change in my pocket so I told the child I would have something for him on my way back. I planned to pick up some biscuits from the tea stall across the street. The neem tree above us swished slightly in the wind and I remembered how my grandmother and mother would come and gather bunches of leaves whenever any of us children fell ill with measles or chicken pox. The leaves were used to stroke our skin. This prevented us from scratching so would have no scars. Of course, in modern times, women resorted to using stupid pink powder puffs.

***

The next Friday being auspicious, I was standing in front of the shore temples of Mahabalipuram, waiting for dawn to break. There was the voice of Doc in my head saying, "Restlessness eventually leads to a kind of rest when the mind is filled only with awareness. This is all one can hope for."

It was high tide when powerful and foamy white surf became an invisible giant hand, an unseen sculptor, shaping gray black rock. The waves hissed and surged and sang their song. The receding waves sucked at my flat and slightly swollen feet. I stood before the two foot carving of Lalita, most benign and beautiful aspect of the divine mother. The design at the base was the Srichakra that represented cosmic energy. It had the power to grant the devotee anything he desired. I reached out with my right hand and caressed this and prayed that my death and reincarnation would go well.

It was not very trendy or fashionable to admit that one was conventional in some ways after all, that one still thought the world had not changed that much. For example, the sounds of thunder and flashes of lightning remained the same. Nature inspired awe and was always seen as God's calling card. If temples spoke to us through a language of symbols, nature too had a parallel—wind, trees, the ocean, mountains. Not to forget things underground—life under the sea and more that the eye cannot see. So many forms of life changing and mutating, so many levels of life. I pictured these spreading out like ripples over earth, planets and the stars. How vast was the universe and how small a man.

When we had a staring contest as children, why was there that urge to blink and look away, what was it that prevented us from looking deep within each other? Were we afraid of something we might find in the other person that we did not have? The other person was more than a mirror image, for we knew instinctively then of the vastness of the universe, the possibilities and dangers that lurked within us and were scared of what we saw there. And because the other person was also like you, this meant we were also scared of ourselves.

Who was this person I was talking to? Never mind, I reminded myself, I talked to myself these days, a sign of intelligence or advancing years,

I did not care, you may choose to believe what you like.

www.ingramcontent.com/pod-product-compliance
Lightning Source LLC
Chambersburg PA
CBHW021012120726
47905CB00009B/2972